DRAMA OF DESIRE

"Sarah."

It was only one word, spoken roughly, in a voice that resonated with need. But it was enough.

Hearing her name on Lord Linton's lips turned Sarah's knees to jelly. As his mouth once again descended to hers, she knew how foolishly she had underestimated the danger of acting out this scene together.

It was impossible to know how long this sweet torture continued, but a blazing oath finally brought Sarah to her senses as Lord Linton set her from him quickly, almost making her fall.

"You have proven your point." A seething undertone in his icy words suggested that he held himself under tight control.

"I do not understand," Sarah stammered.

A demonic gaze condemned her. "A 'light touch' and 'a knowing gaze'—you said they would be sufficient to kindle carnal desire." His smile was bitter. "You were correct, of course. I had not counted on your extraordinary skill and experience. I will rewrite the scene."

He strode through the study door, leaving Sarah to grapple with the emptiness of her Pyrrhic victory and the growing ache in her heart.

A
Passionate
Performance

Eileen Putman

A SIGNET BOOK

SIGNET
Published by the Penguin Group
Penguin Books USA Inc., 375 Hudson Street,
New York, New York 10014, U.S.A.
Penguin Books Ltd, 27 Wrights Lane,
London W8 5TZ, England
Penguin Books Australia Ltd, Ringwood,
Victoria, Australia
Penguin Books Canada Ltd, 10 Alcorn Avenue,
Toronto, Ontario, Canada M4V 3B2
Penguin Books (N.Z.) Ltd, 182–190 Wairau Road,
Auckland 10, New Zealand

Penguin Books Ltd, Registered Offices:
Harmondsworth, Middlesex, England

First published by Signet, an imprint of Dutton Signet,
a division of Penguin Books USA Inc.

First Printing, March, 1997
10 9 8 7 6 5 4 3 2 1

 REGISTERED TRADEMARK—MARCA REGISTRADA

Printed in the United States of America

To the A's in my life:
Alan, Andy, and Abby.
Miracles, every one.

Prologue

London, 1801

The pistol pointed straight at Justin's heart. He knew it was loaded, for he had watched his father prepare the weapon using bullets, measure, mallet, and powder flask from the polished mahogany case.

His father's hands shook, as they always did, from too much drink. His gaze met Justin's over the barrel of the gun.

"Death is a rather permanent state, boy," he drawled, anger etching the lines on his face into deep crevices. "Are you certain you do not wish to retract those words?"

Justin stared mutely at the man who had given him life, the man whose blotched and puffy face made him unrecognizable as the father who had bought him his first pony, taught him to swim, and showed him how to shoot before he could scarcely hold a weapon's weight.

That man was nowhere in evidence. Instead, this ugly stranger stood in his place, smiling a dangerous smile and pointing a trembling pistol at his son's heart.

Like wildly firing cannons, Justin's pulse thundered in his ears. He could not manage even an inarticulate grunt in response to his father's question. Yet moments ago the words had spewed from him in an accusing rush of sound and rage spawned by the image of his mother's bruised face. He had meant to force his father to see the damage he had wrought, to change his ways. But he had gone too far, said too much, and accomplished nothing. He was only a youth, without the skill and strength of a man, even a man such as his father.

Words were the only weapons he had. And they had failed, because they were only words.

"Pity. You have lost your tongue." His father yawned, but

kept the pistol leveled at him. "'Tis just as well. I have no desire to listen to more of your drivel." He gave Justin a penetrating look. "Be careful before you set yourself up as judge and jury, boy. You may not be in possession of all of the facts."

"I did not mean . . ." But Justin's voice cracked, and he broke off in mortification. His father laughed scornfully.

"You are no more than a mewling babe, hardly fit to criticize your elders. That scullery maid I sent you has obviously had no success in helping you find your manhood."

Justin flushed, remembering the awkward exercise he had endured with the smirking maid. He could not imagine his parents engaging in such a crude activity, but he knew they did, for his mother was more than five months gone with child. He wondered about the mistresses whose existence his father never troubled to hide. Did they enjoy such sport? His mother surely did not. He had heard her cries in the night, cries of anguish and pain.

Fury filled him, a man's fury in a boy's body. Smoke darkened his gray eyes as a rush of courage propelled him a step forward.

"I demand satisfaction," he said in a voice that was not quite steady. "On my mother's behalf."

Red-streaked eyes blinked at him. A crude laugh of disbelief echoed around the room. "You!" His father gaped. "You would challenge me to a duel! How old are you, boy?"

"Nearly thirteen, sir."

"Thirteen! That is rich!" The pistol shook wildly as his father nearly doubled up in mirth.

"I can shoot, sir," Justin replied with as much dignity as he could muster. "And I am prepared to die."

A fist crashed upon the desk, sending Justin's heart to his throat. "First you consign me to the devil," his father roared, "then you decide to send me there yourself! Perhaps your mother did not birth such a milksop puppy after all—only an idiot." His father lurched toward him, nearly losing his balance. "Very well, lad," he said, a wild gleam in his eye. "I will accept your challenge. My choice of weapons, of course."

A deck of cards suddenly appeared on the desk. A grin, cunning as it was grotesque, distorted his father's features.

Justin waited.

"Low card loses," his father said softly.

Justin looked from the man to the cards. "I do not understand the stakes."

" 'Tis a simple duel. Whoever draws high is the victor. The owner of the low card will be deemed to have cocked up his toes." His father waved a hand dismissively. "All in pretense, of course, else the hounds of hell will be on my heels. But you and I will know the truth, will we not?" His malevolent smile sent a shiver down Justin's spine.

Now he understood. It was a game, but not a game. Justin nodded slowly, somberly agreeing to the stakes. "Shuffle the cards thoroughly, if you please, sir."

His father's gaze narrowed. "Perhaps I did not raise such a fool, after all." He set the pistol down to take up the cards. Justin breathed a sigh of relief, though he knew that the danger remained. He watched closely as his father shuffled clumsily. The cards were probably marked, although there were no obvious signs.

"Go on, boy." His father tapped the deck. "Choose."

Carefully, Justin took a card from the middle. He put it face-down, covering the back with his palm so his father could not see the markings, if they were there. When he looked up, he read the anger in his father's eyes. Without a word, his father pulled a card from the top of the deck. He turned it over. It was the king of spades. He grinned.

"Your turn, boy." The scent of victory gave his voice a hoarse, breathy sound.

Justin removed his palm. His father's gaze went to the back of the card. A flicker in those bloodshot eyes gave Justin pause. Slowly, he turned over his card.

Ace of spades.

Father and son stared at each other.

"Alas, I am dead." His father's lips curled contemptuously around the blunt words. "I shall find a comfortable grave and watch the lot of you make fools of yourselves for all eternity. My troubles are over. Yours have just begun, however."

"Sir?" Justin willed his voice to calm.

Idly, his father ran a finger over the barrel of the pistol. "Did you think you would escape unscathed, boy?" he asked softly. "That is not how it works."

Justin's blood ran cold at the venom in his father's voice. "I do not understand."

"Surely you know that it is a son's duty to extract revenge for his father's murder?" A strange, glittering look inhabited his father's gaze. "I am dead. By your hand, in a duel. I am afraid that means you must now die. An eye for an eye, you know."

As the boy watched in horror, his father pushed the pistol toward him. "Take it," he commanded, placing the gun in Justin's hand and curving his son's finger around the trigger. His fleshy lips curled in a knowing smile as he maneuvered the weapon so that it pointed at Justin's head.

"Go ahead, *son*," he said in a silky purr. "See that justice is done." His voice dropped to a hoarse whisper. *"It is your duty."*

Chapter One

"Very well, Harry. I shall be your bride," the Honorable Sarah Armistead said in an exasperated voice, "but this is the last time."

Harry shot her a relieved smile. "You've got bottom, Sarah, I will give you that."

She eyed him sharply. Harry's colorful cant was not one of his endearing traits. "I mean it, Harry. I will not do it again."

"With a bit of my luck and your skill, there should be no need to. Do you think you could manage to be increasing? 'Twould be wonderfully convincing."

Green eyes flashed him a look that instantly removed the smile from his face. "That is too much, even from you, Harry," Sarah admonished as a flush swept her features. "I daresay my performances are not *that* good."

Harry had the grace to look properly chastened. "I ought not to have said that. 'Tis just that I keep forgetting my manners around you."

"Hmmph." Sarah gifted him with the stern gaze of reproof she had perfected over many months of delivering setdowns to members of the masculine gender. Men often made unflattering assumptions about her character, but that did not mean she would tolerate such careless disregard of her sensibilities. "There will be none of *that,* sir. Or you can very well go begging to your Aunt Agatha alone."

"She will probably leave everything to Justin anyway," Harry grumbled, "even though he will never wed. No respectable woman would have him."

"Oh?" Sarah flounced into the chair at her dressing table, angry at herself for accepting Harry's offer, angry at the circumstances that had forced her to do it. "Pray, what is your cousin's problem, Harry? Two heads? A weakness for Blue Ruin? An unquenchable thirst for the muslin set?"

"Not two heads. His one is more than a match for most men." Harry eyed her cautiously, wary of her mood. "The latter, perhaps."

"Do you mean to say that your cousin is a rake?" Sarah pretended shock. "Never say I am marrying into a *notorious* family, Harry!"

Harry's chin lifted mulelishly. "I suppose every family has a scandal or two. I have kept *my* branch of the tree spotless, you may be assured."

"Oh, yes," Sarah retorted. "Paying an actress to pretend to be your bride is most aboveboard. I am surprised more young men have not thought of it."

"Justin has a reputation," he conceded, ignoring the barb. "Comes by it naturally. His father was infamous in his day. Aunt Agatha was cross as crabs after Justin's duel with Greywood. She fears his scapegrace ways will result in the title being passed on to me prematurely."

Harry blew a ponderous breath, like a man with many burdens. "She hounded me for months to wed and start my nursery. Wants legitimate heirs, not the bastards Justin is rumored to have spread about the country."

At Sarah's indignant glare, he managed an apologetic smile. "I ought not speak so baldly, should I? Even an actress has standards."

That last comment did nothing for Sarah's black mood as she studied the array of powders before her. It was time to get ready, even though there was not one chance in a hundred that she would get to play Ophelia tonight. Rose McIntosh was exceedingly healthy. An understudy could grow positively ancient waiting for Rose to succumb to so much as a headache.

Sarah could hardly blame Harry for his crude speech and his indelicate assumptions about her character. In a profession where women were viewed as no better than they had to be, upholding her reputation was a Sisyphean task. Her poor parents, were they still alive, would have been scandalized to know that she performed on stage for faceless strangers. They had enjoyed the little plays she had put on in the privacy of their home; for them, however, her talent was not for public consumption.

But they had been dead for five years, and her father's last pie-in-the-sky business investment had removed any possibility of an inheritance. When William was younger, she had scraped by. But now—Sarah sighed heavily. Acting provided a decent living if one were fortunate to get steady circuit work and could tolerate being considered a loose woman. The best money was to be made on the side, however, and most actresses had few scruples where those side activities were concerned. Sarah had long since gotten used to the leering Lotharios who haunted the theater seeking actresses eager to feather their nests in exchange for performances of an entirely different sort.

Sometimes it was hard to hold her head up as she walked past them through the playhouse doors. She was a respectable woman, even if no one else knew it. Her mother had taught her that virtue was its own reward. If only the reward were not so . . . intangible.

William would be mortified if he knew the truth—that his sister was not the sedate lady's companion he believed her to be but a member of one of the most disreputable professions in England. But her brother was tucked safely away at Eton, where a baron's son belonged and where she meant to keep him. He would get the education he deserved, if she had to do every menial job in the theater, including scrubbing floors.

However, that did not include joining the muslin set herself. God had indeed given her a talent, and while she plied it in a forum her parents would not have sanctioned, she would never hire her body out for satisfaction of a man's carnal appetites. For all the worldliness surrounding her, Sarah had only a vague notion of what those appetites involved; she only knew that she was determined to retain her honor.

Though it was not, perhaps, the simplest of tasks. She had recently discovered there were degrees of honor. This was the second time, for example, that Harry Trent had employed her to play the role of his wife for his Aunt Agatha who, with one foot in the grave, was determined that her wayward nephews would marry and produce heirs upon whom she could bestow her fortune. On the first occasion, Harry had driven her to his aunt's estate for tea, and Sarah had played the demure, deferential bride with great skill.

Harry had assured her that the charade was harmless, that Aunt Agatha's wits were dulled, and that Sarah was only helping to brighten the dear lady's remaining time in this life. Sarah's conscience had pricked her mightily, however, when the woman's eyes lit up upon being presented with Harry's "bride." After that, Sarah vowed to restrict her roles to more benign ones, such as the recent job she had taken reading Shakespeare to an earl's sickly wife.

But the earl and his wife had removed to Bath. Then William had written to say that his funds had run out. Another letter had come from the headmaster saying that William was showing great promise in his studies. Thanks to Rose McIntosh's superb health and the dearth of women's roles in *Hamlet,* one of Mr. Stinson's favorite plays, Sarah did not have money to send her brother. Mr. Stinson was extremely stingy when it came to paying understudies for a role they were never likely to perform.

Harry's offer of a substantial sum for one last performance as his bride was a godsend. He did not have the ready at the moment but had promised to pay her upon receipt of his quarter allowance next month.

Aunt Agatha's house party was next week, however, so her performance would be tendered on faith. Sarah eyed Harry dubiously.

"I mean it, Harry. This is the last time. Have you thought about how you will explain my absence from future family events?"

Harry waved a dismissive hand. "I will say you died in childbirth, or some such. She will never know the truth. Aunt Agatha is practically a recluse. She rarely leaves that musty country estate. Telling her you have gone to your final reward will buy me a proper period of mourning. She would not dare pester me to remarry for at least a year—perhaps two, if I am especially heartbroken."

Sarah shook her head. Harry was willing to go to absurd lengths to avoid the parson's noose. "Has it ever occurred to you simply to look for a real wife? That would solve your problem altogether."

"Why would I want a wife? Women are pleasant enough to

look at, and some have delightful, er, talents. But a wife is plaguesome. Why, George Ferguson's bride spent a fortune last year on a wardrobe that she promptly declared to be out of fashion this Season. Who would want to settle down with one woman, when he can have a different one every night? If you will pardon my frankness."

"I will pardon almost anything, Harry," Sarah said evenly, "providing you pay me on time."

"Do not worry. My allowance is due in three weeks. And now that Aunt Agatha believes me to be married, I think I can persuade her to increase the sum." He winked. "Especially if it seems we are starting a nursery."

Three weeks. With luck, William could scrape by until then. He was nearly living on charity as it was—and soon there would be Oxford to think about. Sarah sighed and began to apply Venetian talc to her skin as Harry watched in fascination. She supposed that a proper lady would not have allowed Harry access to her dressing room, but as her dressing area was simply an open alcove off the theater's back hall, the fact of his presence there seemed merely incidental and perfectly acceptable. After all, dozens of people rushed by nightly. A little screen behind which to change was all she had, and that she shared with several other actresses. There was no privacy in the theater.

In the mirror she could see Harry watching as the profusion of freckles on her nose slowly disappeared and the genteel baron's daughter vanished before his eyes. Sarah had learned the artifices of her profession well. She thoroughly enjoyed disappearing into a role; it was one of the pleasures of acting. Pretense took the edge off the harsh realities of life. On stage, she became someone else—a woman with passions that bubbled over without a care for society's strictures, a grand lady with a comfortable life and servants to command, a princess awaiting rescue from a lovestruck knight. Real life was not like that. It was all about changing one's clothes behind a dingy screen and hoping for a modicum of privacy, trying desperately to scrape together the funds to keep William at school, sharing a bed with another actress in a cramped room in a bawdy boardinghouse. And it was about holding one's head up high, no matter what people thought. It was important not to feel the humiliation. For then, all was lost.

When at last Sarah turned to face Harry, her skin was ghostly white and her reddish lashes had been darkened with a preparation of elderberries. Carefully, she tucked her thick auburn hair under a pale blond wig. Her green eyes, the only remaining genuine feature, gleamed with unnatural brightness.

"Good God, Sarah," Harry exclaimed. "You look very unlike yourself. In fact, you look rather . . ."

"Ill? Mad, perhaps?" She gave him one of her best eerie smiles. " 'They say the owl was a baker's daughter,' " she quoted, rolling her eyes heavenward. " 'Lord, we know what we are, but know not what we may be.' "

At his baffled look, she giggled. It was far from a carefree expression of mirth, however, and her eyes remained curiously impassive. " 'Tis not me, but Ophelia," she explained. "Do not worry, Harry. For Aunt Agatha, I shall once more be your demure, devoted bride. Exceedingly healthy and perfectly sane."

He nodded uncertainly.

Justin, Viscount Linton, stepped down from his claret-trimmed carriage with the easy grace of a natural athlete. His keen gray eyes narrowed, hawklike, as he took in the number of carriages waiting in the drive. It was as he suspected. Aunt Agatha was entertaining guests. Predominantly female, if he did not miss his guess.

These duty calls were damned inconvenient, especially now, as he had more pressing concerns in town. But he supposed he could spare a week in the country for the only woman who had never bored him. He was between mistresses, which perhaps accounted for the edgy restlessness that plagued him recently. Agatha had undoubtedly sensed that fact, as very little escaped her attention. She had begun campaigning again. The house party was ample proof of that. The determined woman never gave up hope of transforming her debauched nephew into a paragon of respectability.

The party would undoubtedly include an array of acceptable debutantes with their wary mothers. Justin scowled. Debutantes bored him. Their mothers, on the other hand, occasionally could be most interesting.

Stifling a yawn, he ascended the steps to his aunt's ancient mansion. Married women offered benefits that inexperienced debutantes did not. Once you got past the cat-and-mouse game they were obliged to play, the wives of other men could be most rapacious in their appetites. No one knew that better than a man of his repute.

"Hello, Sidney." Justin clapped his aunt's aging butler on the back with the familiarity of long acquaintance.

The butler allowed himself a slight smile and opened his mouth to return the greeting. Just then, Justin gave a mild exclamation.

"What is this?" he demanded, lightly touching the butler's ear and appearing to pull something from it. "Tsk, tsk," he said, shaking his head. "You ought to be more careful about your toilette, man."

As he beheld the queen of hearts dangling between Justin's fingers, the butler emitted a long-suffering sigh. "It is always a pleasure to see you, my lord."

Justin's laughter momentarily erased the lines of cynicism on his face as he stepped into the house. His aunt would be waiting somewhere upstairs to ring a peal over him. He might as well get it over with. Tolerating Aunt Agatha's tirades was the least he could do for the woman who had practically raised him. His harsh features softened further as he thought of his crusty relative.

Aunt Agatha did not approve of his antics or, indeed, most of his pursuits. Nor did she scruple to say so. It was regrettable that the scandalous reputation he had achieved in London had come to her attention here in Cheshire. In his dealings with the female sex, she thought him frankly predatory. Had the topic been suitable for discussion, he would have told her that he was careful to seduce only those women who wished to be seduced and that most women, in his experience, enjoyed the chase. They wore their virtue like a Sunday frock, pulling it on and off as the occasion warranted.

Except for his aunts—and he was beset by two of the troublesome creatures—Justin had never met a woman he truly liked. For him, congress between the sexes was simply a matter of mutual need.

Which brought him to a pressing problem. At the moment he had urgent need of a woman—an actress, and a very good one at that. One who was desperate, for the role he had in

mind would be dangerous. He had combed the London the-
aters for actresses willing to take the job, to no avail.

And who could blame them? It was not every day a woman
was asked to shoot a man.

Chapter Two

"In a moment you will meet my other nephew," Lady Claremont said. "Doubtless you have never seen him in town. Justin moves in rather exceptional circles."

The frown accompanying that last comment made it clear that Harry's aunt did not approve of those circles. Sarah adjusted her bonnet and smiled politely.

"Harry has spoken admiringly of his cousin," she said carefully, certain that she was not supposed to know of Viscount Linton's unsavory reputation. "You must be very proud of him, ma'am."

Lady Claremont rolled her eyes skyward. "Justin is an unrepentant rake. If Harry has not told you that by now, he is an idiot. Forewarned is forearmed."

Sarah blinked. At that first tea several weeks ago, Lady Claremont had merely regarded her with silent scrutiny as Harry gabbed away like a magpie. Sarah had taken the lady's silence as sign of a placid, perhaps even feeble nature. But the sharp-tongued grande dame who greeted her today did not seem at all feeble or dull-witted. In fact, Sarah had the dreadful feeling that Harry had painted a picture of his aunt that was not entirely accurate. Her stomach lurched queasily. She would have to be very careful not to raise Lady Claremont's suspicions.

Lady Claremont turned to greet the other guests as they entered the spacious parlor. In the whirlwind of introductions Sarah registered the presence of several young ladies and their mamas, an older gentleman who apparently lived nearby, and two men about Harry's age.

As she was trying to commit their names to memory, the back of her neck began to tingle uncomfortably. A strange sensation seized her, as if someone unseen were watching. Sarah felt suddenly awkward, as if she had stepped onstage and somehow forgotten her lines. Surreptitiously studying the other guests, she could not detect that anyone was paying her an extraordinary amount of attention. Still, the uneasy feeling did not go away.

Sarah smiled pleasantly, but her mouth grew dry and her heart began to race. The symptoms were not unlike those of stage fright, and although dozens of performances had inured her to an audience's scrutiny, she sensed that whoever watched her was no benign spectator.

There was a threat here, and it was imminent.

As if to confirm that fact, the space around her suddenly seemed to contract. The sunlight that had poured in through the window behind her vanished, chased by the abrupt appearance of a shadowy presence. With growing apprehension, Sarah turned.

A tall gentleman, his expression unreadable, bowed politely. His glossy chestnut hair was thick and unruly, tousled in the style of the day—although something told her the man had not a care for fashion. His eyes were a cool, unfathomable gray. They regarded her assessingly for a long moment without betraying any hint of the results of his scrutiny. There was about his features an arrogance that proclaimed his class, and while his expression was one of perfect civility, there was an unsettling insolence in his air that suggested his manners were but a thin veneer.

His gaze took in her leghorn bonnet with the pink ribbons, moved downward to her pink spencer and sedate cambric frock, and settled on her left hand, which held the glove she had removed in order to show Lady Claremont the opal ring that had once belonged to Harry's mother and which she now wore.

"So it is true, after all." He shook his head. "My condolences, madam."

"I beg your pardon?" Sarah managed, trying to ignore the hammering of her pulse as the intense gray eyes held hers. To her dismay, her breathing had grown strangely shallow. She was almost panting for air, like an actor who had run out of wind before his soliloquy was finished.

Her odd reaction seemed to interest him. His gaze held hers rather longer than was polite, and his lips curled in an unsettling smile.

"I take it you are my cousin's new bride, though I could scarcely credit that Harry had decided to wed." A brilliant shard of ice gleamed within those gray depths. "Now that I have seen you, I quite understand the appeal."

At her blank stare, he cocked his head consideringly. "How remiss of me. I am Linton, Harry's cousin. No doubt he has been filling your head with all manner of scandalous things about me. Most of them true, unfortunately."

The half smile that accompanied this last comment sent shivers down her spine.

"I am pleased to meet you, Lord Linton," Sarah said uncertainly. The queasiness in her stomach grew, as did the doubts about the wisdom of her masquerade. Even if Lady Claremont suspected nothing, there was still this man to get around—and he appeared to be extremely sharp-witted and not a little dangerous.

"To think that Harry has turned responsible," he continued blandly, with a slight shake of his head. "To be sure, our aunt's dictates can be most persuasive." He paused for a heartbeat. "But I imagine that Harry was not thinking of Aunt Agatha on his wedding night." This last comment was uttered with such polished civility that Sarah was completely taken aback.

It was undoubtedly acceptable for a man to flirt with a married woman, but all the nuanced performances Sarah had ever witnessed had not prepared her to penetrate the layers of meaning beneath his words, or indeed, to fathom his intent. She stared at him uncertainly. She had the notion that a proper young matron might take offense.

"I believe you are being impertinent, sir," she said with what she hoped was the right amount of sternness.

He nodded approvingly at her reprimand, although his eyes narrowed. "Quite right. You will forgive me, Mrs. Trent. I am not very respectable, you see." He eyed her mournfully and took her hand, squeezing it lightly.

Sarah's palm tingled as it met his cool, dry fingers. Her own skin was excessively damp and warm—to her great mortification, as she was certain that a proper young bride did not perspire when a man other than her husband touched her palm. Hers was an entirely inappropriate response. Something told her that he took great satisfaction in eliciting it.

"Good God, Justin! Leave the girl alone," commanded Lady

Claremont, who approached as Sarah was wondering why she could not seem to pull her hand from his. "Sarah has but just arrived. She must be longing to exchange her traveling clothes for something more comfortable. You must not bombard her with your rakish charm. And do not play all innocent with me," she admonished as his brows rose in a fair imitation of astonishment, "for I know that you are always looking for trouble."

"Not at all, Aunt," he replied gravely. "In my experience, it is the other way around." He gave Sarah a glittering smile and bowed deeply. "Adieu, madam, for the nonce."

Sarah almost expelled a sigh of relief at his departure. But as he turned to leave, Lord Linton abruptly halted and pulled something from the flapped pocket of his dove-colored tailcoat.

"I believe this is yours, Mrs. Trent," he said.

Sarah stared. In his hand was her glove. The same glove she had held most securely during their encounter. "How did you . . . ?" She broke off in utter confusion.

"Illusion, Mrs. Trent." He eyed her steadily. "The world is full of it, you see."

With that comment, he left the room. The sun came streaming cheerfully through the window again, but Sarah felt suddenly and decidedly ill.

Justin eyed his cousin over the rim of his glass. "Forgive me for not offering my congratulations sooner, old man. Your bride is a beauty. Most charming."

"What? Oh, er, thank you, Justin." Harry drank deeply of his port but did not meet his gaze. "Yes, Sarah is very talented."

Justin arched a brow. "Talented?"

Snickers were heard from one of the young men at the other end of the table. Harry eyed him blankly. Then a flush spread over his face, and he glared at the culprit. "See here!"

"We all know what you meant," Justin put in smoothly, "—that Mrs. Trent is a master of all the many details of running a home." Casually he stroked the stem of his glass. "I assume you are still living in London?"

"Er, yes." Harry shifted uncomfortably and took another sip of his port.

"You have given up your bachelor's rooms, then?"

"Not precisely. That is, ah, I have let them to a friend."

Justin nodded. "I see. You must give me your new direction.

I will say it was considerate of you to spare us the spectacle of a lavish ceremony at St. George's." He studied his cousin, intrigued by Harry's uneasiness with the topic. "How long have you been married, exactly?"

Harry spilled a drop of wine on the table, and his thumb made rapid, irregular circles as he rubbed the spot absentmindedly. "Two months. The wedding was, ah, very sudden."

"Anticipated the vows, eh, Trent?" This knowing comment came from Mr. Throckmorton, Aunt Agatha's elderly neighbor. "Nothing to feel ashamed of—you married the gel, after all. Often wish I had done the same with my Ellen. That long betrothal nearly drove me mad. Now she is gone these two years and more. What I wouldn't give to have had those few extra months in her arms."

Horace Throckmorton had had too much to drink, Justin decided as he watched tears spring to the older man's eyes. Throckmorton had always been a mawkish sentimentalist—hanging on to his wife's sleeve and never bothering to hide his dependence on his lady's affection. God save a man from such a fate. It was embarrassing enough to watch, never mind the mortification of enduring such a lowering condition.

Justin doubted very much that Harry was in similar thrall to the lovely Mrs. Trent. Harry was not the sort of man to feel deeply about any woman—even if she came with an extraordinary pair of emerald eyes. His cousin might be enamored of his wife's indisputable charms, but his heart almost certainly had not been touched.

That was fortunate for Harry, as Mrs. Trent's affections did not seem overly engaged either. Oh, Justin had seen the warm smiles and affectionate glances she shot Harry over dinner. And when the ladies had withdrawn, she bestowed a look of tender regret on her husband. These gestures seemed completely genuine. But his senses had given him other signals as well: the rapid intake of her breath and widening of her pupils when Justin greeted her, the dampness of her skin when he had taken her hand, and the air of distraction that had made her such an easy target for his parlor trick with the glove.

Those were not the responses of a woman who only had eyes for her husband. Curiosity filled him. Perhaps Harry had not satisfied her. He could not imagine that his cousin was a terribly skilled lover. And though she dressed demurely enough, with her reddish hair tamed into a sedate bun at her neck, Justin had a notion that Sarah Trent was a woman of passion. Perhaps Throckmorton was right and that passion had once gotten out of hand. Perhaps she regretted being shackled for life because of that momentary indiscretion. Or perhaps she simply had hopes of becoming a viscountess. Justin smiled grimly. If all went as planned, she might get her wish rather quickly. He tried to imagine her with the Linton emeralds draped around her swanlike neck, then frowned as he realized the dazzling sight would be wasted on Harry's untrained eyes.

The lovely Mrs. Trent was an intriguing mystery. His senses tingled at the thought of unraveling her secrets. Whether she knew it or not, she was sending out signals that ordinarily he would have seized upon. But even a man of his repute would not stoop so low as to seduce his cousin's wife, no matter that the woman might not be the chaste young bride she appeared. None knew better than he that appearances could be deceiving, especially when it came to women; some women, however, were best left alone.

Justin drank deeply from his glass. She was a luscious eyeful. As long as he restricted himself to the simple acknowledgment of that fact, everything would be fine.

Nighttime in Lady Claremont's house was quiet—too quiet, for it meant that every noise came to Sarah's attention with startling clarity. She had been given the room adjoining Harry's in the family wing, while the other guests had rooms on the opposite side of the house.

Lady Claremont always retired early, so only Harry and Lord Linton moved about in this part of the house at night. Harry imbibed freely with the gentlemen, and his presence in the hall typically was accompanied by loud whistling or humming that woke her from a sound sleep. A decisive slamming of his door customarily marked his return to his room.

Lord Linton, on the other hand, moved with the stealth of a cat. She never heard his footsteps—even though his room was across from hers—or the closing of the heavy door to his chamber. He seemed to walk in ghostly silence, like some restless soul seeking surcease from ancient burdens. She wondered where he had learned such furtive habits.

A crashing noise startled Sarah from this disquieting reverie.

There was nothing ghostly or silent about the accompanying loud oath and the heavy thud against her door. With some trepidation, she rose from her bed and peeked out into the hall.

Harry, obviously very much in his cups, was leaning against the wall, scarcely able to hold himself upright. His face brightened as he saw her.

"Ah, m'blushing bride," he mumbled in a slurred voice. He turned and spoke to someone over his shoulder. "Didn't I tell you, Justin? Sarah always waits up. Devoted to me, she is."

Sarah had not noticed Lord Linton's presence in the hall. Her gaze met his, and she flushed. Her sedate flannel nightgown revealed far less of her than the gown she had worn to dinner, but his obvious awareness of the fact that she was in her bed clothing made her blush to the roots of her hair.

There was no drunken leer on his face, however, no intimate caress in his eyes—only a wary narrowing of his gaze. He looked very much the sober gentleman, in stark contrast to her thoroughly foxed husband.

Harry was not handling himself well. Sarah doubted very much he would negotiate the few feet to the door of his room without assistance. Lord Linton appeared to come to the same conclusion.

"Come, Harry. Let me summon a servant. In your condition, you will not manage to undress yourself." He put one arm under Harry's and urged him toward his room.

"Not so fast, Justin. If I need help with my clothes, Sarah is here." Harry cast her a leering smile. "What is a wife for, anyway, if not to see to one's needs?"

Lord Linton shrugged and removed his arm, evidently content to leave Harry at her door. Sarah gave a little cry of dismay.

"Oh, no!" She put her hand to her mouth as both men looked at her in surprise. "That is, 'tis late, Harry. We both need our sleep."

Lord Linton eyed her curiously. Harry's mouth pursed in a childish pout. "Now, now, Sarah. What will Justin be thinking if you refuse to take me into your room like a proper wife?" He gave her what was clearly intended to be a meaningful look; to her eye it was merely a drunken smirk. Sarah's temper flared. She would not be intimidated by an inebriated lout.

"You will get no consoling from me in your state. If Lord Linton will not assist you, you can very well sleep there in the hall." She turned her back in what she hoped was a reasonable imitation of wifely outrage. She had every intention of slamming the door in his face when a clumsy hand clamped down on her shoulder.

"See here, Sarah. You ought not talk to me like that. I have a right to claim what is mine."

Harry might be out of his senses, but that did not mean he was harmless. His hand felt heavy on her shoulder, and his other arm snaked about her waist. Sarah bit back a sharp rebuke and forced herself to remember how much she needed this job. She could not make a scene and risk raising Lord Linton's suspicions about the true nature of their relationship, but neither did she intend to allow Harry to manhandle her. Paralyzed with indecision, she stood motionless at her door. Harry took her stillness as assent.

"There. I told you she would come around, Justin." He took her hand and made to pull her into her room. That act finally snapped Sarah's temper.

"Stop it, you odious man!" she cried. She jerked her hand free, but Harry simply fumbled for the other one.

"Your bride does not appear to hold you in particular regard at the moment, Harry," Lord Linton drawled. There was something in his tone that made Sarah eye him sharply.

Harry glowered at his cousin. "This is between a man and his wife, Justin," he grumbled belligerently.

"Perhaps." Steel glinted in the gray gaze. "And perhaps not."

For a moment Harry watched his cousin uncertainly. Then he scoffed derisively. "That is rich! The infamous Linton playing a lady's defender. I suppose if I live long enough, I may even see *you* take the parson's noose!"

"I should not count on it," came the sharp reply. "At the moment, your life expectancy is exceedingly short."

With that, Lord Linton grabbed Harry by his neckcloth and propelled him down the hall. At the door of Harry's room, he thrust his hapless charge inside. Sarah heard a resounding thump as Harry landed on the floor.

In the next instant Lord Linton stood before her. "Your husband finds himself in more need of sleep than he realized at first," he said gravely. "He has informed me that he is not to be disturbed further tonight. You will comply with his wishes in this?"

"Y-yes, of course," Sarah stammered.

The viscount bowed politely and turned to leave. "Wait!" she cried. He halted, arching a brow. "That is, I—thank you, Lord Linton." Sarah flushed, feeling supremely awkward and greatly aware of her dishabille.

An expression of irritation crossed his harsh features. "I am in no mood for thanks, Mrs. Trent. You have just caused me to break two of my rules."

Sarah eyed him in confusion. "Rules? What rules, sir?"

"One of them is never to interfere in a dispute between a man and his wife. Unless I happen to be the cause of that dispute, of course."

"I see. And the other?"

His gaze swept over her, and this time there was nothing veiled in his raw appreciation of her state of undress. As she watched, mesmerized, he reached out and straightened the shoulder of her gown, which had slipped during her skirmish with Harry.

"The other," he growled as his fingers withdrew abruptly, "does not bear discussing."

Breakfast was an informal arrangement. Guests accustomed to country hours could be found doing justice to a plate of kidneys and ham long before the others even thought of bestirring themselves. Since Lord Linton was used to town ways, Sarah decided there was little chance of encountering him at this early hour. She had no wish to see him so soon after last night's mortifying episode.

When she stepped into the dining room, however, he and Horace Throckmorton were sitting at the table. Mr. Throckmorton nodded a cordial greeting and resumed his attack on his food.

Sarah felt Lord Linton's speculative gaze as she helped herself from the covered dishes on the sideboard; he was still staring as she slipped into a chair at the far end of the table. Though he nodded and made agreeable sounds throughout Mr. Throckmorton's monologue on new farming methods, his eyes remained on her.

Thoroughly unnerved by his silent scrutiny, Sarah brought the coffee cup shakily to her lips, only to have some of the liquid spill on the white damask cloth.

Her cheeks grew warm as the small brown stain spread steadily outward. She was not usually so clumsy, nor so easily embarrassed. Surely she was making too much of things. Lord Linton had probably forgotten last night's incident altogether. If his gaze lingered on her this morning, it was merely his insolent way. By now, he had undoubtedly found something else to interest him.

Sarah took a deep breath, keeping her eyes on the stain. Slowly, she felt her composure return and with it a calmer state of mind. Reason told her that Lord Linton was not the sort of man to occupy himself with thoughts of his cousin's marriage or, indeed, of her. He would see nothing remarkable or suspicious in the fact that she and Harry had quarreled. Many couples did, she was certain. She was also quite certain that Lord Linton saw women in their nightgowns rather often. All in all, last night must have barely registered with him. There was no reason to feel this strange and fearful excitement in his presence. Her mother had always told her that her imagination was entirely too fanciful. Her mother had been invariably right.

Sarah looked up, confident that his attention was now elsewhere.

Lord Linton's gaze had not wavered. Lazy speculation—and something else besides—filled those enigmatic eyes. That something else made her heart lurch in her chest.

The ham felt dry and tasteless in her mouth. Sarah gulped her coffee, trying to ward off the growing panic. Her imagination had not led her astray. Her initial instincts had been right. There was danger here, and it was gazing at her from depths as murky as a storm-tossed lake.

Some of the coffee went down the wrong way. A coughing fit seized her, and the two men halted their meal to look at her. Sarah managed a weak, reassuring smile. Mr. Throckmorton immediately returned to his plate of kidneys. Lord Linton did not.

"You seem disturbed this morning," he observed quietly when she had herself under control. "I trust everything is well?"

Sarah flushed beet red. He was obviously asking if she had slept unmolested by her husband.

"Yes. Thank you."

He frowned, as if unsatisfied by the brief reply. For a moment he looked as if he would pursue the matter, but in the end he did not.

In fact, he did not say another word for the rest of the meal.

Chapter Three

Glumly Sarah fingered the daisy chain she had fashioned from the pale yellow flowers in a meadow near Lady Claremont's stables. Neither the daisies nor her walk through the woods had lifted her troubled spirits.

Many of the guests—and to Sarah's dismay, Lady Claremont herself—had joined a hunt organized by one of the neighbors. A demanding chase over hill and dale was not the act of a feeble woman with one foot in the grave. The more time she spent with Lady Claremont, the more Sarah became convinced that the woman was not only fit but awake on every suit. This knowledge made her realize just how foolish was Harry's plan. She did not think Lady Claremont suspected anything yet, but it would take all her skill to carry off this masquerade for the balance of the visit.

Unfortunately, her acting abilities seemed utterly useless when Lord Linton was around.

Sarah had been intensely aware of him from the beginning, but since the night he rescued her from Harry's boorish advances, he had never been out of her mind. She could not think straight in his presence; she responded to him on some visceral level her will could not control. Still, she might have fared well enough had not he suddenly become inordinately attentive. And while it might appear to others that Lord Linton was merely making his new relative feel welcome, Sarah doubted that the viscount had ever acted out of altruism.

There was no need for him to volunteer to partner her in whist when Mr. Throckmorton was perfectly happy to do so. They won every rubber, of course; Lord Linton had a way with cards. Nor was there any need for him to escort her into dinner. Lady Dressmire was the highest-ranking lady and by rights should have had his arm. Such was Lord Linton's charm that

the countess merely beamed at him when he left her to the sal-
low Sir Peregrine.

Nothing in Sarah's experience had prepared her for the effect
Lord Linton had on her senses. She could see why his reputation as a rake was well deserved. He had a way of looking at a
woman that made her blush to think of the thoughts behind
those intense gray eyes. They radiated a magnetism that left her
powerless to turn away when he came toward her.

What made her especially uneasy was the fact that he was
something of a conjurer. One night he entertained the group for
hours with dazzling card tricks. Sarah knew there was nothing
truly magical about them, but she could not discern his secrets
no matter how hard she tried. Moreover, Lord Linton seemed to
be familiar with all manner of mysterious arts. When Mr.
Throckmorton had complained of the toothache, the viscount
handed him a powder he said would relieve the pain. For Lady
Dressmire's gout, he recommended a potion from wolfsbane, a
purplish flower which, he warned, could be poisonous if taken
in excess.

The man was too shrewd by half. His eyes were too knowing, too changeable—hard as stone one moment, soft as velvet
the next. Sarah had no idea there could be so many shades of
gray. Watching Lord Linton converse with one of the young
debutantes and then turn to greet her was to witness alchemy—
the transformation of dull gunmetal into luminous silver.

Although there was nothing unseemly in his conversation,
those eyes conjured bewitching, mysterious images that re-
pelled, yet drew her. She prayed that the viscount was not a
reader of minds, as some of the charlatans she had encountered
on the circuit had claimed to be, for her thoughts were occupied
more and more with him, and in ways that were not at all
proper.

Had her gaze lingered on him at dinner last night? Had she
blushed when his eyes held hers over his wineglass? Had Lady
Claremont noticed these things? Sarah vowed to be more careful. An actress ought to be able to put aside such distractions.

Lord Linton knew precisely what he was doing, of that she
was certain. His mastery of the cards was nothing to his skill
with ladies. Did he suspect that she was not Harry's wife? Was
there something in that hallway scene that had alerted him?
Was he trying to expose her, to draw her into making a mistake

that would spell disaster? Or had he simply formed the intention of seducing his cousin's bride? Sarah had encountered men like that in the theater, men with no morals and no concern for the effect of their actions on others. Was Lord Linton such a man?

"You look exceedingly troubled, Mrs. Trent. Has Harry abandoned you for the charms of the fox?"

Sarah jumped. The viscount was propped against a tree not ten paces before her. Oddly, she had not sensed his presence. It was as if he had suddenly materialized from the air around her.

"You do have a way of sneaking up on people, Lord Linton," she said irritably.

He bowed. "I apologize, madam. Since I know precisely where I am at any particular moment, it never occurs to me to impart the information to others."

Sarah shot him a dubious glare, hoping he did not sense how his sudden appearance had unsettled her. "Harry has indeed gone off with the hunt," she said haughtily, "but I assure you, I am not bereft. I was just enjoying my solitary walk." She looked him a challenge, making certain he understood the point.

"And I have interrupted it. I apologize." A smile hovered about his lips. "That is the second time I have been forced to make my apologies in as many minutes. What do you make of that?"

"I make nothing of it, my lord," Sarah snapped as she made to pass him by. Without warning, his hand snaked out and caught hers. He gripped her gently, but his touch felt like fire on her skin, and his eyes shimmered with the force of an intense power only lightly restrained. Involuntarily, Sarah gave a little shiver.

"You are cold," he observed, the pupils of his eyes contracting, then widening as his hand moved almost imperceptibly to her waist.

Never had she felt so alarmed in his presence. The sense of danger was almost palpable. Strangely, it was not fear for her safety that troubled her but something else, something unknown and wickedly tantalizing that held her rooted to the spot like a frightened rabbit.

Defiantly Sarah lifted her chin. Not for nothing was she an actress. "Cold?" she echoed in a frosty tone. "Not at all. But I must ask you to remove your hand from my person, Lord Linton. I cannot think your constant handling at all appropriate."

"Handling?" His brows shot skyward. "My dear Mrs. Trent, whatever are you talking about?"

Sarah's patience snapped. Anger at his insolent guile put reckless words on her tongue. "I understand what you are all about, my lord. I have seen men such as you. I know your type quite well."

His mouth twitched derisively. "Oh? And what type is that? From your vast experience, of course."

Aghast, Sarah realized she had revealed too much. "I only mean to say that you are far too attentive," she said, flushing. "I find your manner unsettling and your impudence insulting. Since that night when Harry was . . . indisposed, you have singled me out. I do not think it fitting that you look at me quite that way, nor escort me into dinner instead of Lady Dressmire, nor suddenly appear from the woods like a wizard when I am very much alone. I am your cousin's wife, and there is nothing amiss with my marriage, no matter what you may think you saw that night."

"You are plainspoken, madam." His gaze was unreadable, although his tone bore more velvet than steel.

"I value the truth," Sarah retorted, hoping lightning would not suddenly descend from the clouds and strike her dead. "And the truth is that I welcome your friendship, but nothing more. Harry has his foibles, but he is everything I could want in a husband." She held her breath. If he was going to challenge her statement, now would be the time. She might as well know what she was up against.

"You think I seek to seduce you, Mrs. Trent?" His eyes remained shuttered, but now she detected a faintly predatory gleam in those silvery depths.

Sarah's color deepened, along with the certainty that she was woefully unmatched in this game of wits. He had indeed challenged her, but on a level she had not anticipated. The mere fact that he had uttered the word *seduce* had given weight to the concept, like a sinful thought suddenly spoken aloud in church over the vicar's rambling sermon. Now he was waiting to see how she would respond.

"It is *you* who are guilty of excessive plain-speaking, Lord Linton," she insisted, summoning every ounce of bravado that was in her. "I would never make such an accusation." She paused, lowering her gaze. "My experience of the world is not broad like yours. I am no London sophisticate. I do not know the art of flirtation, nor am I comfortable with it."

"And yet you manage it exceptionally well."

"I beg your pardon?" Baffled, Sarah stared at him.

"Perhaps it is a skill that comes to you naturally," he said in a low voice.

"I do not know what you are talking about," she insisted, wondering whether he meant to expose her after all. "I only want your friendship, sir."

He cocked his head and his lips curled disdainfully. "I do not have friendships with women."

"I see. Then we have nothing further to discuss." Sarah wrenched her hand away and started toward the house.

"Wait."

What was it about that one-word command that made her halt in her tracks like some docile filly schooled to his voice?

"What is it?" she asked, not daring to turn toward him.

"I may not have friendships with women, Mrs. Trent, but I am capable of conversations with them." He paused. "And of apologizing most sincerely for any discomfort I have caused you."

Now he was at her side. To her surprise, he did not touch her but kept himself at a respectable distance. Sarah ventured a look at his face. His eyes were solemn. She had no way of knowing if he was sincere but fervently prayed that he was.

"I appreciate your apology, Lord Linton. Perhaps I have been too quick to take offense."

He grinned suddenly, and Sarah nearly caught her breath at the vitality in his face. It occurred to her that it was the first time she had seen him smile. "I should not be so quick to retract your accusations, madam. You have made me thoroughly ashamed of my behavior, a rarity, I assure you. Surely you would wish to make me grovel as long as possible."

"I have not retracted them," Sarah said warily, for she could feel herself being drawn to this devilishly charming side of him.

"Of course not." His smile vanished. "May I escort you back to the house? I imagine the hunt will be over soon."

Sarah did not elect to take his arm, but she did not object when he fell into step beside her. "How is it that you did not go

off with the others?" she asked politely, trying to fill the silence
as they walked.

"I do not hunt small animals," he replied. "It is not worth
even the little effort involved. I prefer bigger game."

"What sort of game, Lord Linton?"

"The kind with two legs, Mrs. Trent."

Sarah eyed him in confusion. "I do not understand."

He gave her a thin smile. " 'Tis just as well, madam. I would
not wish to unsettle you further."

"I declare, Justin, you are the plague of my old age."

Justin gave his aunt a wryly affectionate smile. "I suppose I
must accept your characterization of me, Aunt. You, however,
are far from old."

"Pish! Spare me your flattery." But a pleased flush spread
over Lady Claremont's features.

" 'Tis true. Any woman who can ride as you do is hardly
doddering. You are a welcome addition to the field at any age."

With a regal nod, his aunt accepted the compliment. "My
neighbors have never objected to my hunting with them, although Horace continually warns me about the dangers. Poor
man! Just because his wife fell and broke her neck does not
mean that every female rider is so doomed. I have not fallen off
a horse in years. We had a good run yesterday, Justin. Why did
you not join us? You used to love a good hunt."

Justin sighed. As always, Aunt Agatha came to the point in
her own inimitable fashion. He had had several such "chats"
with his aunt since his arrival, although they had been the usual
good-natured harangues about how it was past time he find a
wife. This time, however, she wore a somber expression. He
had the sense that he was about to learn why she had summoned him from London.

"I have no interest in running a fox to ground at the moment,
Aunt. More pressing matters command my attention."

"I hope you are not referring to Harry's wife," Lady Claremont said severely. "I understand the two of you were spotted
yesterday emerging from the woods together. I have seen the
way you look at her. I warn you, Justin, I shall not stand for
your rakish ways here."

An unaccustomed warmth spread over his features. His aunt
was alone in her singular ability to make him feel like a small

boy again. She was right, of course. Since seeing Harry's wife in that silly tent of a gown the other night, he had been unable to rid his mind of the image of her in more revealing bed-clothes—or none at all. For the first time in his life he envied his cousin.

Usually he had more control over himself than his behavior of the last few days had indicated. In London, no one expected restraint of him—nor, he supposed, did he expect it of himself. No one looked askance at his dissolute behavior, nor imagined him anything other than a rogue and a scapegrace. Only he knew how hard he had worked to achieve his reputation, and to what end. Justin frowned. Perhaps he had allowed appearances to blur the edges of reality. Perhaps he had become that rogue in truth. Perhaps that was why he could not keep Harry's wife from his mind. That scene outside her room had made him ex-ceedingly curious about Harry's relationship with her, and he had conveniently forgotten his vow to avoid a flirtation. Obvi-ously he had been making a cake of himself. The lady herself set him aright just yesterday. And now, his aunt.

Justin sighed. "I have committed no impropriety with Mrs. Trent. It pains me to see how low your estimation of my honor has sunk."

"My estimation of your honor is as it always has been, Justin," she replied sharply. "You have your own code in these matters, and I have yet to puzzle it out. I do know that you are not above angling for another man's wife. Even in Cheshire, word of your activities reaches me."

He smiled. "I am certain that any reports you have received are greatly exaggerated."

She turned to pick up her tea. "You deny that you fought a duel with young Lord Greywood over his wife?"

So this was the bee in Aunt Agatha's bonnet. He might have known. He let her words go unanswered in the long silence that followed them. Finally, he spoke. "I do not deny it," he said carefully.

"The dowager is a family friend, Justin." Amid the reproach in her voice was an odd note, and Justin wondered whether his aunt knew the whole truth about the elder Lady Greywood. "How could you do such a thing? To seduce Evangeline's daughter-in-law, then nearly kill her son in a duel . . ."

"I did not seduce her daughter-in-law," he said coolly. "The lady has strayed before and will do so again. I merely happened to be there when she decided to wander."

"Do not insult my intelligence," his aunt said quietly.

Anger surged through him. Justin rose. "This topic is entirely unsuitable. At all events it is my affair alone." He paused, then added in a clipped voice, "I regret any harm to your friendship with the dowager. It is not my intent to wound you."

Gnarled hands gripped the cup and saucer so fiercely that they rattled. "That is just the point, is it not?" she demanded, her faded blue eyes piercing his. "You do not think these things through. You cannot do just what you wish and then step back and disclaim all responsibility. People *do* get hurt. That is something I have learned in my life."

Justin forced himself to remain silent. God willing, his aunt would never know how agonizingly thorough his mental calculations *had* been—or how costly. There was no art so demanding as the art of illusion.

"I simply cannot reconcile your behavior with the sober young man who grew up in my house." His aunt shook her head. "What did I do, Justin, to have failed you so?"

Her voice trembled, and Justin moved instantly to her side. "Do not despair, Aunt," he said lightly. "Had you not taken me in, I daresay I would be in Newgate by now." He gave her a bolstering smile, but she did not seem consoled.

"I have not seen you so . . . so unhinged since your parents' deaths." Her voice trailed off, and he knew she was thinking of those black days, the ones that had made him far older than his years. "I know I was no substitute for your parents, but when you grew into a confident and diligent young man, I assumed you were content, at least."

Content. Now that was a nice irony. The state was as foreign to him as flying. "You must not blame yourself for my behavior," he said gruffly. "You were father and mother to me, far more than . . ." He paused. "Than I deserved," he finished. But his aunt had the bit between her teeth. It did not surprise him when she refused to let things be.

"Reports reach me weekly of your outlandish activities," she said sternly, setting her tea aside again. "Dueling, wenching, flaunting one disreputable mistress after another, seducing other men's wives, drinking deeply at gaming hells . . ."

"Your sources must be quite exhausted simply keeping track of my nefarious deeds," he said dryly.

"It is not like you," she insisted. "You are behaving just like your father. And look where it got him—into an early grave."

His father. Now she had the nub of it. "You talk as though you believe my father deserved his death," Justin said in a tight voice.

Aunt Agatha's face seemed to collapse. "Your poor father was a wretched and tormented man, but he deserved to live. As did my sister—God bless her weak soul."

Memories washed over him. His mother's tearstained face and the bruises that did not fade, her gently rounding stomach and its promise of new life. His father's bloated features contorted with rage. A game that was not a game.

A sigh, heavy and burdensome as a shroud, filled the air. For a moment, he thought it was his. Until his aunt spoke in the same heavy tones.

"What's done is done, Justin," she said wearily. "You are twenty-eight years old. If your father were here, I am certain he would tell you that he regretted his own behavior and that it is past time for you to put your dissolute ways behind you."

"Ah, yes. And to set up my nursery." Now they were on familiar, more manageable ground. He smiled grimly. "I have no time for such foolishness, Aunt. The future will take care of itself."

She threw out her hands in exasperation. "What torments you so, Justin? Have you gambled away your fortune? Everything I have is yours. Your reputation can be restored, providing you change your behavior. All I need do is whisper a few words in the right ears and all will be put right again."

Justin bent stiffly and kissed her cheek. "I appreciate your concern, Aunt, but I do not need your assistance." Yet the truth weighed on him, along with the sorrow in her lined face. He hesitated, then added, "You ought not put so much faith in those reports, Aunt."

Aunt Agatha dabbed her eyes, then quickly looked away, and he knew she was embarrassed by her momentary display of emotion. She eschewed sentiment and all displays of it, public or private. When next she met his gaze, she had herself under control. All trace of emotion had vanished. Her tone was matter-of-fact.

"I do not truck with gossip, Justin, but one cannot ignore certain things that come to one's attention."

"Promise me that you will believe nothing until you see the evidence with your own eyes. It is important that I have your word."

Her eyes narrowed. "What is this about, Justin?"

"Just promise, Aunt."

"Very well." She sighed. "I promise."

"Good. That is settled." He exhaled deeply, feeling the weight of his burden. "Now, if you will excuse me, I have things to attend to."

She frowned. " 'Pressing things,' if I recall. But I still have no idea what they are. You say this does not concern her?"

"Her?" His brow furrowed.

"Sarah."

His face relaxed. "Of course not."

The house party was over, thank goodness. Sarah's nerves were stretched almost to the breaking point. She could not wait to see her little rented room next to the Chester playhouse and to plunge back into her own life—where one learned one's lines and delivered them and that was that. The company would move on to Shrewsbury next week. With luck, Rose would be wearying of Ophelia by then.

With that buoying thought, Sarah gave Harry a cordial smile as he handed her into his carriage. Her good-byes were said. Lady Claremont had even unbent enough to allow Sarah to plant a kiss on her cheek. Sarah was certain the lady had suspected nothing.

Lord Linton was another matter, however. Though he had been all that was proper since that day she encountered him in the woods, she could not escape the feeling that he was very curious about her relationship with Harry. The man was as shrewd as he was handsome.

With a sigh of relief, Sarah settled back against the squabs. She would soon be home, or what passed for it to an itinerant actress. She forced from her mind thoughts of the dear little house in Surrey that had been her family home.

As the carriage rolled over the rutted road, the tension left her body. No longer did she have to carry on a civil conversation with Harry, and he did not seem to mind her silence. He said little, and within a few miles was snoring loudly. Sarah smiled. He really was not such a bad sort. She closed her eyes. Soon she, too, was asleep.

She was still groggy when Harry deposited her at her door. "Another week and I shall be able to pay you," he promised.

"I shall depend upon it," she said sternly as he set her little valise inside her room. The trunks containing the fine clothes he had provided her for the house party remained with the carriage. He would probably give them to a mistress, not that she cared. Harry's concerns were no longer hers. She removed the opal ring from his left hand and returned it to him.

Putting it in his pocket, he made as if to leave. For a moment he looked at the floor. Then his gaze met hers. "Your performance was very good, Sarah," he said sheepishly. "I am sorry to have been such a trial."

"Never mind, Harry. We are quits now." She gave him a bracing smile. "At least we learned that we are not a good match, did we not?"

"Quite." He grinned. "But I still say you've got bottom."

Sarah sighed wearily. "Good-bye, Harry."

After he left, Sarah sank gratefully into a chair, suddenly beset by a persistent headache and even more persistent memories.

No matter how she tried to control her thoughts, they were filled with images of a pair of intense gray eyes, unreadable except for the odd light there that made her skin ripple in forbidden pleasure.

Her reaction to him puzzled her. To be sure, Lord Linton was wickedly sure of himself and devastatingly skilled with the ladies. His easy confidence and knowing charm ought to have been offputting. Instead, Sarah found herself entertaining all manner of inappropriate thoughts. She wondered whether he would be so sure of himself if he were courting a woman in earnest. Had he ever done so?

Probably not. Lord Linton was a jaded rake, not the sort to fall victim to Cupid's arrow. Nor would he be in thrall to any woman. He would always be in control, always in charge. The world danced to his tune, and women were just partners in the dance. One woman was as good as another. If his eyes had studied her a bit longer than necessary, if his fingers had lingered overlong at her waist, it was nothing to flatter herself about.

Why was she dwelling on such things? To him she was Harry's wife, not an eligible female. By the time Harry announced her unfortunate death to the world, Lord Linton probably would not even recall what she looked like. At all events, she would never see him again. That, surely, was for the best. A woman like her had no business mooning over a man like that. No matter that she was as wellborn as he, he would never see an actress as anything except a female to be used and discarded at the first sign of boredom.

Sarah felt her face grow warm at her foolishness. With renewed energy, she threw herself into the task of cleaning her room, which had accumulated a fair amount of dust in her absence. Her roommate, one of the other actresses in the company, was not one to exert herself with a broom or mop. At last Sarah sat down at the little table and began to compose a letter to her brother. Slowly, her headache began to vanish.

The peremptory knock at the door fractured the peaceful atmosphere in the little room. With irritation, Sarah rose from her chair. It was probably Mr. Stinson informing her of her new role and the paltry sum he intended to pay her for it.

She threw open the door.

Lord Linton stood there, his mouth curved in a sardonic smile.

"Mrs. Trent. Or should I say Miss Armistead? Allow me to say how very much I enjoyed your recent performance. I, for one, found it most inspiring."

And with those daunting words, he crossed the threshold into her room.

Chapter Four

Anger settled over him like a well-worn mantle, its familiar touch keeping dangerous thoughts at bay. Chief among them was disappointment, he realized in chagrin.

Why should he taste disappointment at this proof of her perfidy, when it was no more than he had come to expect from the female sex? He had known all along that Sarah Trent was hiding something beneath her demure, respectable exterior. His imagination had provided tantalizing images of a woman with powerful yearnings, a woman who—despite her married state—still waited to be fully awakened to the passionate side of her nature.

But he had been wrong. The charming Mrs. Trent was merely a fraud. That was her secret—not some burning, unquenched desire. The only secret desire Sarah Armistead possessed was for money. She had taken them all in.

Even now, she had the temerity to stare at him as if he had committed some grave impropriety by invading her room—as if she had the slightest notion of what constituted proper behavior. She was an actress, all right, and a damned good one. Moreover, her natural assets aided her immeasurably. Looking at that dusting of freckles on her nose and the errant auburn tendrils curling around her heart-shaped face, Justin found it nearly impossible to believe that she was an impostor.

But she was. And he was an idiot for allowing himself to be taken in. For wishing, even for an instant, that it was not so.

With a resounding thud, he closed the door. He rounded on her, pleased to see apprehension spring to her face. Vengeance sharpened his senses, staving off all else.

Except for one tiny thought. Could Sarah Armistead be some diabolical answer to his prayer? His gaze narrowed thoughtfully. It was no worse than he deserved.

                    *   *   *

"Do tell me again how much you value the truth, Miss Armistead," he snarled. "It was one of your most effective lines."

Involuntarily, Sarah took a step backward. The viscount filled the space around him like an actor with the uncanny talent of consuming an entire stage. Lady Claremont's large rooms had not allowed her to fully appreciate the way his imposing form could dominate his surroundings. Then again, perhaps it was his eyes that gave him such presence as they gleamed with the fury of an avenging angel—a fallen angel, at that, with a gaze as hard as perdition.

"I knew actresses were mercenary creatures, but I thought it was customary to ply your talents with the masculine sex." Even his voice was hard, brittle, like the fractured veneer that thinly contained his all-too-evident rage. "Tell me, Miss Armistead. When did you turn to bamboozling elderly ladies? And how much did my foolish cousin pay you for that charming little masquerade?"

"Not enough to put up with your theatrics, Lord Linton," she retorted, indignation at his high-handed invasion of her sanctuary giving her courage. "And I do *not* recall inviting you in."

Smoky anger darkened his eyes, and a dangerous gleam in their depths made her wish she had not been so impudent. "Who are you, little minx?" he demanded, stepping closer. "Other than an enticing bit of muslin without sense enough to know when the game is up?"

Sarah's face reddened. "I will not have you calling me names, Lord Linton. I am entirely respectable, and as well-bred as you, I might add."

His dark brows arched skyward. "Do I look the fool, Miss Armistead? I assure you I am not."

"Very well, sir. You are not a fool. You merely behave like one." Sarah's chin tilted mulishly. She was sorely overmatched in this game of wits, but her own temper had made her reckless. Bit of muslin, indeed!

A muscle tightened in his jaw, and Sarah wondered if she had gone too far. For a moment he said nothing. Then an intriguing light appeared in his eyes.

"I ought to summon the magistrate."

"The magistrate?" Sarah's eyes widened in alarm. "You have no grounds!"

"On the contrary, Miss Armistead," he said coolly. "You have conspired to fool a wealthy widow into believing that you are her nephew's wife, a condition that would make you a beneficiary of her considerable largesse." He paused to allow his words to sink in. "My aunt will be heartbroken to learn of your deception. Who knows what it will do to her fragile health?"

"Fragile health?" Sarah was incredulous. "Oh, no, sir. Harry had me believing that tarradiddle for a time, but you will no more persuade me that Lady Claremont is frail than you will tell me the moon is made of green cheese."

A sly smile swept his features. "You miss the point, Miss Armistead. It is not necessary to persuade *you* of these facts. It is only necessary to persuade the magistrate. Whom do you think he will believe? A peer of the realm or a second-rate actress of dubious repute?"

In the silence that followed this bald statement, Sarah realized the truth. All was lost.

Helplessly she eyed his stern features, willing the tears not to come. He was right. There was no charitable interpretation to place on her behavior. They would throw her in jail. She would lose everything, even the self-respect that had kept her sane. William would have to leave school. He would learn the sordid truth about the sister he adored. She should never have agreed to Harry's ill-conceived plan, nor believed his blithe assurances that it could do no harm. Slowly, she sank into her chair.

"What do you want, Lord Linton? I warn you, I shall languish in Newgate before I submit to your advances."

"An intriguing notion—but quite beside the point. I have a plan, you see."

"A plan?" Sarah eyed him suspiciously.

Lord Linton wandered over to the fireplace and poked a log with the toe of his burnished leather boot. "Yes, indeed, Miss Armistead," he drawled. "And unlike my cousin, I am willing to advance you a substantial sum before the job is completed."

Sarah flushed. "How did you know that Harry . . . ?"

"My cousin is always under the hatches," he said dismissively. "You will be fortunate to see even a farthing of what he has promised you."

"His allowance is due next week," Sarah insisted, trying to stem her rising panic. "He will pay me in full."

The viscount yawned. "Before he settles his gambling debts and mollifies his tailor?" He shook his head in mock pity. "Tsk. Tsk. I believe *you* now stand bamboozled, Miss Armistead."

"I shall tell Harry that I will go to Lady Claremont and tell her the whole," Sarah said angrily.

"Blackmail?" He nodded, as if he had expected as much. "You see? I knew you were a conniving bit of muslin."

Mortification swept her from head to toe. How could she have entertained such a thought, even for a moment? Thoroughly dejected, Sarah stared at the surface of her writing table, where the letter to William lay unfinished. She had behaved despicably. Proclaiming her virtue when she had fallen to such a deplorable state was laughable.

"Perhaps you ought to tell me about your plan," she ventured with as much dignity as she could muster, which was not a great deal.

The devil himself could not have looked at her with as much demonic glee. "It is very simple, Miss Armistead," the viscount said in a stage whisper, quickly moving toward her and leaning so close that his breath tickled the back of her neck. "And what's more, it is perfect."

Stiffly, Sarah held herself away from him. "There is no need to be encroaching, Lord Linton. Nor so dramatic. I am certain that if you have devised a plan, it must be very nigh perfect. But perfect or no, will you simply spit it out?"

At her impudence, one corner of his mouth quirked upward. His brows drew together in a fearsome glower. Sarah calmed herself with the knowledge that if he was going to do her violence, he would have done so already. Indeed, his next words removed all such thoughts from her head.

"I have a juicy role for you, Miss Armistead. One that will not be too much of a stretch, I imagine. I wish you to play the part of my mistress."

Sarah rose abruptly, her face pink with embarrassment and fury. "I told you, Lord Linton, I would rather take my chances in Newgate . . ."

"And you will get your wish rather soon," he put in smoothly, "if you do not agree to my proposal. But it is not what you think." Scorn filled his eyes. "You need only pretend. And say a few lines that I will write for you."

"That is all?" Sarah slanted him a suspicious gaze.

"Not quite," he said casually. "The final act of my little play requires you to kill me. I imagine you will enjoy that."

Her mouth dropped open. "You are a Bedlamite."

"On the contrary. I know precisely what I am doing." His voice was cool, dispassionate. "I have planned everything, right down to the words that will fall from your mouth as you pull the trigger of one of my best Mantons. Do not despair. You will not be charged with murder. I shall see to it that you disappear. And, of course," he added, almost as an afterthought, "I will not really be dead."

"There must be something terribly wrong with my hearing." Sarah rubbed her now aching forehead. "I am to kill you, but you will not be dead?"

"It will be an illusion, Miss Armistead. Do not worry. Illusion is an art at which I excel. I am merely asking you to play a small part."

"I do not understand. To what end?"

For the first time, Lord Linton looked away. He walked over to the solitary window in her room and stared through the cracked pane. He did this for so long that Sarah wondered whether he had forgotten her question. At last, however, he spoke. "I do not explain myself to those in my employ."

"I understand that a man of your arrogance is loath to explain himself under any conditions, sir," she replied evenly. "Nevertheless, I must insist."

His swift, sharp glance revealed that he was not pleased by her defiance. But his next words surprised her. " 'Tis a good thing you are not Harry's wife," he muttered. "He could never keep you in line."

"What an impertinent thing to say."

The wicked curve to his mouth told her she would get no apology. "Impertinence is not a hanging offense, Miss Armistead. You wish to know why I stage my little drama?" He studied her intently. "Very well. I am trying to catch a killer. If you agree to take the job, I will tell you the rest. That is all I care to divulge at the moment. What is your answer?"

Sarah stared at him, wondering why nothing he said was

making sense. Her head pounded. She wanted nothing so much as to drink a comforting cup of tea and take to her bed.

"I cannot think," she said wearily. "I must have time."

Cynicism leapt to his eyes. "I see I have failed to mention the most important fact, Miss Armistead. I will pay you one thousand pounds."

Numbly, Sarah sank into her chair again. "One thousand pounds?" She had never seen such a sum in her life.

"Fifty pounds immediately, the rest after the job is done. But you must follow my instructions completely. I am most particular about the way this part is to be played. There will be no room for error, nor improvisation. The stakes are too high."

William's education would be taken care of. She could set up her own establishment, even hire a companion to give her countenance. His offer seemed too good to be true.

It probably was.

What did she know of Lord Linton, other than that he had a gift for artifice? She would be a fool to trust such a man. Did he honestly think she was naive enough to believe that he only meant her to "pretend" to be his mistress? She might be poor as a church mouse, but she was undoubtedly better off than as one of Lord Linton's cast-off women. The man had a cruel streak, she was certain. Who could believe that Banbury tale about catching a killer?

And yet, what was the alternative? The magistrate? Newgate? Sarah massaged her temples.

"I must have time, Lord Linton."

"Very well. I will expect your answer tomorrow."

"Tomorrow?" She rose in alarm. "But I cannot . . ."

A loud knocking at the door made her jump.

"Now what?" Sarah groaned. She looked at the mantel clock. The afternoon was all but gone, and with it that cup of tea she so craved. With a sigh, she threw open the door.

"About time you got back from your little holiday." Mr. Stinson's impatient gaze settled into a knowing smirk as he spied Lord Linton. "Smart girl. Held out for a plum, did you?"

Sarah blushed. "What did you wish to see me about, Mr. Stinson?"

"Rose has tumbled down the stairs. You must come right away."

Sarah stared at him blankly. "I will do what I can, but I am no doctor. Perhaps you ought to summon one."

There was a stunned silence. Then he slapped his knee. "Damn it, woman. 'Tis no quack I need. 'Tis you. You must play Ophelia tonight." He stared at her in sudden horror. "Never say you have forgotten your lines?"

"N-no." Sarah stared at him. "That is, I do not think so."

"The noise in the pits will cover most of your mistakes. Tell your gentleman friend here he can have the first box. Good for business to have quality in attendance."

"Lord Linton is not my . . ."

"No time for chitchat, girl." Mr. Stinson grabbed her hand and pulled her out the door. "I have got a performance to put on. And the devil of a headache, to boot."

Sarah scrambled after him, leaving Lord Linton alone in her room. Presumably, the dreadful man would show himself out.

"I know precisely what you mean, Mr. Stinson," she muttered.

Why did it have to be *this* play? It was enough to live and breathe revenge. Must he partake of it for entertainment?

Justin shifted uncomfortably in his chair. The Chester playhouse was not a luxurious facility, nor did its intimate size make up for the lack of amenities. The shabby furnishings appeared to have been salvaged from some recent fire. A tattered green curtain hung over the players. The stage scenery had been painted by someone with no apparent artistic skills. Wobbly chandeliers provided the lighting, the unevenly placed candles dripping wax onto those unfortunate enough to find themselves below. And while one could easily hear the performers onstage, it was also possible to discern practically every remark from the pits.

Those were minor inconveniences, however. What was deuced hard to take was the sight of a half-foxed company of players making a mockery out of lines he had no wish to hear in the first place. That fellow Hamlet was too much of a ditherer, and he listened to far too much criticism.

"Your father lost a father, that father lost, lost his, and the survivor bound in filial obligation for some term to do obsequious sorrow," admonished the King, whose bulbous red nose owed nothing to an actor's paintbox, "but to persevere

in obstinate condolement is a course of impious stubborn-
ness."

Hamlet did not deserve a scolding from that drunken sot,
Justin thought glumly. Death spawned many sorrows. Who
could say how long it might take to put them to rest?

Cheers went up from the pit when the Ghost finally arrived
to proclaim in a sonorous voice: "I am thy father's spirit;
doom'd for a certain term to walk the night, and for the day
confined to fast in fires, till the foul crimes done in my days of
nature are burnt and purged away."

Perhaps the fact that it was the company's last night in
Chester explained why so many of the actors appeared to have
imbibed freely before taking the stage. The Ghost hovered pre-
cariously near the edge of the platform, and several young lads
in the pits occupied themselves with reaching for his robes to
see if they could topple him. Though the actor dodged them
manfully, despite his castaway state, Justin knew it would be
only a matter of time before his lack of balance worked in their
favor.

Justin found it easier to occupy his mind with these goings-
on than to think about the words that echoed through the playhouse. For all his foibles, the actor playing the Ghost had a
forceful voice, and his stentorian tones resonated with ghostly
indignation. Again, Justin shifted uncomfortably in his chair.

Ghosts did not exist. They did not walk the night waiting to
be avenged. People simply died, and their lives ceased to exist.
Their deaths, if unnatural, were sometimes avenged. Usually
they were forgotten.

Justin had not forgotten. Every word he had spoken to his father on the day of his death was inscribed in his memory. Every
tear his mother had shed was imprinted on his brain. Every
fiber of the bedsheet that had wrapped around her neck was as
vivid to him as the players before him. Memory was a useful
thing. Cleverness was better. His plan was very clever. And the
woman who would help him carry it out was even now taking
the stage.

"My lord, I have remembrances of yours, that I have longed
long to redeliver; I pray you, now receive them." Her voice was
melodic, slightly trembling as her character hailed her lover,
uncertain of her reception.

"I never gave you aught."

"My honored lord, you know right well you did," she replied, startled, "and with them words of so sweet breath composed as made the things more rich . . ."

She made a perfect Ophelia. A wig covered her luxurious auburn hair, and she had done something with her complexion, made it whiter, more ghostly, such that she radiated an ethereal—albeit disturbing—beauty. And although Miss Armistead had seemed to him in possession of a healthy dose of common sense and sanity, he found himself readily believing in this Ophelia's burgeoning madness. Her distress at Hamlet's denial of his love was palpable, despite the fact that few of the audience had ceased chattering long enough to pay her any attention.

"Get thee to a nunnery," Hamlet commanded, and Ophelia sank to her knees in anguished despair.

Justin wondered idly whether she would have bruises from the bare wooden floor. He could not imagine her in a nunnery, but the role of mistress would suit her perfectly. She had all the right physical assets—fiery green eyes, flaming hair, sensually swaying hips—and she used them expertly, especially the eyes. They had their own language. Here, in her most emotional scene, they were limpid pools of sorrow as her "woe is me" rang to the rafters.

She was a superb actress. And she was his. He had no doubt that she would accept his proposition. Any woman who would hire herself out as Harry's wife would not cavil at the role he had to offer. She might need a bit of polish, but he would train her. He would put every word in her mouth, give her every action. She would be good. Very good.

With supreme satisfaction, he settled into another position in the rigid wooden chair and listened to Hamlet's soliloquy. That Danish fellow was not such a poltroon after all. He knew that revenge delayed was revenge denied. He even had a few good ideas. Like using a play to catch a murderer.

Sarah Armistead was perfect. He could not wait to start training her.

"I will not do it, Lord Linton."

Incredulous, Justin stared at her. "You must be joking." But she did not look it. She was standing in the center of her tiny room, her arms crossed like some rebellious termagant. From the looks of her bloodshot eyes, she had not slept well.

"On the contrary, I have never been more serious," she insisted. "I cannot take part in your havey-cavey plan."

"You are willing to cast your fortunes with the magistrate? I assure you, Miss Armistead, that would be a mistake."

She sighed heavily. "Summon the magistrate if you wish. There is nothing I can do to stop you. But I do not think you will call him."

"No? Why not?" he demanded indignantly.

"Because it will not gain you an actress. My decision is final, whether you haul me before a magistrate or no."

Daring to call his bluff was she? The little trollop. " 'Tis no more than your appalling behavior deserves. It would be a most fitting revenge."

"Revenge," she echoed, studying him intently. "And that is important to you, is it not?"

Justin saw the disdain in her eyes, and it angered him. "Do not be so quick to judge that of which you know nothing, Miss Armistead."

"Do not be so quick to assume that I know nothing of such dark passions, sir. I am an actress, after all."

"A good one," he agreed, thinking of her performance last night. That comment brought an attractive flush to her cheeks, but he hardened his heart against the appealing picture she made. "I do not doubt that your knowledge of passion is vast," he added sardonically.

Her flush deepened to scarlet. "One does not have to experience passion to convey it, Lord Linton."

"That is a ridiculous notion."

Sudden sparks in her eyes told him what she thought of his words, but just as quickly they disappeared. "You may believe what you wish about me," she said evenly, "as long as you leave me alone."

Women could be so difficult. Justin willed himself to be patient. One did not pull in every fish on the first try. "If you mean to wait until Harry pays his debt to you, I am afraid you will starve," he pointed out charitably. "The man has been an irresponsible fribble since my father's brother was struck dead while listening to one of Mr. Wilberforce's sermons. The one thing Harry learned from his father was that nothing is to be gained from virtue."

"I have thought about your insight into your cousin's character," Sarah said, her teeth gnawing pensively on her bottom lip. "I believe it would be wise for me to travel to London to collect what is due me. With the extra money I earned for last night's performance, I have just enough for the Mail."

"You are a fool."

This time she did not bother to hide her anger. "That may be, my lord, but at least I am not your mistress—even in pretense."

Abruptly he closed the space between them, stopping mere inches from her charming person. "There are worse things, Miss Armistead," he murmured, brushing a lock of hair away from her face. He was pleased to see that this brought a slight tremor to her lips. "None of my mistresses ever had cause to complain," he added provocatively.

Although he had clearly unnerved her, she stepped calmly out of his reach. "I would be the first, I am certain," she replied with mock sweetness. "Who knows? Perhaps I should even shoot you in earnest."

"That is not funny."

"No. It is not," she agreed, walking over to the door and pointedly holding it open for him. "So you see, we are best quit. I do not need your money, Lord Linton. I have every faith in Harry."

"If Harry Trent is to be your salvation," he retorted, striding angrily through the doorway, "then I shall see you in hell, Miss Armistead."

A shocked gasp told him his words had hit home.

Chapter Five

H arry welcomed her about as much as the plague. Or rather, his manservant did. Harry himself was indisposed, Sarah was told, and could not see her.

"I demand that you rouse him," she told the haughty servant who tried to close the door in her face at Harry's bachelor quarters just off Oxford Street. It was a seedier location than Sarah had imagined, which added credence to Lord Linton's dismal assessment of his cousin's finances.

Harry's servant looked her up and down, his disdainful expression eloquently conveying his opinion of unescorted women who had the temerity to demand entry to a gentleman's private quarters.

But Sarah had spent a most uncomfortable two days, traveling first by rackety cart to Gloucester, where she picked up the Mail, then sitting alongside the driver all the way to London, the inside seats being beyond the reach of her meager funds. She had no money to pay for a night's lodging in town. This business had to be settled now or never. She returned the servant's contemptuous gaze with an equally haughty one of her own.

"Inform your master that his *wife* requires a word with him, if you please," she demanded with a confidence she was far from feeling.

The man's eyes nearly bulged out of their sockets. He disappeared, and within two minutes Harry himself was standing at the door, bloodshot eyes and all. His buff-colored breeches and parrot yellow waistcoat looked as if they had been slept in.

"Sarah!" he exclaimed with a nervous laugh. "I hope you ain't telling that clanker all over town. Most indiscreet, you know."

"I do not have the luxury of discretion at the moment," Sarah replied irritably. "Will you let me in, or must I stand here until I drop?"

Alarmed, Harry shook his head vigorously. "Not the thing to be entertaining females in one's rooms. Think of your reputation."

"An actress has no reputation," she snapped, "leastwise not one that is in any danger of being damaged. Especially not after spending a week masquerading as your . . ."

"Hush!" Quickly he pulled her in. Sarah found herself standing in a dingy parlor with frayed carpets. The draft from the open door sent dust floating up from the windowsills. "Confound it, Sarah!" Harry admonished. "Are you dicked in the nob? First you send my man into a tizzy claiming to be my wife, then all this loud blabbering about queer masquerades. What will people think?"

"I do not care what people think, Harry," Sarah retorted, "as long as I get my money. *Now*, if you please."

Harry's sudden pallor said it all. With a sinking heart, Sarah realized that Lord Linton had been right. The man had no intention of paying her. "Did you receive your allowance, Harry?" she asked quietly.

"You must understand, Sarah. I had some pressing debts." Harry mopped his brow with his handkerchief. "A man can't welsh on his vowels, you know."

"*I* am one of your pressing debts, Harry." Sarah drew herself up indignantly. "And I demand my money."

Harry kicked the threadbare rug. "I will pay you as soon as I can, you know that."

"I know only that I have been a fool to take you at your word."

"Now just a minute!" He managed a credible expression of outrage. "The word of a Trent is just as good as any man's."

Sarah eyed him contemptuously. "Maybe to another man, Harry. I imagine the women to whom you have made promises find themselves less than pleased."

"What does that mean?" he demanded sourly.

"It means that I am leaving."

"What are you going to do?" The bloodshot eyes suddenly opened wide. "Are you going to Aunt Agatha?"

Sarah sighed. "I have already served your aunt one bad turn, Harry. It would not be an act of kindness to crush her with the disappointing news that her younger nephew is a despicable cad. I will allow her to discover that fact in her own time." She eyed him sternly. "Or perhaps one day you may grow up and spare her the ordeal. Good-bye, Harry."

As exits go, it was a grand one. Sarah was able to keep her voice steady, and the indignant turn she executed on the way out was perfect. It was only when she reached the street that the tears welled in her eyes. Without money, her situation was dire. She would have to find a way to catch up to the theater company and hope that Mr. Stinson would forgive her latest absence. But how could she do that without funds? She had counted on being able to pry at least a few pounds from Harry.

Pinning her hopes on Harry had been one of the more foolish mistakes of her life. The meager sum she saved for the Mail was gone, thrown away on a fool's mission. Now she was standing alone on the street like a fallen woman. But then everyone knew that actresses were not respectable. And she had no place else to go.

Sarah walked slowly, eyes down, trying to ignore the stares and rude calls that were beginning to come her way. Above, threatening skies loosed their hold on a few drops of rain, adding to her misery. She wondered what William was doing. She hoped it was something fun and carefree. Soon enough, he would have precious few carefree moments.

Her thoughts wandered to the little house in Surrey, where she had spent most of her twenty-two years. Squire Gibbons had promised to find a tenant, but that was ages ago. She had heard nothing from him, despite her repeated entreaties. Either he was pocketing the rent or had allowed the place to go to ruin. The last few years had taught her that people were capable of such cruel deeds.

Sorrow turned the sights and sounds of London into a dirge for the placid, decent life she had abandoned to make her own way and provide for William. That little house held memories, good ones, and its loss was symbolic of how her life had deteriorated. Perhaps she ought to have stayed in Surrey, even if it meant that William would never get the proper schooling. She had been wrong to think that she could earn her own way and keep her self-respect. To be sure, she had tried to hold her head high and maintain her honor, but apparently that was also a fool's mission. What did it matter that she adhered to her standards, when the world thought her a fallen woman, when people like Harry used her so cavalierly, when men on the street taunted and jeered and spoke of things that made her blush?

Respectability was but an illusion for her now. The Honorable Sarah Armistead was only a second-rate actress of dubious repute—just as Lord Linton had said. She could rejoin her company, but nothing would change. Mr. Stinson would stint on her wages, and she would continue to fend off the advances of men who, like Harry and his odious cousin, thought females could be bought and sold.

What would happen to her?

Sarah did not feel the tears that coursed down her face, so it was a great surprise when a snowy white handkerchief began to blot them away. Startled, she looked up into eyes the color of the rain.

"Lord Linton."

That was all the speech she could muster for some time as he wiped her cheeks and lashes, a somber expression on his face. No man had ever touched her so, and she was surprised by his gentleness. His eyes gave away nothing of his thoughts, and Sarah studied him in a daze, wondering whether she was imagining compassion in that gray gaze. When he extended his arm, she took it without questioning where he meant to take her. He walked her to a large closed carriage, and the driver respectfully opened the door. With her thoughts all a muddle, it seemed the most natural thing in the world to allow Lord Linton to hand her in.

"You mustn't blame Harry, you know," he said in a surprisingly gentle tone. "I learned long ago that some people will never change, no matter how much you wish it." He hesitated. "Can I drop you somewhere?"

Sarah shook her head. "I must return to the company," she said slowly. "They should be in Shrewsbury by now."

"Miss Armistead, it is four o'clock in the afternoon. It will take you two days to make Shrewsbury under the best of circumstances, and as you can see, a storm is brewing." He paused to gauge her reaction to this news, but Sarah said nothing. What was there to say? "It would not be wise to travel alone," he added softly. "I daresay you must stay in town tonight. Do you have a room?"

Her awkward silence spoke for itself, as did the new tears

that sprang to her eyes. Turning into a watering pot in front of the viscount was acutely embarrassing. She closed her eyes in mortification against that steady, knowing gaze.

"My offer still stands," he said at last, his words softly resonant in the confines of the carriage. " 'Tis the role of a lifetime, you know."

Her eyes flew open. Now she understood the reason for his sudden kindness. He meant to take advantage of her destitute, helpless condition. "You are despicable, sir," she declared.

Like a curtain descending on the stage, hooded lids suddenly shuttered his gaze. "So I have been told. But perhaps you can set your feelings aside and accept my proposition even so. The money would come in handy, would it not?"

Sarah did not speak; she merely turned to stare out the window, her mouth set in a bitter line. What he said was no more than the truth, but somehow the truth chafed when it came from those sensuous lips. She felt powerless in the face of his knowledge, frustrated and helpless in the face of her penury and his wealth. She wanted to consign him and his offer to perdition, but she dared not. How many compromises must she make before all was said and done?

Lord Linton allowed the silence to endure for several minutes, during which Sarah bleakly studied the darkening skies as the raindrops collected on the glass. Abruptly, he tapped on the roof to get the driver's attention.

"Lintonwood, John. By nightfall, if you please."

A crack of the whip told Sarah that his orders were being carried out immediately and were not, perhaps, unexpected. She stared at him in surprise. Certain details began to register for the first time. He wore a greatcoat and was dressed as if for traveling. The rattling of baggage on the roof as the coach picked up speed down the Oxford Road confirmed her dawning suspicions.

"You knew this would happen," she said accusingly. "You followed me to town and lay in wait for me outside Harry's rooms. You knew he would not pay me. You knew you would be proven right. What are you, some kind of sorcerer?" To her dismay, her voice broke on the last sentence.

"There is nothing sinister or magical about my behavior, Miss Armistead," he replied calmly. "I simply predicted the correct turn of events based on my excellent understanding of human nature."

"Your arrogance is appalling," she sputtered.

"One has confidence in what one knows. Being prepared is half the task of creating an illusion. The rest of artifice hinges upon successful prediction of human response."

Sarah blinked rapidly, trying to stem tears of frustration. When he attempted to blot her cheek with his handkerchief once more, she turned her head away. Gently but firmly, he pressed the cloth into her hand. Shooting him a speaking look, Sarah snatched the handkerchief and dabbed violently at her eyes. Lord Linton watched her silently, his steady gaze cool and calm in marked contrast to her flustered discomfiture. Finally, he spoke again in a voice that was maddeningly complacent.

"As an actress you learn your lines and deliver them in a manner designed to elicit a predictable response from your audience. I do the same in orchestrating the events in my life."

Sarah closed her fist around the tight ball of his handkerchief. "Am I to assume that I am such an 'event,' my lord?" she demanded bitterly. "For I seem to have been orchestrated to a fare-thee-well."

"At the moment you are the most important event in my life, Miss Armistead." His lips curved in a half smile. "I believe that puts you at center stage."

Defeat sapped her remaining energy. Sarah sagged against the squabs and slanted him a weary gaze. "For some reason, Lord Linton, that makes me very uneasy."

He merely arched a brow and said nothing.

Lintonwood stretched out before them like a lazy, well-fed cat, supremely content with its verdant perch on the top of a gently rolling hill. Even in the encroaching dusk and fog, the house sparkled, its brick and stone polished to perfection, its windows gleaming with newly lit lanterns, bidding them welcome.

It was a friendly house, Sarah realized in surprise. Somehow she had expected something dark and gloomy, as befitting the viscount's dubious character. Servants busy with an ancient traveling coach in the drive quickly turned to greet them, opening the carriage door and watching without a sign of curiosity or speculation as Lord Linton helped Sarah descend. The but-

ler, of some exotic heritage and inscrutable mien, bowed deeply
and led the way into a cozy parlor, where two older ladies were
in the act of taking tea. Apparently they were newly arrived, for
the wore traveling gowns.

"Lady Claremont!" Sarah exclaimed, then bit the words back
in embarrassment. One of the women eyed her sharply, but the
elder lady in a pink turban who bore an uncanny resemblance
to the viscount's Aunt Agatha did not seem to hear her. Sarah
saw that although there was indeed a family likeness, this lady's
mouth was softer than Lady Claremont's. Her eyes were a startling shade of violet, and they did not possess the same keen-
ness. She wore an abstracted air as she bobbed her head at the
newcomers.

"Aunt, allow me to present Miss Sarah Armistead," Lord
Linton said. "Miss Armistead, this is my aunt, Miss Clarissa
Porter, and her companion, Miss Harriet Simms." As Sarah
curtsied, he whispered a curt command in her ear: "Not a word
about Aunt Agatha, if you please. They do not speak."

Before Sarah had a chance to ponder that strange statement,
Miss Porter smiled. It was a rather giddy smile, and it was accompanied by a small giggle.

"Will wonders never cease?" she said gaily. "*I*, of all people,
playing chaperon! Miss Armistead, did you know I am the
black sheep of the family?"

There seemed no appropriate response to that statement, so
Sarah merely smiled politely. She was intrigued—and relieved—by the thought that the viscount had seen fit to have her
properly chaperoned. Somehow she had envisioned him keeping her captive in some stark, cheerless room until she learned
her lines. The knowledge that she was to have female company
heartened her enormously. She wondered what Lord Linton had
told his aunt to explain her presence. She did not have to wait
long to find out.

"So this is the poor orphan from America, is it? The young
woman whose relatives you are endeavoring to find?" Miss
Porter eyed her sympathetically. "I must say, Miss Armistead, it
was too bad for your uncle to pack you off to England in such
a fashion. The thought of a young woman traveling such a long
way! And to find that your relatives here have moved without
leaving their direction! How dreadful."

Sarah shot the viscount a sharp look. "Thank you, ma'am,"

she said cautiously. "I do not know what I would have done if it had not been for Lord Linton."

"Oh, yes," Miss Simms muttered dryly. "Linton is known far and wide for his kindness to young women." More loudly, she added, "You have not said how you met the girl, Linton."

"But, Harriet," interjected Miss Porter, "do you not remember? Justin told us that Miss Armistead's uncle, whom he met on his travels, had instructed her to seek him out if something went wrong."

Miss Simms rolled her eyes, and Sarah could not blame her. It was a farfetched story. The viscount obviously knew that his aunt would not question it. Miss Simms, however, was another matter. Her eyes were sharp with suspicion, and her mouth was set in an expression of distaste. Each time she spoke, she pointed her long, bony fingers at Sarah as if she were some sort of spectacle at a carnival.

"Is there any progress in finding Miss Armistead's relatives, Justin?" Miss Porter asked.

"No, Aunt," he replied easily. "But in the meantime, Miss Armistead will make her home with us."

"But of course," his aunt murmured in delight.

Her companion, however, narrowed her gaze. "When you said she was an orphan, Linton, I envisioned a child." Miss Simms looked Sarah up and down. "If you ask me . . ."

"No one did," Lord Linton snapped.

Evidently used to such treatment from the viscount, Miss Simms merely gave him a speaking look. "A strange business, Clarissa," she muttered, but Miss Porter was seemingly without any awareness of the fireworks brewing in the room. She simply smiled beatifically, ignoring her dour companion.

"Charming, simply charming," she said happily, staring at Sarah. "I declare, Justin, if you do not find her relatives, you must keep her for yourself."

Sarah flushed in embarrassment as she met the viscount's gaze over the head of his aunt. To her surprise, he appeared a bit taken aback. At that moment, the butler handed him a glass of brandy, which Lord Linton tossed off gratefully in a single gulp. He made no reply to his aunt, not even the sort of light-hearted remark one would make to such a joke, and for the first time Sarah wondered if the woman were not a bit addled in her thinking.

Sarah accepted a glass of sherry from the butler and stood uncertainly in the parlor, wondering what her position in this household would be. Lord Linton's Banbury tale had made her a guest of sorts, and perhaps even a respectable one, but Sarah knew that in reality she was little more than a servant. During the carriage ride, the viscount had pressed fifty pounds in bank notes into her hand, to her great amazement and delight. Honor demanded that she fling the money into his face, but Sarah knew that was only wishful thinking. With no money, she was fast losing all illusions about her respectability. Simply put, she had no choice but to accept Lord Linton's offer. She could wish that it was otherwise, but wishes would not keep her clothed and fed and William ensconced at Eton.

Was this how it happened, how an honorable woman was corrupted and degraded until she no longer knew what was proper behavior and what was not? Was this how the world conspired to limit women's choices until they became what everyone assumed they already were? Sarah steeled herself against that unhappy thought. This job would assure her independence and her future. For that, and for William, she would do almost anything.

Then again, perhaps this job did not truly compromise her values. Perhaps she could view it as but another role she had taken on—one that she might not like, but which would pay her bills. There was nothing wrong with that—was there? She was properly chaperoned, and her behavior would be above reproach. She could still face herself in the mirror each morning.

Sarah took a bracing sip of sherry and immediately felt better. She was only required to memorize her lines and learn to shoot Lord Linton's pistol. Those things, at least, she could do without compromising her honor.

Something told her that the viscount would not be content with that, however. His diabolical mind was full of schemes. At least her virtue was not in jeopardy, thanks to the presence of these ladies. In a world of increasingly narrowed choices, Sarah was supremely grateful for that. Yet something nagged at her. Lord Linton must have known that bringing his aunt here would protect her, perhaps even make his plans more difficult. She could not imagine why he had done so. An uneasiness swept over her, akin to the feeling she had had at Lady Claremont's of being overmatched in this game of wits.

"I wish to thank you for coming at such short notice, Aunt," Lord Linton was saying. "I trust that Anh has arranged everything to your liking."

Miss Simms eyed the butler dourly, but Miss Porter positively beamed. "Mr. Anh is the most amazing man, Justin. Why, he can do all sorts of magic tricks, just like you. Did you teach him?"

Amused, the viscount glanced at the silent figure who was clearing the tea tray. "It was the other way around, Aunt. Anh is an exceptional teacher. I did not know he had been entertaining you with his tricks. How interesting."

"Barbaric, rather," snapped Miss Simms. "Heathen magic does not belong in a decent English household."

"Miss Simms . . ." Lord Linton began irritably.

"Oh, no, Harriet! It was delightful," trilled Miss Porter. "I have been trying to explain the mirror trick to Silvester, but he does not seem to understand. Ghosts have a peculiar loathing for mirrors. Or is that vampires? I do forget these things."

The room fell into an immediate and profound silence. Miss Simms pursed her lips, but did not say a word. The viscount elected not to finish whatever reproof he was about to issue to Miss Simms. Only the butler continued about his activities, smoothly removing the tea tray without a sign that anything out of the ordinary had been said. Sarah tried mightily not to stare at Miss Porter, who was smiling in apparent fond recollection of her recent conversation with the ghost.

At last Lord Linton broke the silence. "You will be wishing to change before dinner, Miss Armistead. Anh will have someone show you to your room."

"But I have nothing to wear," Sarah protested. She had come to London with only a small bandbox and the dress on her back.

His smile surprised her. "I imagine the maid who has spent the last half hour unpacking your trunks would disagree."

Trunks? Sarah recalled the rattling of boxes on the roof of the carriage. He must have brought her a wardrobe. Her face was burning. She felt like a kept woman.

"I could not accept . . ." she began, but he cut her off.

"I believe you will find in your closet everything that is *necessary* for your stay here," he said meaningfully, and Sarah understood that he regarded the garments merely as costumes essential for her new role. Mr. Stinson made his actors and actresses furnish their own costumes, but Sarah could hardly afford to do so for this part. Like Harry, Lord Linton was simply providing her with what she needed for the job. Still, she was embarrassed. How did he know her size? Had he selected intimate clothing for her as well?

Undoubtedly he had. The man thought of everything. Something else suddenly became horribly clear. His aunt and Miss Simms might be at Lintonwood for form's sake, but Lord Linton would not have invited them if he had thought they could hinder his scheme. Miss Porter was obviously a bit addled; it was no great challenge to pull the wool over her eyes. Miss Simms was sharper, but she was only a companion, with no real power to affect events in the household. The two women were simply window dressing. The viscount would do whatever he wished with her, and no one would stop him.

Once again, Sarah had the distinct impression that Lord Linton had played her for a fool.

Her pulse thundering in her ears, Sarah sipped the last of her sherry, wondering why the amber liquid that trickled down her throat no longer gave her courage. Then she met his gaze over the rim of her glass and knew the answer.

The devil himself was looking at her from within those gray depths.

Poor Aunt Clarissa had been short a sheet for years, but Justin had forgotten how much of a trial she could be. As for that prune-faced Harriet Simms, she'd be fortunate if he did not throttle her before too long. Her only redeeming quality was her devotion to his aunt.

They were respectable ladies, however. Miss Armistead's stay under his roof would not be marked by any appearance of impropriety. To be sure, he had not made the arrangement for her sake. An actress's reputation was nothing to concern oneself with, and Miss Armistead knew it. She had entered his carriage freely, readily accepted his money, and thought nothing about traveling alone with him to Lintonwood. She had no expectations that the proprieties would be observed. He had seen the surprise in her face when she realized that his aunt and Harriet Simms were provided for that purpose. Her reaction had provoked in him an unexpected twinge of pity. Her life had not been easy. She could not be much above twenty, an age when most ladies of his circle were settling into the role of pampered bride. But she had never seen the sort of luxury that kept those women in lavish gowns, featherbeds, and wetnurses for the babes they produced to secure their husbands' lines. She was used to fending for herself.

A woman like that was after the main chance. Justin had brought in the chaperons more for his benefit than hers. Otherwise, what was to stop her from laying claim to his entire fortune, rather than the one thousand pounds he was paying her? Better men than he had been trapped by conniving women crying compromise and demanding a wedding. Not that he would have to marry an actress—they could be bought off easily enough. But he had a feeling that Miss Armistead's price would be higher than he cared to pay. The woman had spunk; who knew what hue and cry she would raise? And, of course, by the time they were quits she would know his plan. He could not allow anything to jeopardize his scheme—especially not a designing actress.

The thought of marriage under any circumstances made him ill. His parents' loveless union had wrought nothing but tragedy. Even love, were one so foolish as to believe in that exalted state, was no guarantee of happiness. Justin had seen a number of his friends make fools of themselves over one infatuation or another. He prided himself on never having succumbed to such an inane state. Marriage was for idiots.

There were not enough tricks in Anh's vast store of knowledge to make him think otherwise. Women had little to offer a man besides their physical charms, and any passion after a time grew old. It galled him that he felt the need for female companionship rather more often than he wished.

Like now.

Unbidden, Miss Armistead's image appeared in his mind's eye. It was a strange fantasy, as she looked every inch the grand lady. A diamond ornament nestled in the auburn hair that was piled gracefully upon her head. Her shimmering emerald gown was the elegant product of a fashionable modiste's skilled needle. Yet she was not concerned about wrinkling it as she reclined on the satin comforter that covered a plump featherbed. Her smile was gentle, yet provocative, as he moved toward her.

Warning signals flashed in his mind, instantly obliterating the ridiculous image. The blasted female was nothing but a lightskirt, an actress with no scruples and no standards to speak of. The closest she could hope to come to respectability—if she were lucky—would be as some gentleman's mistress. He had not been thinking about protecting her when he invited his daft aunt and the eternally miserable Miss Simms to invade his household.

Certainly not.

Women like her were after only one thing: a way to feather their own nests at some man's expense. It had happened to his father.

It would not happen to him.

Chapter Six

It was fortunate that Sarah did not believe in witchcraft, for Lord Linton's library would have greatly unsettled her.

As it was, she found it only a bit unnerving—and not a little fascinating. There was, for example, an engrossing book by Thomas Hill, entitled *Naturall and Artificiall Conclusions,* which seemed to be an English translation of an Italian work from the sixteenth century. In it, Mr. Hill described many ways of astonishing one's friends with skills that ranged from preserving roses fresh through the winter to using a loaf of bread to locate a drowned person. Sarah could not believe that Lord Linton subscribed to those notions, but she did not know what to make of the fact that he had such a book on his shelf.

Another sixteenth-century treatise appeared to be a bit more practical. The author, Reginald Scot, wished to debunk certain myths about witchcraft by pointing out that what was often taken to be magic—especially in the art of healing—was merely the skill of matching an illness to the appropriate cure. That made sense to Sarah, but she did not quite follow Mr. Scot's argument that the cure must needs bear some similarity to the nature of the illness. He cited a Biblical example, wherein Jacob peeled twigs to give them a streaked appearance and showed them to sheep as they copulated. As a result the lambs were born with streaked and spotted coats. Sarah absorbed this information in amazement. Her mother's Biblical instruction had somehow omitted that particular passage from Genesis.

There were books on necromancy, alchemy, and astrology, as well as a copy of the *Malleus Maleficarum,* several herbals, and an intriguing article on one Dr. John Lambe from the last century, who was known as "the Duke's Devil." Dr. Lambe was renowned for curing diseases, finding lost things with the help of his familiar, and using magic potions to bring about death. He was apparently an egregious rapist as well, but escaped being called to account for his crimes due to the influence of his master, the Duke of Buckingham. Sarah was not at all dismayed to read that a London mob finally caught him in the streets and beat him to death.

Thinking to find a temporary refuge for her turbulent thoughts, Sarah had sought out Lord Linton's library on the first morning of her stay. She became so engrossed in his book collection that it was afternoon before her rumbling stomach gave her a reason to tear herself away.

No one had missed her, she realized as she put *The Tragical History of Doctor Faustus* back on the shelf. Apparently Miss Porter and the other members of the household were busy with other things. Lord Linton had not summoned her, although she knew he would eventually. That prospect filled her with a mixture of impatience and trepidation. She wanted to learn her part and be done with this job, but she was also greatly relieved not to face him today. Idly, she ran her fingers over the *Faustus* binding.

"Thinking of selling your soul to the devil?" a silky voice said from the doorway, startling her into a tiny shriek of surprise. "I warn you, Miss Armistead. It will not relieve you of your obligation to me."

Chagrined that his unexpected appearance had provoked her into betraying fear, however slight, Sarah willed her racing pulse to calm. She was not really afraid of him. The peculiar reading material in which she had been absorbed for so many hours undoubtedly lent something sinister to Lord Linton's presence, but that was all there was to it. He was no sorcerer. He could not possibly believe in the black arts, much less practice them. Still, his eyes *did* hold something of the devil as they regarded her steadily.

"On the contrary, Lord Linton," Sarah said calmly. "I begin to think that I have already done so."

His gaze slid to the bookshelves, then returned to study her, as if to determine whether she had indeed taken the books to heart. "You do not strike me as the superstitious sort."

"Nor am I, sir," she returned. "But I do find such material provoking. Your interest in the magical arts appears to be . . . consuming."

There was an odd pause. "I am interested in many things, Miss Armistead," he replied at last. "I am consumed, however, by only one."

Yes, Lord Linton was consumed by something. Sarah wondered that she had not realized that fact earlier, for it explained much: the steel in his eyes, the tension in his voice, the rigidity of his bearing—as if forces he could barely control were at work in him. Sarah wondered what was so powerful as to obsess a man like the viscount. Did some dark episode lie buried in his past, some heinous crime, some unforgivable wrong? Whatever it was must have something to do with his strange plan. He had never shared the details with her. Perhaps now he would.

"And what would that be, Lord Linton?" Sarah prodded. "That thing that consumes you?"

"Justice," he replied, holding himself stiffly against the strength of emotion that lent his voice an undertone of violence. "I want only justice."

An answering tremble, born of fear and fascination, shot through Sarah. She stared at him, wondering why he affected her so. What, after all, did she know of this man and the shadowy forces that drove him? Clearly, more than a simple craving for justice held him in its sway.

"In Chester you spoke not of justice, but revenge," she observed, her voice softly challenging.

Slowly, his lips curled into an unpleasant smile. It was as if Lucifer himself had stepped out of the pages and off the shelves to stare her down in Lord Linton's library.

"Revenge, justice—they are the same, are they not?" Velvet warred with steel in his riveting gaze. "As a woman, surely you understand that. Nothing is sweeter to a woman than revenge."

Sarah tried to marshal the thoughts that had scattered the moment he turned those smoky eyes on her. "You can have no understanding of women if you believe that."

"Oh?" His brows arched, and Sarah was put to the blush as she realized that a man of his reputation must have a far greater understanding of women than she. "What is sweeter to a woman," he softly demanded, "than to destroy the man who has wronged her?"

"A woman is no more apt to seek revenge than anyone else," Sarah said, a defiant tilt to her chin. "Perhaps she is even less inclined to do so. A woman wronged would still rather have love than vengeance."

Bitter amusement leapt to his eyes. "You are either refreshingly naive or incredibly stupid, Miss Armistead."

"And you, sir, are exceedingly rude," she snapped.

"Perhaps." But his admission held no repentance. "Let us just say that I am intrigued by your notion of love as an emotion that does not include the darker passions."

Sarah frowned. "I did not say that, exactly."

"Oh, but you did," he corrected, crossing the room to stand next to her. His sudden nearness sent a shiver down her spine. Carefully, Sarah took a step away from him, but Lord Linton did not appear to notice. Instead, he idly scanned the shelves. "Evidently, the alliances in your life have lacked a certain . . . flair."

"I beg your pardon," she began, flustered at the sudden personal turn of his remarks.

"But surely," he continued, taking no notice of her protest, "you have the poets and playwrights, whose lines you so blithely recite on stage, as a guide. Think of the tragedies they have penned, the paeans to love and loss. And revenge." He turned to her. "Do you not see how capable of vengeance is the human soul?"

Sarah felt decidedly out of her element. "Yet Ophelia did not seek revenge for Hamlet's ill treatment," she persisted.

"Ophelia was weak, able only to throw herself into a pond in despair. It was left to that brother of hers to exact revenge for her death—and for his father's," he added softly.

Sarah searched his gaze, intrigued as the dark currents yielded momentarily to sorrow. "A sorry business it was," she pointed out, "with innocent lives lost."

Lord Linton merely shrugged. Whatever softness existed in those stormy depths immediately vanished. Dismayed, Sarah studied him, wondering what had triggered that momentary yielding and what could bring it back.

"Misery begets misery, my lord," she insisted, sensing that it was somehow important to make him understand. "As for revenge, I believe it is the impulse of a deformed soul."

Granite eyes held hers. "In that, Miss Armistead," he said with a self-mocking sneer, "we are in complete agreement."

* * *

There was no getting around it. Sarah looked up from the pages in her lap and cleared her throat. The viscount, who had been perusing another sheaf of papers, eyed her expectantly.

"Well?" he demanded. "What is it?"

Sarah pursed her lips. Lord Linton would not like what she had to say, but she considered herself a fair judge of such matters and owed him the benefit of her opinion.

"This is dreadful."

He eyed her in disbelief. "What?"

"These lines." Sarah fingered the pages he had given her. "No one would say such a thing— 'If I cannot have you, I vow that no other woman can.' " She shook her head. " 'Tis not realistic. I could not say such words convincingly."

"Your judgment is of no concern," he said coldly. "At all events, you apparently spared no thought to verisimilitude when you were endeavoring to persuade me of your wifely devotion to my cousin."

Sarah flushed. "That was different."

"Nonsense." He rose, ripping the pages from her hand. "You will not persuade me that you find my lines more difficult to say than 'Harry is all I want in a husband,' " he mimicked. "If you did not choke on those words, I imagine you will manage these easily enough."

Sarah tried to curb her rising temper. "Be reasonable, Lord Linton. You wish me to say these dreadful lines, then shoot you in front of dozens of people. Ladies do not have such violent notions. Certainly they would never act upon them in company."

"You are not playing the part of a lady," he pointed out. "You are playing my mistress."

"That may be," Sarah replied, wishing fervently that it was not, "but I do not think you would have selected a mistress as coarse as a fishwife. Or one who did not know the rules of society."

"Fortunately, you know nothing of my taste in mistresses." A wicked smile flitted over his mouth. "Although I am certain you know a great deal about the topic in general."

Swallowing insults was just another aspect of her job, Sarah told herself. The viscount seemed bent on reminding her that she was beneath him in station and repute. It infuriated her that a man like that was sitting in judgment of her, a man who by all accounts was himself something of a satyr. With an effort, Sarah bit back the sharp retort that sprang to her lips.

"Nevertheless," she said evenly, "you mean for this woman to move in the first circles, do you not? A woman like that would be compelled to abide by the rules of behavior."

The papers fluttered impatiently in his hand. "We are speaking of a woman consumed by anger, a woman sufficiently out of control to shoot a man. She would not give a fig for the rules of behavior."

"I cannot accept that," Sarah insisted. "Mistress or no, women do not shoot their lovers. At least not before the entire *ton*."

There was a muttered oath, and then the script sailed past her to the desk. Its loud thump resonated in the uncomfortable silence between them. On her earlier visit to the library, Sarah had thought the room pleasantly cozy, but now she wished that they were not in such close confines. Both the subject matter under discussion and Lord Linton's temper made her exceedingly uncomfortable.

"What in the world do you know of such things?" he demanded, glowering. "The *ton,* or fine ladies, or any of it. You are just . . ."

"Just an actress?" Eyes blazing, Sarah finished the sentence for him. One could tolerate only so much abuse. "I am a baron's daughter, Lord Linton," she said with as much frosty self-possession as she could manage, given her flaming temper. "I know as much about that world as anyone."

"A baron's daughter?" He stared at her incredulously. "What nonsense is this?"

"You may choose not to believe me, as is your right," she said coolly. "But you are foolish to imagine that this scene you have written smacks of anything credible. 'Tis clear you know nothing of women. Or their passions."

"And you know a great deal," he replied sardonically. "A baron's daughter, my foot. As if a respectable lady would be exposed to such things."

Sarah's frigid gaze met his. "A respectable lady is exposed to a great deal when she has not a feather to fly with," she said in a tightly controlled voice. "Your arrogance chief among them."

His fist banged suddenly on the desk, and Sarah nearly

jumped out of her chair. "I will not tolerate your rebelliousness, Miss Armistead. I told you before that there is no room in my plan for improvisation. You will play this scene exactly as it is written."

If she gave in now, she would never have the courage to raise the issue again. Oh, well, Sarah thought. In for a penny, in for a pound. She took a deep breath.

"You also said you would tell me exactly why you are staging this little drama, my lord, and you have not done that." She rose and straightened her skirts, as if to leave. "I do not believe I will give you the benefit of my considerable insight into theatrical matters until you do so." She gifted him with her haughtiest gaze.

"Damnation, woman!" he thundered. "I do not need your insight, only your performance."

Part of her was vastly enjoying this scene, Sarah discovered. For the first time she realized that he needed her as much as she needed this job. It would be time-consuming for him to find another actress at this point, after he had already established her in his household with that elaborate cover story for his aunt's benefit.

"You need a *believable* performance, sir," she corrected. "There is a difference. And I shall not do it unless you tell me what this is about. At the moment, it smacks of vulgar comedy, not drama. I demand that you tell me the whole."

"You are in no position to make demands," he growled.

"Nevertheless, I am making them. And I will have answers before I continue." She tilted her head consideringly. "It has occurred to me that it is rather improper for me to be here alone with you. Do you wish me to find your aunt and ask that she join us? Or better yet, Miss Simms. I am certain she would be happy to oblige."

His glare would have brought the most defiant hellion to heel, and Sarah wondered whether she had gone too far. But this was a matter of honor. After the afternoon's talk about revenge, she needed some assurance that she was not involved in anything criminal.

A great angry sigh filled the room. Lord Linton's brows knitted together like some wrathful god. He walked over to the window and exhaled deeply.

"I am attempting to duplicate an event that happened many

years ago." His voice was flat, disembodied, as if he were distancing himself from his words.

Sarah waited. When he did not continue, she prodded, "A shooting?"

"A woman killed my father fifteen years ago. She was also responsible for my mother's suicide. I intend to force her to confess to those crimes."

If he had said that pigs could fly, Sarah would not have been more stunned. "H-how are you going to manage that?" she stammered.

"By recreating everything about that night in precise detail. My father was shot at a masquerade very much like the one at which you are going to put a period to my existence—or appear to, anyway. The woman who killed him was dressed as Marie Antoinette. As you will be."

Sarah frowned. "Was she not apprehended?"

"She fled immediately afterwards. She was never arrested. Nor did she come forward."

"Then how can you hope to find her?"

"The woman was my father's mistress, Lady Evangeline Greywood. She is presently residing in London."

Sarah's brow furrowed. "How do you know that?"

"The day after my father's death," he continued, ignoring her question, "my mother hanged herself. She took her own life, and that of her babe yet unborn." His eyes were hard. "Lady Greywood has much to answer for."

The silence that followed this statement weighed heavily between them. Lord Linton stood at the window, his eyes unseeing as he gazed out onto the sloping valley, where evening mists were beginning to enshroud the colorful array of carefully tended spring bulbs and, beyond them, the scrub heather. Sarah watched his powerful shoulders shake slightly with some untold emotion, and she felt immeasurably saddened by the sight.

"The lady has kept silent, then, all these years?" she ventured.

He nodded curtly. "After the shooting, her husband whisked her from the country. By the time they returned, the scandal had blown over. Lord Greywood died several years later. I understand that Lady Greywood is a very unhappy woman, given to megrims and the like. At the moment, I believe she is dangerously unstable."

"Why is that?" Sarah did not like the ominous chill in his voice.

Lord Linton turned, his bleak gaze suddenly transformed by a malevolent light that made her wish she were anywhere else. The devil himself could not look so fiendish.

"I have gone to considerable lengths to duplicate the events that led up to my father's shooting," he said in a voice as remote as the ends of the earth. "I believe I have the lady on the verge of breaking down and confessing."

Sarah's eyes widened in sudden understanding. "Dear God," she said slowly, staring at him in horror. "You mean to destroy her."

Her blunt assessment seemed to take him aback, for he made no immediate reply. But after a pensive moment, he nodded.

"My 'murder' will be the coup de grâce," he declared softly.

His words floated through the room, past the shelves filled with witchcraft lore and stories of men consumed by black magic and deviltry.

I am interested in many things, Miss Armistead. I am consumed, however, by only one.

Revenge. Revenge was the thing that consumed Lord Linton, drove him, spawned his diabolical plan. And he would carry out that plan, no matter what she thought or said. If she refused to help him, he would find another actress who would. No matter what it took.

His cause, perhaps, was just. No one should be allowed to get away with murder, not even a member of the *ton*. But Lady Greywood's wrong could not be undone by her destruction.

Sarah was appalled by the viscount's single-minded, unfeeling pursuit of a woman who had probably suffered much over the years for her crime. His anger weighed heavily on Sarah's spirit. He was imposing a relentless, merciless code upon himself—and now, upon her.

"Are you certain that Lady Greywood was the one who killed your father?"

There was no compassion in his implacable gaze, no hint that he had ever held a doubt. She wondered whether he would even deign to answer her question, but he must have thought that she deserved that bit of reassurance.

"It was well-known that Lady Greywood was my father's mistress," he said matter-of-factly, as if reciting a familiar story he had told himself over the years. "He spent many hours at her London town house, until he was discovered there by Lord Greywood. There was a duel. It caused quite the scandal."

"But are you certain that Lady Greywood was the woman dressed as Marie Antoinette?" Sarah persisted. "If your father's assailant fled, how can you be sure?"

"Greywood found the blood-soaked costume in his wife's chamber. It is a mark of his own foolishness that he did not turn her over to the authorities. I would have washed my hands of a woman who had played me false and made me the laughing-stock of London." There was a pause.

"No, that is not quite the truth," he added slowly. "I would have killed her with my bare hands."

Inadvertently, Sarah's hands flew to her own neck. The image was not a pleasant one, yet Sarah was suddenly angry at this unforgiving man who dared to take so much upon himself. Who was he to mete out such deadly justice?

"I am certain no wife of yours would dare to commit such a transgression, my lord," she said coolly.

A smoldering gaze nearly black with rage—and, oddly, de-sire—met hers. Sarah whirled away, turning her back on that dark visage and the vengeful soul it betrayed. With great dignity she left the room, carrying with her the burning questions she dared not ask.

Had his desire for revenge thoroughly destroyed him? Or merely sent him part way down the road to perdition? She yearned to find out. She had seen enough of Lord Linton to know that he was a man of contradictory impulses. He had no obligation to protect her, yet he had arranged for a chaperon during her visit. He never intervened in marital disputes, yet he had rescued her from Harry's advances. He never apologized, and yet he did so three times when he believed she was Harry's wife. He was bent on destroying an enfeebled woman, yet he was apparently not an unfeeling man. Within him warred opposing forces—velvet and steel, desire and rage, charity and raw vengeance.

What would it take to upset the balance, to free that weighted soul of its dark bindings, to send it soaring beyond its shackles and into the light?

* * *

Aunt Clarissa had been discovered in the kitchen, talking to the pots and pans. She claimed she was showing Justin's modern new oven to her dear Silvester, but there was no mollifying Cook, who did not take kindly to an invasion of her realm by a woman who was, as she put it, "as queer as Henry's hat."

To Justin's knowledge, there was no Henry in his household, but dinner was ruined nevertheless, Cook being too distraught to manage the tasks necessary to produce a meal following such a disturbing event. Miss Simms launched a harangue about servants being allowed to rule the household.

All in all, Justin found himself wishing he were elsewhere. His aunt was batty, his aunt's companion was a crosspatch, Cook was on a rampage, and the actress he had hired to complete his revenge had the temerity to tell him his lines would not fadge.

That was what happened when a man turned his house over to women.

At least they had not invaded his study, Justin thought morosely as he accepted the brandy Anh silently offered him later that night. His butler always managed to exude a serene air, no matter what the crisis.

"You are fortunate to have escaped having women interfere in your life," Justin said, casually shuffling a deck of cards.

The butler bowed, eyes narrowing as his employer dealt the cards upon the table in what had become a nightly ritual for the two of them. "I am accustomed to the solitary life, my lord. Your premise that it is by choice is erroneous."

Justin nearly misdealt, so rare was it to hear such a confession from his butler. Anh's life before entering Justin's employ had been a bit of a mystery, and Justin had never pressed him for details. He had met Anh on his travels years ago and had been mesmerized by the man's knowledge of arts Justin had never encountered. When Anh readily agreed to come to England, Justin had not asked why it was so easy for him to pick up and travel a world away to a country he had never seen. He had never known Anh to seek female companionship. The man seemed to prefer a monkish existence. Justin always assumed it had to do with Anh's religion, an eastern philosophy that centered around stoicism.

Carefully, Justin placed a new card facedown on each of the

columns he had previously dealt. Anh did not appear to be studying the arrangement, but Justin knew better.

"You will not persuade me that you allowed a woman to get the best of you," Justin said lightly. "I have never known you to permit anything to jeopardize your judgment, certainly not an excess of feeling."

Anh's face was impassive. "Perhaps when you reach my age, my lord, you will realize that there is much you do not know."

It was a gentle setdown, but Justin did not mind. Indeed, it only whetted his appetite for information about his butler's mysterious past. "Well put," he said with a rueful laugh. "You have taught me that appearances can be deceiving. You have also taught me that asking is the best way to find out something."

"*One* of the ways," Anh corrected. "And only if the other person wishes you to know the thing which you seek."

Justin put down the deck and sighed. "Very well. I can see that there is something you wish me to know, and it involves your past. And a woman. Would you care to tell me before I expire from impatience?"

"Impatience has always been your weakest suit, sir. A little more discipline would serve you well." Anh's eyes followed Justin's hands as they left the deck.

"Damnation, man," Justin growled. "Out with it."

Anh bowed his assent, his calm demeanor both an eloquent contrast to his employer's glaring eyes and a silent reproof. Before he spoke, Anh pushed the deck slightly off to the side of the table.

"Long ago I loved a woman," he said in an emotionless voice. "I was not of her class. Her parents did not approve of the match. They sent me away."

As Justin waited, Anh tapped the deck of cards lightly and brushed a speck of dust from the table. Then he sat back, regarding his employer impassively. The silence between them lengthened, broken only by the steady rapping of Justin's knuckles on the table. Finally, Justin gave a sigh of disgust. "That is *all*?" he demanded. "That is what I have been waiting with bated breath to learn?"

Anh's brows rose almost imperceptibly as he met Justin's incredulous gaze. "It is not quite all. The daughter grew sick and died."

Justin stared. He knew he was missing something. "That is tragic, of course, but—damnation, man, *this* is what is responsible for your . . . reticence with women?"

Anh's face seemed to deepen in hue, and Justin wondered if he had overstepped himself. His butler was a private man who would have no wish to discuss such things.

But apparently he did not mind another word or two on the topic. "I loved her," he said simply. "I was eager to be her husband, to explore our love on a deeper level. But she was young, unable to go against her parents' wishes."

"How long ago was this?"

"Thirty years."

Justin could not believe his ears. "And you have not enjoyed a woman since then?"

"I have never known a woman in the way that you mean, my lord," Anh replied quietly.

Stunned, Justin gaped at him. "You have allowed this event to rule you for thirty years? Nay, to *ruin* your life?" He threw out his hands. "One woman is not worth thirty years of misery."

"I have not been miserable."

"But her parents. You must have hated them."

"Hate is an excessive emotion, my lord. I do not experience hate."

"And yet you say you loved," Justin pointed out. "That is an excessive emotion, if ever there was one."

Anh bowed his head slightly, which made Justin want to shake him, for it was the butler's sign that he would speak no more about the matter. The man was impossible. Well, in one thing at least, Justin would have the upper hand. Anh had been so intent on his story that he had not paid attention to Justin's handling of the cards. One day he would best Anh with this card trick. He had a suspicion that tonight would be the night.

"Very well," Justin said. "I shall require no more answers if you can find me the queen of diamonds."

The trick relied on a deft combination of skillful dealing, memory, and distracting one's opponent. Tonight, Justin had achieved all three. Anh would undoubtedly go to the fourth column of cards, where each night this week Justin had secreted the object of the game in order to set up tonight's unexpected switch.

Without so much as a blink, Anh picked up the deck and

plucked a card from the bottom. He flipped the card over to display it, then calmly rose to complete his nightly duties.

Justin stared at the diamond queen Anh had chosen as effortlessly as he did everything else.

"I do not understand," he said in amazement. "I did not put it there. It was in the third column, under the ace." But the ace, Justin quickly discovered, had somehow become the two of clubs. He eyed Anh in frustration. "What in blazes have you done?"

"Only confounded your expectations, my lord. And demonstrated that there are many different ways of seeing."

"Every damn night you show me different ways of seeing," Justin grumbled, for he had yet to best his teacher in this or any other card trick.

Anh sighed heavily. "Yes, my lord. Fortunately, I have hopes that one day you may learn."

Chapter Seven

S arah did not know what to make of Lord Linton's story. It was the stuff of great tragedy, yet so utterly fanciful she wondered whether even Mr. Kean could have produced a believable performance from such a tale. The notion that a woman would shoot her protector in front of the entire *ton* was farfetched, to say the least.

And yet, it *had* happened—to Lord Linton's father.

A frown brought tiny lines to the corners of Sarah's mouth. Something about the viscount's story did not ring true. A woman scorned might wish to humiliate a man, but would she commit murder before scores of witnesses whose testimony might send her to the gallows?

If Lady Greywood's actions were illogical, however, Lord Linton's plan did not suffer from that flaw. His script detailed in practical and precise fashion the shooting and the events leading up to it. Sarah studied the sheaf of pages on her lap. In their first week in London, they were to make the rounds of parties so that everyone knew her as Lord Linton's latest mistress. He would flirt outrageously with several other woman; they would stage a few public arguments over that fact, making it clear to observers that trouble loomed on the horizon.

By the time Lady Hogarth's masquerade arrived, the *ton* would be primed for Sarah to pull a pistol from her muff and, in a murderous rage, shoot Lord Linton before the horrified Lady Greywood and scores of other spectators. He would see to it that Sarah escaped being seized and clapped into irons, although he had not shared that particular aspect of the plan with her. It seemed that he preferred to reveal only what she needed to know at any given moment.

Such as the fact she was to wear a dampened petticoat for her first society appearance.

"Botheration," Sarah grumbled as she absorbed this telling detail. The page she was studying began at the point where she and Lord Linton encountered one of his flirts at a party. Sarah wondered which of his many female admirers he would choose for this honor. Her own role was to be outrageously provocative in an obvious effort to compete with the society beauty. Once again, the script noted that she was to be sure to wear dampened undergarments.

"What business does he have dictating the condition of my petticoat?" Sarah muttered in disgust.

"If you are referring to Linton, the answer should be obvious."

Sarah gasped. Harriet Simms towered over the garden bench, her disapproving countenance betraying complete condemnation of the young woman before her.

Hurriedly, Sarah scooped up the pages, inwardly cursing her foolishness in allowing the sunshine and fresh garden fragrance to seduce her into straying from the privacy of her own room while studying her lines. She should not have risked discovery by the suspicious woman now looking so censoriously down her prim nose.

"Pray, what is *that*?" Miss Simms said, her beady eyes fixed on the script.

"Miss Simms," Sarah acknowledged, hoping that if she ignored the question the woman would not pursue it. "I did not hear you approach."

"A woman preoccupied with Lord Linton and the state of her undergarments is undoubtedly unable to manage even a rudimentary awareness of the civilized world around her," came the acid reply.

So taken aback was Sarah that she could not immediately formulate a response. Undaunted, Miss Simms promptly sat down on the bench and regarded Sarah with a penetrating look.

"You may have fooled Clarissa," she said, wagging a bony finger in Sarah's direction, "but Harriet Simms is a different kettle of fish."

"I beg your pardon?" Sarah strove for an air of baffled innocence, for despite Miss Simms's suspicions, the woman could have no solid evidence that anything was afoot.

"Do not play the innocent with me, missy," Miss Simms said sternly. "I know what is what. Linton thinks to fool everyone by ensconcing his light-o'-love under the very nose of his aunt, but even he cannot turn a sow's ear into a silk purse."

Had Harriet Simms just called her a pig? Sarah was torn between indignation and the need to deflect the woman's suspicions—if such a task was possible.

"Perhaps it is not fitting to dignify such a comment with a response," Sarah said with as much frosty composure as she could manage, "but I must inform you, Miss Simms, that I am no one's 'light-o'love'—*certainly* not Lord Linton's."

Miss Simms's thin brows arched to the heavens. "Do you take me for an imbecile, girl? If anyone besides Clarissa believed that orphaned-American tale, I will eat my hat. Even Linton is capable of devising a better story than that."

Oh, yes, Sarah thought. Lord Linton was capable of devising very good tales, but that was beside the point. Her immediate problem was to stop this woman from causing a ruckus over what they both knew to be a bold-faced lie.

"I *am* an orphan," she said evenly. At least that much was the truth. "Lord Linton has kindly taken me in until I can find a better situation." *That* was almost the truth. The rest Miss Simms would have to fill in with her imagination. Sarah was not about to start creating her own set of lies. One tangled web was enough.

"I see." Miss Simms's lips pursed thoughtfully. Evidently she decided that Sarah was telling the truth. "Then perhaps, child," she said a bit more kindly, "you are merely a victim of your own ignorance. Perhaps you do not realize what sort of a monster Linton is."

"There is no need . . ." Sarah began, but Miss Simms cut her off.

"I realize that you do not want to hear evil of your protector, but you must understand that Lord Linton is truly an enemy to womankind. He is a rake and a debaucher, and he does not limit his activities to those loose women who brazenly invite such attention. He is a threat to the innocent, ignorant, and unknowing girls of the land who think that a rakish grin and twinkling blue eyes . . ."

"Gray," Sarah corrected. "Lord Linton's eyes are gray."

Miss Simms scowled at the interruption. "As I was saying, that sort of man has no qualms about seducing an innocent young woman . . ."

"Lord Linton did not seduce me."

". . . and leaving her to fend for herself, without a care for the reaction of her family, her friends, and every tradition and privilege she held dear."

"Miss Simms," Sarah interjected, "how is it that you know these things about Lord Linton?"

Abruptly, Miss Simms clamped her mouth shut. Her pale hazel eyes, which had warmed to her tirade, suddenly became blank. "Linton has a reputation," she said tersely.

"A reputation," Sarah conceded, wondering why she felt the need to defend him. "But we do not know what is fact and what is not, do we? Is there someone you know who has personally suffered at the viscount's hands? For I assure you, I myself have not."

Miss Simms shook her head sadly. "You do not even realize it, do you, girl? That you are his next victim. Like all of them, you fall prey to a pleasing countenance and those devastating periwinkle eyes. When will you realize that you are merely co-operating in your own victimization?"

"Perhaps your vision is failing, Miss Simms," Sarah ventured, "but Lord Linton's eyes . . ."

"I am afraid you must give it up, Miss Armistead. There are certain matters Harriet Simms does not see clearly. I, unfortunately, am one of them."

Sarah started. The viscount stood at the edge of the garden, surveying them both with an air of contempt. She had not seen him since yesterday's contretemps over his script. A day's respite had not chased the militant look from that stony gaze.

Rising abruptly, Miss Simms made as if to pass him by, but Lord Linton stepped neatly in front of her, blocking her escape.

"Miss Armistead is my guest," he said in a voice that brooked no argument. "I expect you to extend to her all of the courtesy such a position demands."

But Miss Simms was no hen-hearted spinster. Her sharp gaze met his. "Do not think you can pull the wool over *my* eyes, Linton. I know well enough what she is to you."

"I grow weary of your insinuations," he said in a cold voice. "If they continue, I shall be forced to expel you from this house, my aunt notwithstanding."

"You will do no such thing," Miss Simms retorted, though her eyes were wide with alarm. "Clarissa would not allow it."

"No doubt Aunt Clarissa would be greatly disturbed should events call you away," he said blandly. "Since you are devoted to my aunt, I know you would not wish to have anything disturb her. I shall count on your conduct to prevent such a possibility."

Miss Simms's lips pursed tightly until they were nearly white with rage. Sarah wondered at the hostility between Lord Linton and his aunt's companion. Her own presence had exacerbated it, to be sure, but the tension between them had obviously existed for some time. Miss Simms was practically old enough to be Lord Linton's mother, so it could not be that there had been anything of a romantical nature between them. Despite the woman's harsh temper, Sarah could not help but feel sympathy for her. She had no home of her own but was dependent on the goodwill and financial support of people like Miss Porter and Lord Linton. Miss Simms's fate might very well be hers someday, Sarah realized. That knowledge caused her to shoot daggers at Lord Linton as Miss Simms scurried past him, her bony shoulders stiff with anger.

"You are very harsh, sir," Sarah said.

His gray gaze—how *could* Miss Simms have mistaken those eyes for blue?—met hers. "You would prefer that I allow her to insult you?" His voice was cold as ice. "Or could it be that her insinuations do not offend you?"

Sarah flushed. "Miss Simms was overset. She is obviously a troubled woman. I believe her lot in life is not an easy one."

"Harriet Simms lives a life of ease," he said, scoffing. "As my aunt's companion she has every comfort, everything she wants."

"Except independence."

"What?" He looked puzzled.

"Miss Simms has nothing of her own," Sarah explained. "She is dependent upon Miss Porter for a roof over her head and the clothes on her back. For some women, perhaps, that is quite acceptable. I do not imagine that Miss Simms is one of those women."

"She enjoys her position. She holds my aunt in great affection."

"Even so, there are some things that affection cannot purchase, Lord Linton."

Pondering that, he studied her for a long moment. Sarah

shifted uncomfortably on the bench. "Are you one of those women?" he asked at last.

"One of *what* women?" Sarah echoed cautiously.

His lips curved in a speculative smile. "One of those females who do not like being dependent upon others for their daily bread."

"I am my own person," she said, a defiant tilt to her chin. "I have had to make my own way in the world. I do not expect you to understand what that means."

"What does it mean?" he asked, his eyes unreadable.

"It means living in the attic of a rowdy boardinghouse, sharing a bed with a woman who constantly reeks of spirits and snores like a farm animal. It means subjecting oneself to the advances of every foxed male who enters the theater expecting to find fawning actresses eager for whatever favors he deigns to dispense. It means enduring leers and jeers from the pit and scorn from every well-dressed female in the house."

Sarah rose to face him. "In short, sir, it means making compromises. I do not expect you to understand that. You have doubtless never had to make a single compromise in your cossetted life."

"You know very little of my life, Miss Armistead," he said quietly.

"That may be, but you know even less of mine."

"You are wrong. I know a great deal about you."

Sarah stared at him blankly.

"You have spirit and fire," he explained, an odd reflective note in his voice. "The kind of fire that made Ophelia come alive on stage, not as a fragile martyr, but as a woman whose final response to her lover's repudiation defiantly deprived him of the prize he once sought so fervently."

"You are mistaken," she insisted. "Shakespeare did not see Ophelia as a rebel."

"No," he agreed. "But you do, do you not? That is why your performance was so compelling. *You* are a rebel, Miss Armistead. Through and through. That is why your Ophelia had fire. That is why you have not hired yourself out as a companion, as Miss Simms has done, as would any woman of genteel breeding who had come upon hard times." He paused. "You have not had an easy time of it, have you?"

His penetrating gaze bore no pity as it held hers, and Sarah was glad of that. She could not have endured his pity.

"My lot is no better nor worse than that of many women," she said stiffly.

"Like Harriet Simms?"

"Yes."

"Harriet is no rebel, Miss Armistead. She has a sharp tongue and a cross disposition, but she would never put a bullet through my heart."

"And I would?"

He studied her, amusement flaring in his eyes. "I believe you might. I shall have to remember to watch your aim at Lady Hogarth's ball."

"That is nonsense." Sarah retorted. "I have already told you what I think of such an implausible scenario." She picked up the sheaf of papers.

"Ah. The script. We are back to that again, are we?"

"Yes, indeed," she said, glad for the distraction. "This scene, for example. I would never wear dampened petticoats to any function. As for draping myself around you like some doxy, merely to compete with another woman, that is utterly ridiculous. I would never do such a thing."

"You keep forgetting that we are not talking about how *you* would conduct yourself, Miss Armistead. This is a role, that of my mistress. I cannot fathom why you are having such difficulty accepting that."

Sarah tried to control her temper. "I accept it well enough, my lord. I simply think her behavior here is not plausible. A mistress of yours would not be so . . . coarse."

His brows rose. "Your continued interest in the type of mistress I require is most flattering."

Biting back the retort that sprang to her lips, Sarah met his gaze evenly. "I only mean to say that the mistress you *require*, my lord, would probably have more sense than to risk her death in soggy muslin and create a scandal by throwing herself over you like a tablecloth."

"You seem to think I have little understanding of a woman's nature, Miss Armistead."

"I merely suggest that you are looking at things through a man's eyes, Lord Linton. You do not see what a woman sees. You do not really know a woman's world."

That remark seemed to take him aback, as well it might, for

a rake like Lord Linton surely considered himself an expert on all things concerning the female sex. He looked momentarily disconcerted as he considered her words.

"Perhaps you are right," he said at last.

His concession caught her by surprise. "What?"

"I have recently been accused of not seeing certain matters properly," he said in a musing tone. "Perhaps you can help me rectify that."

"I do not understand."

Warily, he studied her. "I might consider rewriting *certain* portions of my script—providing you help me."

Sarah stared at him. "I am no writer, my lord."

"But you are a woman," he said easily, his gaze roving over her in a disconcerting manner. "We will begin this afternoon. In my study, while the ladies are napping."

"Begin?" Suddenly, her pulse raced alarmingly. "What will you wish me to do?"

His lips curled in a sardonic smile. "I need a woman's perspective, Miss Armistead. You will show me how a real woman fights for her lover."

"Oh, my," was Sarah's faint response.

A mistress should not have freckles. That was Justin's first thought as he watched Sarah Armistead sail into his library and seat herself in a green leather wingback chair that brought out the brilliant emerald of her eyes. Unlike many women, she did not try to hide the freckles that danced over her pert nose and sprawled merrily over slightly flushed cheeks. Her auburn hair was pulled artlessly back from her face, but a few errant tendrils had escaped the hair combs to display her features with the richness of a costly frame on one of Turner's landscapes. Turner was especially good with sunlight, and that is what Miss Armistead looked like in a dress of yellow jonquil and matching shawl that perfectly complemented her coloring.

A sunbeam. Good Lord. Had he lost his mind?

Justin's frown caused her to sit a bit straighter in her chair and tilt her chin upward in that defiant manner he was coming to know quite well. The woman had entirely too much spirit for someone in her position. A militant spark in her eyes bespoke a stubborn wariness, even as an appealing openness shone within those green depths. With that freckled nose, honest gaze, and artless hairstyle, Miss Armistead projected a thoroughly wholesome look.

It had to be an illusion.

No one was more skilled at manipulating her image than an actress, and Miss Armistead was an extraordinarily good one. Unfortunately, she was also a most troublesome one, with the unbridled temerity to criticize the way he had written her part. It was a damned nuisance to have to deal with this rebellious termagant, but he had come too far to abandon his quest. Moreover, a nagging question had recently niggled at his thoughts.

What if she were right? Her knowledge of drama—and, yes, of females—might be worth considering, especially if it could prevent a mistake that would jeopardize his plan. But he had made no promises. None at all.

"Very well, Miss Armistead. Let us begin at the party scene, where you encounter my latest flirt." She waited expectantly, blushing slightly. "What, precisely, is wrong with the way I have envisioned your actions, other than the excessive 'draping' of your person over mine that you have already criticized?"

Her freckles almost disappeared in the flush that spread prettily over her face. She cleared her throat.

"The nibbling," she stated firmly.

He blinked. "Nibbling?"

Nodding, she regarded him with a determined look. "No respectable woman would nibble at a man's ear in public."

" 'Tis for an obvious purpose," he explained, wondering why the conversation had suddenly veered onto the entirely irrelevant topic of respectability. "You are demonstrating to the other woman your prior claim and reminding me of our shared carnal delights."

"Yes, well." Her face deepest scarlet, she cleared her throat again. "It is far too brazen. Perhaps your mistress could accomplish the same thing by lightly touching your arm and sending you a knowing gaze."

Justin almost laughed out loud. "You expect a man to respond to such subtlety? A light touch on the arm hardly evokes the far more personal intimacies one enjoys with a mistress."

It was fascinating the way those freckles kept appearing and disappearing amid her blushes. For a woman of Miss Armistead's broad experience, her obvious embarrassment was something of a wonder.

"On the contrary, my lord," she said stiffly. "I rather imagine that the merest touch from a woman you loved would be sufficient to kindle the, ah, spirit of desire."

"Who said anything about love?" Justin waved his hand impatiently. "This is a relationship based on carnal instinct—not love. You seem to confuse one with the other. Perhaps that is your difficulty with this scene. Let me say it plainly, Miss Armistead. You are playing the part of my mistress, a woman I bed. You are not playing the part of a woman I love."

"I am aware of the distinction, Lord Linton," she snapped, embarrassment giving her voice a strained tone. "But you have written this too broadly. The intensity of the scene will come from the undercurrents between the characters, as demonstrated by subtle cues, not by any coarse actions that would simply brand your mistress as a common harlot."

There was a moment of silence as Justin weighed her argument. "Show me," he commanded, irritated at having to take lessons from such a female.

"What?" Her voice held a note of alarm.

"You have offered a reasonable argument to support your view, Miss Armistead. You will show me just how you would carry off this particular scene in a believable fashion."

Regarding him dubiously, she rose and looked somewhat hesitantly around the room—for inspiration, he supposed. Evidently she found it in the statuette of a falcon that stood on a bookshelf. Her face was a picture of frowning concentration as she picked it up.

"We will pretend that this is the other woman," she said, her hand on the bird. "The one you have unwisely chosen to flirt with. I, your mistress, see this woman as a threat. I do not want to lose your affections—your *protection*, I should say," she quickly corrected, "so I will try to make myself as amiable as possible."

"That will not work," Justin said blandly. "I do not like amiable women."

She eyed him suspiciously. "You are trying to make this difficult for me, are you not, Lord Linton?"

"Not at all, Miss Armistead."

"Very well," she replied, her tone brisk. "As your mistress, I wish to engage your attention, so that you will remember the, er, delights we have shared and forget about the other woman."

"You will have to get closer than that, Miss Armistead. I have difficulty remembering delight from halfway across the room."

"Of course." Despite her sudden flush, she set the falcon down and moved decisively toward him, stopping a foot or so away. "Is this better?"

"Eminently." Justin discovered that he was vastly enjoying this particular scene.

"Perhaps I would put my hand on your arm like so." Tentatively, she allowed her hand to rest on the sleeve of his jacket.

"Surely you can do better, Miss Armistead. I can barely feel that."

Chewing her lip with pearly white teeth, she considered the matter. As he studied the small indentations in that smooth, rosy mouth, Justin felt a sudden pang of desire that owed nothing to the scene on the pages but arose from an entirely different one in his increasingly lurid imagination. What was it about this woman that spawned all manner of odd fantasies?

Just then, the pressure on his arm increased. Her fingers pressed firmly, provocatively, in the crook of his elbow, and he could feel his pulse point there throbbing with awakening need. She moved closer, her body mere inches from his, so close that he was aware of the warmth she generated, so far that he ached with frustration.

Only her fingers touched him, lingering tantalizingly at his elbow as they made an impression in the fabric. Kerseymere and fine linen shielded his bare skin from her touch—so flimsy a barrier that he easily felt her heat, yet so complete his clothing might as well have been forged steel. Justin studied those fingers. Long and delicate, they possessed a sensuality that hinted of hidden talents. Bemused, he allowed his gaze to wander upward to her face. From cool brilliant jewels, her eyes had transformed into limpid pools of emerald fire. Yet they held no naked desire, nothing that he could identify as a woman's raw craving for her lover. They radiated only a mesmerizing awareness of him, a spark that ignited the space between them and made it suddenly difficult to breathe.

Like a drowning man lured toward uncharted seas, Justin felt her eyes draw him in. He stared mutely at her, unaccustomed to this feeling of utter helplessness. Dimly, one part of his brain realized what had occurred.

Sarah Armistead had turned the full force of her sensual power on him, and it left him breathless with wonder and longing.

"Good God," he muttered.

Chapter Eight

L ord Linton was going to kiss her.

To Sarah's amazement, that stunning realization did not horrify her as it should have. Moreover, since disappearing into the role of cajoling mistress, she had made a number of other momentous discoveries. Such as the fact that touching his arm jolted her like a thunderbolt. Meeting that enigmatic gaze threw her pulse into erratic flip-flops. Watching the bemused curl of his lips sparked wild speculation as to how they might feel on hers.

Anticipation hovered in the wordless moment between them. The silence bespoke a clamoring readiness, like the unnatural stillness of an audience waiting expectantly for the actors to begin. Sarah told herself that this was but a performance. And yet, she did not imagine the singular shared awareness that sucked the breath from her lungs.

It was as if they were playing out a powerful fantasy that had taken on a life of its own. In the real world Lord Linton would never look at her this way. She did not possess the power to ignite his passion simply by touching his arm. Only in plays did such things happen, and Sarah had seen enough of life to know it bore little resemblance to art. A man did not respond to such subtlety, he had said. Besides, her touch had been clumsy, artless. He must have wanted to laugh at her lack of skill.

Mere inches separated them. Sarah's fingers still rested awkwardly on his coat sleeve. So painfully acute were her senses that she could feel the individual threads of the fabric. Underneath the fine wool, the muscles of his arm flexed against her touch. She knew she ought to remove her hand, but the same tension that electrified her nerve endings left her immobile.

Her mouth was dry. Without thinking, she licked her lips. Instantly, Lord Linton's gaze darted to her mouth. Sarah's face burned. She had not meant to do such a provocative thing.

Or had she? She did not know the answer.

Within those brooding eyes, dark pupils radiated a passion so palpable it set off answering tremors inside her. As he bent toward her, a muscle twitched in his jaw, and an uneasy tension about him suggested he was not entirely comfortable with the way this scene was playing out. Yet there was nothing ambiguous about the message of unfettered desire in his eyes.

Alarm bells pealed wildly in her brain, but the first touch of his lips muffled them quite thoroughly. His kiss was surprisingly gentle, his lips dry and cool. Sarah had been kissed before, mostly by the theater Lotharios as she dodged their gropings, once on stage by a mischievous actor broadly embellishing his role as her lover. But nothing in her past experience prepared her for the wild racing of her heart as Lord Linton's mouth covered hers. When his lips began to tease from her a shy gasp of pleasure, Sarah knew she was entirely out of her element.

This was no clumsy groping, but the consummate performance of a polished artist. His hands stole around her waist with disarming ease as he pulled her to him. His embrace held just enough pressure to give Sarah freedom to pull away, but not enough so that she wanted to. Indeed, she found herself straining for him, frustrated by the tentativeness of his kiss, which was undoubtedly calculated to drive a woman to distraction.

The sly rake knew precisely what he was doing, Sarah thought in irritation. She could feel the solid musculature of his chest and knew he was receiving a more than passing acquaintance with a similar part of her body. Mortified, she put her hands up in a belated attempt to establish a respectable distance between them.

Immediately, he severed the kiss.

"What is the matter, Miss Armistead?" Under the familiar sardonic tone was a strained note she could not identify. "Did you forget your part so soon? A man's mistress would not cavil at a chaste kiss like some unschooled virgin."

"I see nothing chaste about this," Sarah responded, trying to steady her runaway pulse. "And I am *not* your mistress."

He arched a brow, a rather *rakish* brow, Sarah decided. His hands still lingered about her waist, effectively preventing her from stepping out of the circle of his arms. Danger lurked within his eyes, but Sarah could not muster the will to flee. Amid the peril was a solid strength that was actually quite comforting. Rather than leave this masculine fortress, Sarah wanted to remain, to lean on someone other than herself, if only for a while.

Despite his mocking words, Lord Linton seemed to be experiencing a similar bout of indecision. For a long moment he studied her with a slightly quizzical expression. And while he did not let her go, he did not increase the pressure of his embrace. Perhaps she was wrong about the danger he posed. Any man who could kiss a woman with such tantalizing control and then hold her without making further demands was a man who could restrain himself, who could accept the limits she set.

Contenting herself with this thought, Sarah almost forgot that his hands rested at her waist, that she stood within the shelter of his powerful arms. It all seemed so natural, so pleasant, so harmless. Feeling slightly foolish for worrying so, she smiled up at him.

"Sarah."

It was only one word, spoken roughly, in a voice that resonated with need. But it was enough.

Her smile froze.

Hearing her name on his lips turned her knees to jelly. As his mouth once again descended to hers, Sarah knew how foolishly she had underestimated the danger.

When had that smoldering gray gaze become a blazing inferno? When had his thumbs begun massaging the rise of her hips? When had he eased her against him, bringing their bodies into scandalously intimate contact? And when, dear Lord, had he learned to kiss in such a fashion?

For this kiss was quite different from the other. This was sorcerer's work, deeply embedded with some mystic masculine power. Whatever its source, Sarah had never experienced anything like the scorching fire that suddenly seared her mouth, making it unusable for anything but this urgent meeting of flesh on flesh.

Panic flared, then fled, replaced by her own reckless need. Under that blazing kiss, her behavior grew quite wanton. Pressing herself to him, Sarah found she could not get close enough.

When his tongue sought entry to her mouth, she quickly granted it, discovering to her surprise that even that shocking intimacy was not sufficient. Lord Linton's kiss summoned a strange, blinding desire from some part of her that consigned respectability to the devil and wanted only to plunge headlong down the path to perdition.

It was impossible to know how long this sweet torture continued, for time had also become enslaved to Lord Linton's kiss. As he caressed her bare shoulder, Sarah wondered fleetingly when the bodice of her dress had been rearranged. As the masculine warmth of his hand closed over her breast, she realized she did not care. Her helpless whimper might have been a protest or a plea.

A blazing oath finally brought her to her senses, as did her lambswool shawl, which Lord Linton abruptly flung over her with a string of curses that would have bruised any lady's sensibilities.

He set her from him so quickly that Sarah would have fallen had not a chair been nearby.

"You have proven your point." A seething undertone in those icy words suggested that he held himself under tight control.

"I do not understand," Sarah stammered, trying desperately to straighten her clothing under the protective covering of her shawl.

A demonic gaze condemned her. "A 'light touch' and 'a knowing gaze'—you said they would be sufficient to kindle carnal desire." His smile was bitter. "You were correct, of course. I had not counted on your extraordinary skill and experience. I will rewrite the scene."

He strode through the study door, leaving Sarah to grapple with her disorderly clothing and the emptiness of her Pyrrhic victory.

"My, what a nasty rash you have, my dear. I declare it must cover your entire neck."

Clarissa Porter's unexpected greeting came just as Sarah emerged from Justin's study, wanting only to flee unnoticed to her own chamber and horrified at being discovered in such a state of disrepair. The older woman merely gave her a friendly smile.

"There is no need to distress yourself," she said, taking

Sarah's elbow. "I believe I have some cream that might help. Would you like to come to my room?" She gave no sign that there was anything unusual about Sarah's demeanor and the chafed spot on her neck that provided eloquent testimony as to her recent activities.

Sarah followed in Miss Porter's wake with a prayer that the woman's wits would prevent her from discerning the truth. Peering into the mirror in Miss Porter's room, however, Sarah moaned in dismay. The scarlet burn was visible even in the dim light that filtered through the closed drapes. Sarah recalled the rough sensation of Lord Linton's chin as he trailed kisses down her neck. At the time she had found it incredibly stimulating, but now she closed her eyes in mortification. The entire household would know of her indiscretion. Everyone would assume, as Miss Simms had, that she was Lord Linton's mistress.

"Now, now. You must not be overset," Miss Porter said. "Harriet told me she saw you in the garden earlier. I declare, the bindweed is as coarse as an elephant's hide this season. You must have brushed into it, just as I did the other day. I have been meaning to ask Justin to have that hedge trimmed. It wants discipline."

Sarah sent a silent prayer heavenward for the lady's blissful ignorance and her previous encounter with the nefarious bindweed. "Thank you, Miss Porter, but I . . ."

"You must call me Aunt Clarissa, dear. Everyone in the family does."

Uncertain as to how Aunt Clarissa came to consider her kin, Sarah nevertheless gave her a tentative smile. "Certainly, ma'am. But I can see you have drawn the drapes for your afternoon nap. I will just retire to my room and tend to my complexion."

"Oh, no, dear," Aunt Clarissa replied gaily. "I am not tired in the least. I keep the drapes closed because Silvester prefers darkness to light. Besides, I have the perfect cream for what ails you."

No cream could repair the damage to her pride and self-esteem wrought by Lord Linton's scathing denunciation. No mere cream could erase her shame. She had submitted willingly to his scandalous advances—nay, she had *invited* them by touching his person provocatively. She deserved whatever punishment fate handed her.

"That is quite a burn, my dear," Aunt Clarissa observed, applying a fragrant ointment to Sarah's neck.

With her emotions in a turmoil, Sarah could scarcely appreciate the soothing cool of the salve. How could she hope to hold on to her respectability when she had so eagerly aroused a man everyone knew to be a dangerous predator of females? Fortunately he had developed a sudden disgust of her; otherwise, who knew what liberties she might have permitted in her demented state?

Why had she permitted them, more to the point? Had she simply fallen prey to a skilled seducer's art? Or was there something within *her,* something of the rebel, as he had said? Something that yearned to abandon the uphill fight to retain her virtue and, instead, dance to the devil's tune? Sarah closed her eyes against her reflection, against the new awareness, the vulnerability that Lord Linton had awakened. If she continued to stare at that swollen mouth and chafed neck in the mirror, she would have to concede that there was something else in her eyes—something very like the desire and lust she had seen reflected in his own.

"I would suggest applying this three times daily. You might also consider wearing a high-necked gown for the next day or two. Just until the chafing disappears."

The violet eyes held no sign of censure. Indeed, Aunt Clarissa seemed most solicitous. Sarah desperately wanted someone to turn to, another woman who might understand. Her mother's axioms had long guided her, but they had always painted the world in starkest black and white. Since leaving the comfort of that little house in Surrey, Sarah had discovered that things often cast themselves in shades of gray. And though she was not Justin's mistress, for a moment in his study she had become that fantasy woman. Giving in to sinful lust had not repulsed her, as she had always imagined it must. Instead, it had thrilled her beyond her wildest dreams. She could not confide that to anyone. Even the generous-hearted Aunt Clarissa would not accept such a wanton woman.

"Now, dear, there is an hour or so before dinner." Aunt Clarissa tucked the pot of cream into Sarah's hands. "Why do you not retire to your chamber for a bit? If you do not feel well enough to come down later, I am sure everyone will understand."

Succumbing to her blue spirits was tempting, but Sarah had never had the luxury of retreating from difficulty. "Thank you, ma'am, but there is nothing wrong with my health."

"That is the spirit." Aunt Clarissa beamed her approval. "You must not let a little setback get the best of you. Silvester told me that from the very beginning, and he is invariably correct."

Sarah had the distinct impression that she was missing much of the import of the conversation. Then again, much that Aunt Clarissa said was beyond fathoming. Sarah smiled uncertainly, but before she could slip out of the room Aunt Clarissa touched her elbow.

"I understand your distress, my dear," she said kindly. "You must not imagine that I have never known such emotions. I told you I was the black sheep of the family—remember?"

Warily, Sarah nodded.

"Even now, sometimes at night, the feelings wash over me such that I can almost touch them." Aunt Clarissa's gaze took on a faraway expression. "Silvester is a comfort to me, but he is maddeningly thin of substance, you know," she added forlornly. "That is my chief regret."

Tears shimmered in the older woman's extraordinary violet eyes. Aunt Clarissa must have been a most beautiful woman at one time. Sarah could not imagine what had caused her tears, but she did not doubt that Justin's aunt was intensely moved by something. She touched the other woman's hand encouragingly. Aunt Clarissa smiled.

"You did not come here to listen to an old woman's ramblings."

"You are not old, ma'am."

Aunt Clarissa shook her head and gently stroked a tiny bouquet of dried violets near her bed. "I am old enough, my dear. I am old enough."

"It is beginning." Anh held out the bamboo stick for inspection. Justin eyed the butler in irritation.

"*What* is beginning?"

"The change."

Justin pointedly ignored the bamboo. He palmed a deck of cards, deftly shuffled them with one hand, and tossed back a glass of brandy with the other. The liquid seared his throat, a familiar and predictable sensation from which he drew some comfort since there had been precious little of the predictable in his day. First there was that disastrous and profoundly unsettling encounter with Miss Armistead. Then he discovered that his aunt had seen fit to decorate his study with a riotous assortment of sweet-smelling flowers. Now his butler had chosen this of all nights to retreat into his mystical ramblings.

Incense assaulted his nostrils. Justin had never cared for the smell but tolerated it because Anh liked to indulge in such rituals from time to time, and, truth be told, they were invariably interesting. Tonight, however, Justin was not in the mood for ancient fortune-telling. Studying the hollow bamboo stick, which itself contained a number of smaller sticks, he glowered.

"I have no need to learn about the future."

Unblinking, Anh continued to hold the stick out to his employer. At last, and with a sigh of resignation, Justin took the bamboo and gave it an angry shake. One of the smaller sticks fell onto the carpet. Anh studied the odd markings on it, but did not immediately comment on their import. Instead, he tossed up a pair of wooden blocks shaped like the two halves of a nut—one side convex and the other flat—and watched them fall onto the carpet.

"Ah," the butler replied as the blocks landed, one facing upward and the other down.

Justin was quite familiar with this part of the ritual. If both blocks had landed facing the same way, he would have had to choose another stick. The present configuration signaled that his choice was correct. He wondered what Anh had up his sleeve. For as much as Justin had come to believe over the years in the efficacy of things beyond his ken, this particular ritual had always struck him as pure hokum, subject to the whims of his wily butler. At least Anh would be so occupied with the divining rods that he would not divine the key to his card trick, Justin thought as he removed a vase of daisies from the card table and began to deal.

"A member of the fair sex is thinking of you."

The cards squirted from his hand onto the floor—to Justin's amazement, for he had not displayed such clumsiness since he was a raw youth. With a curse, he gathered them up and reshuffled. "You forget that I am generally considered one of the most incorrigible rakes around," he said dryly. "I daresay that some foolish woman must waste her thoughts in such a manner."

Anh gave no sign that he was surprised, either by Justin's awkward dealing or by his declaration. Instead, he stared more intently at the bamboo stick on the floor.

"She is to be the instrument of change."

Justin had no doubt to whom Anh was referring. Indeed, he suspected Anh of using the rods to reproach him for his treatment of Miss Armistead. He had not confided to his butler the details of his scheme to avenge his father's murder, but very little slipped past Anh. Nevertheless, any change would be exceedingly unwelcome. Justin's plan was set in stone. He wanted no last-minute revisions.

Other than the one he had been forced to make this afternoon, of course, after the little minx had showed him that he had indeed written her part too broadly. Who would have thought that he could respond so explosively to the merest touch from a conniving actress? Justin prided himself on being attuned to the subtleties of a woman's seductive arts, but she had done more with her fingers than all the skilled courtesans he had ever encountered. It defied credibility that a man of his reputation could be brought to heel by a second-rate actress.

No, he amended, there was nothing second-rate about her acting skills. For that one glorious moment in his study, she had made him believe she was his for the taking. He had tried to resist the impulse to kiss her, but it was impossible to resist the siren call of those lips, the mesmerizing appeal in those eyes. She had driven him to distraction, and he had behaved like some primitive creature staking claim to his mate.

Miss Armistead was good. Very good. She had forced him to change his script, but he would be damned if he would change anything else for her. There was nothing magical about kissing those lips, about running his hands over those smooth, bare shoulders. . . .

"You may choose again."

Anh wore that maddeningly impassive expression that could mean a thousand things. Justin snatched up the bamboo, shook it, and threw another stick onto the floor. Again the choice was approved in the ritual with the wooden blocks. Anh studied the markings on the new stick. Sadly, he shook his head. Against his better judgment, Justin found his interest caught.

"*What?* Damnation, man, out with it." As Anh's pitying gaze met his, Justin reminded himself that he did not believe in this silly ritual.

"The change will destroy you."

"That is quite comforting, of course."

Anh eyed him steadily. "You would do well not to take this lightly."

"Oh, I do not," Justin retorted. "You tell me that a woman is about to change my life and that the change will destroy me—no, that is not a thing that I take lightly. Now, may we forget about this nonsense and get on to the cards? This time I have hidden the two red queens. A guinea if you can find them."

Anh refused to take the bait. "Sometimes destruction is necessary," he said quietly. "It is the process of change. When the sun goes, the moon comes. When the moon goes, the sun comes. Sun and moon alternate. Thus light comes into being. Similarly, the past contracts. The future expands. Contraction and expansion act upon each other. Hereby arises that which furthers."

It was one of the longest speeches the butler had ever made. Justin stared at him, wanting to wring the man's neck but knowing that Anh truly believed his words.

"Very well, then. I am about to be destroyed. What do you suggest I do about it?" Justin could not keep the sarcasm from his voice, and again Anh shook his head.

"You must travel ten thousand years and ten thousand miles to find the answer to that question."

Justin hid a smile. Ten thousand of anything was Anh's way of saying merely that the distance was substantial. Sometimes, he was not referring at all to distance or time—only to the enormity of the task at hand. Anh's comments were often indecipherable.

"Let us hope I am up to it, then," Justin said lightly.

Without a word Anh carefully collected the bamboo sticks and tucked them inside the larger stick. He wrapped the stick in a frayed mat covered by many symbols. Finally, he turned to the table and studied Justin's cards.

"The diamond queen will not help you," Anh intoned, turning up a card. "You ought to prefer her more amiable companion." He turned up another card, the heart queen.

Justin stared at the two red queens. He had painstakingly hidden them in an intricate configuration. Never in a thousand years should Anh have known where they were—never in *ten* thousand years.

Sometimes, Justin reflected as he studied his butler's retreating form with narrowed eyes, an enormous task could be accomplished very quickly.

Chapter Nine

The blast shattered the meadow's morning calm. A flurry of pigeons and pheasants took to the air, squawking frantically as if the hounds of hell were snapping at their tails. Sarah, who had just barely avoided shooting off the toes of her right food, stood paralyzed in shock.

"Damnation, woman! I told you the thing has a hair-trigger!" Lord Linton ripped the smoking pistol from her hand.

"And I am supposed to know what that means?" Sarah retorted, trying to calm her nerves, though the gunshot still rang in her ears. "*You* are the expert, my lord, not I."

Dark brows met ominously above stormy eyes, and for a moment Sarah wondered if he meant to give up on her. Teaching her to handle a pistol was proving more difficult than either of them had thought.

"The gun is too heavy for you," he said, studying her slender wrists. "You will have to hold it in both hands."

Sarah eyed the weapon dubiously. "Why can I not use one of those tiny pistols I have heard about? Once one of Rose McIntosh's gentlemen friends showed us a clever little gun made to resemble a fork. Surely that would be easier to manage than this monstrosity."

"Unless you mean to shoot me across the dinner table, I can see no use for a weapon that resembles a fork," came his dry response. "Moreover, this 'monstrosity,' as you call it, is a masterpiece. Perfectly balanced and deadly accurate—in the right hands, of course."

Glumly, Sarah sat on a nearby rock. "But can you not see? I do not have the right hands. The weapon is too cumbersome . . ."

"It was my father's dueling pistol, a Manton—the best made. More to the point, it is the gun that killed him."

"I see." And she did. Everything about that event fifteen years ago must be the same. The debate was closed. "But how did Lady Greywood obtain your father's dueling pistol?" she asked, puzzled. "Surely he kept it at his house?"

"I do not know," he snapped. "It does not matter. May we continue?"

Sarah sighed. Lord Linton was surly as a bear this morning. There was certainly no sign of the man who kissed her so warmly yesterday. Other than to criticize her handling of the pistol, he had said very little and seemed to wish to keep as much distance between them as possible.

He must have a thorough disgust of her, Sarah thought morosely as she got to her feet. Well, he could scarcely think less of her than she thought of herself. She had not wanted to face him today. Dinner last night had been strained, but at least Aunt Clarissa and Miss Simms had been present. Now there were just the two of them in this wide meadow. Sarah had faced hostile audiences before, but none had intimidated her like Lord Linton.

"Normally," he was saying, enunciating clearly as for a small child, "a gentleman fires as soon as he brings the pistol up. But you must take the time to be certain of your aim. Fortunately, the lock is a fast one, so you will lose nothing by waiting. Here." He handed her the weapon. "Hold the pistol with two hands. Feel the weight. You will not find another with such perfect balance. It will come up easily, with the barrel perfectly horizontal."

Although Sarah did not see why one pistol should merit so much praise, she dutifully held it with both hands. To her surprise, it no longer seemed so heavy. Concentrating, she brought the gun up just as he had demonstrated. But when she looked over at him for approval, he was scowling.

"No, no. You must not bend your elbows. You will have no control. Hold the pistol at arm's length. Keep your elbows almost straight."

Sarah's wobbly effort elicited an impatient oath and a growl as he abruptly closed the distance between them. From behind, he reached in front of her and placed his hands over hers, guiding the pistol into position.

"There," he muttered into her ear. "Now all you need do is pull the trigger. Move only your forefinger, nothing more.

Above all, do not put pressure on the trigger until you are ready to fire."

Acutely conscious of the fact that his arms were wrapped around her, Sarah tried her best to follow his instructions. Swallowing hard, she squeezed the finger. The gun fired, propelling her backward against his broad chest. Had his arms not supported her, she would have fallen.

After bearing her weight for an awkward moment, Lord Linton gingerly set her on her feet.

"That was much better," he said stiffly, taking a step backward. "Do you think you can manage it on your own?"

"I will try," Sarah said. "But I do not know if I can hit the target." The target measured twelve feet high and three feet wide and was supposed to represent a curtain. Next to it stood a wooden shape cut to resemble a man, which represented Lord Linton. In the scene, Sarah was to point the gun at him but move it slightly to the right just before firing, so that the bullet lodged harmlessly in the wall behind the drapery. No one watching would be the wiser. He would fall to the floor, seemingly mortally wounded. A preparation of pig's blood hidden in his waistcoat would enhance the scene's believability.

Steel glinted in his gaze. "If I thought that you were not up to the task," he said in a measured tone, "I would not have hired you. You need only practice. You will find that the pistol will grow lighter and the control of your aim greater. Let us continue, if you please."

While he occupied himself with priming and reloading the weapon, Sarah watched his muscled arms and finely tapered fingers. To be sure, Lord Linton was in excellent physical condition, but there was a mesmerizing grace in his performance of a task that required more art than brute strength. Perhaps that was why he was so skilled at those clever card tricks—and at coaxing a woman into revealing a sensual nature she had not dreamed existed.

Was it her imagination, or was he missing a bit of his customary aplomb this morning? Sarah doubted it had anything to do with those kisses in his study. They would not faze a man like him. Rather, he was probably having second thoughts about relying on her dubious marksmanship. Handling a pistol for the first time had made her appreciate the enormity of the task before her, and she wondered at the sort of man who could risk so much on an untrained novice. Then again, Lord Linton left nothing to chance. If he said she was up to it, then she must be. But Sarah eyed the pistol nervously as he handed it to her.

"I will be beside myself at the ball, knowing that that thing is hidden in my muff. What if I am jostled accidentally? The gun might go off."

"Leave it at half-cock. It will not fire until you pull the pistol out and draw the hammer back fully."

Sarah eyed the little hammer. "What if I cannot do it properly? What if I forget my lines? What if I cannot remember any of this?" She bit her lip in agitation.

At his heavy sigh, Sarah braced herself for a scathing lecture about nervous females. Instead, he set the pistol on a rock and turned to her, a somber look on his face.

"I accept responsibility for the state of your nerves this morning," he said quietly. "I apologize for allowing myself to become too . . . involved with the scene we were rehearsing yesterday. It will not happen again. We must both remember that we are actors performing parts. It is dangerous to allow illusion to take the place of reality."

"Yes. Of course." Sarah stared at those unreadable eyes. He was telling her that there was nothing personal in his kiss, nothing real about the moment they had shared in his study. It was all an illusion, a scene they were acting out with the larger goal of capturing a killer.

"I do not know what I can do to rectify the situation," he said, studying her, "except to have faith in your ability to manage your nerves that night. Surely you have dealt with stage fright before?"

Unsure of his mood, Sarah nodded. "Sometimes I feel nervous before going on—especially if it is a new part. But the moment I begin to speak my lines, the fright goes away. I have no reason to believe this will be different, only . . ." She broke off.

"Only the stakes are a bit higher," he finished, an odd gleam in those murky gray depths.

Sarah bit her lip. "If I forget a line onstage, my lord, some other actor rushes into the breach. Or the noise from the pits is such that it does not matter. But what if I make a mistake that night? What if my aim is off? What if I do not hit the curtain but . . ."

"Kill me, instead?" He smiled, and Sarah's heart caught in her throat at the sudden brilliance in his eyes. "Then I am afraid it will fall to you to hear Lady Greywood's confession," he said wryly, "for *I* shall not be in a position to do so."

"That is not amusing."

"Do not worry, Miss Armistead. I have faced more deadly opponents than you and lived to tell the tale." Abruptly he turned away. "Shall we continue the lesson?"

For nearly two hours, Justin watched her lift the pistol with both hands, aim it at the target, and squeeze the trigger. The first few times she tried it alone, the report propelled her backward and down onto that portion of her anatomy he had cradled so reluctantly when he was instructing her in the proper firing technique. Although he rushed to her assistance, she merely scrambled to her feet, dusted herself off, and waited patiently until he reloaded.

Her determination was impressive. Sarah—somehow he now thought of her as Sarah, not Miss Armistead—had grit, that much was certain. She would need many more days of practice, but he could see definite progress this morning. Justin breathed a sigh of relief. For a few long moments he had wondered whether it was foolish to entrust his life to a woman who had never before handled a firearm.

Sarah was a fine actress, willing to work hard. She would shine in the role of his mistress. She would pull it off. Revenge would be his. He could almost taste it.

Oddly, it did not taste as satisfying as her lips had yesterday afternoon, but that had been a momentary lapse. Revenge was sweeter by far than anything else—even Sarah's charms. But he had learned yesterday that he must keep her at arm's length if he were to fully concentrate on his plan. Considering the time they must spend together, that might prove difficult, but Justin never doubted his supreme control. Just because she looked perfectly charming at the moment with dust on her hands and smudges on her face, there was nothing about her to challenge the iron grip he had on his will. He watched her wipe her mouth with the back of her hand. Squinting carefully against the midday sun, she aimed his father's pistol and gently squeezed the trigger.

For the first time, she hit the target dead-on.

At her whoop of joy, Justin could not stifle the broad smile that spread across his face. It was the most natural thing in the world to grasp her about the shoulders and give her a congratulatory pat, and most unnatural to suddenly pull his hands away and stuff them in his pockets.

"I think that is enough for today," he heard himself say gruffly. At her look of disappointment, he added in a more gentle tone, "It is quite acceptable to rest on one's laurels for a bit, you know."

Her delighted laugh was so captivating he did not mind when she took his arm on the walk back. He did not think she intended the gesture to be provocative. She had understood when he explained earlier that the attraction between them was only an illusion. Sarah appreciated plain-speaking. They would deal well with each other now that the matter of those kisses was out of the way.

Justin found himself caught up in her natural enthusiasm as they strolled back to the house. Her hand nestled in the crook of his arm; it was a perfect fit. With some alarm he realized that he had never felt more comfortable with her. It would not do to get too close to a woman like Sarah.

"I declare, I am almost ready to charge out and fight a duel myself," she said breathlessly. "How satisfying it must be to put some nasty boor in his place. I almost envy you men—demanding satisfaction and exacting it in such a dashing fashion."

A forgotten bitterness rose in his throat. Her words spawned the long-buried image of a green lad righteously demanding satisfaction from a man too mean and drunk to do anything but play deadly games with a youthful conscience.

"Dueling is the purview of fools and bullies. It permits men of breeding to kill each other politely and thereby protect some incomprehensible code of honor inaccessible to the lower classes. The fact that it is outlawed has done little to stem the unfortunate practice."

Puzzled, she studied him. "But *you* have fought duels, have you not?"

From a very early age. Justin's muscles tensed at the memory of that scene in his father's study. He forced his voice to remain dispassionate, for he must appear to be the dashing rake, cool master of the codes of male honor.

"Yes, of course," he drawled in a bored voice. "Lord Greywood challenged me after discovering that I had a somewhat intimate acquaintance with his wife."

Embarrassment and confusion swept her features. "You fought over Lady Greywood, the woman you are trying to trap?"

"Not the dowager," he corrected. "Her wayward daughter-in-law. My opponent was the dowager's son, the present earl."

Silently, she absorbed this information. "Did you kill him?" she asked at last.

"No. I deloped. As did he. The duel was a formality, intended only to allow the earl to salvage his position by appearing to avenge a wrong done him by the miscreant who dared take his property."

"His property?"

Justin turned a sardonic gaze on her. "Surely you are aware that a man's wife is as much his property as his cattle? Until the integrity of the line is assured, she belongs to her husband. The young countess has only produced one child—a girl. The heir has yet to come forth, and I assume the earl will want one or two to spare. Until then, I imagine Greywood will be forced to fight a great many duels, for he is cursed with a wife who cannot curb her wayward appetites. I advised him to take her away to the country, but he is the sort to eschew advice from his wife's erstwhile lover."

This speech was intended to shock her—and to forestall further questions about a subject he did not care to discuss. But as she stared at him in stunned silence, the intent look in her eye revealed that her mind was a whirlwind of activity.

"It can be no coincidence that you fought with the son of the woman who is your sworn enemy," she persisted. "Everything you do is part of your plan, is it not?"

Her astuteness irritated him. "The dowager's husband—the late Lord Greywood—fought a duel with my father under similar circumstances," Justin conceded. "My father also deloped, although he was a crack shot and could easily have killed his man."

"And since you are attempting to duplicate everything about that time," she said slowly with dawning horror, "you managed to get the present Lord Greywood to challenge you. The dowager must have been beside herself."

Justin merely shrugged.

"The extent of your single-minded pursuit of revenge is appalling."

Her condemnation angered him. In amazement, Justin realized that he wanted her approval.

"You could have been killed," she added, her concern further infuriating him.

"Oh, I am a passing shot," he responded coldly. "It is more likely that Greywood would have cocked up his toes."

"You are a monster."

Angered, he rounded on her. What did she know of him, his past, his character? Had her father ever handed her a pistol and demanded that she blow her brains out?

"No more monstrous than a cunning wench who would trade her favors for a thousand pounds," he retorted.

Outraged, she took a step backward. "If you are referring to yesterday, rest assured that the money you are paying me for this farce had nothing to do with what occurred between us in your study."

The little witch. Justin grabbed her arms, imprisoning her so that she could not retreat. Bringing his face close to hers, he let her see the full extent of his contempt.

"No," he agreed smoothly, his voice dripping with scorn. "I could have had you for free, could I not?"

Justin had been consigned to the devil before, but never with such eloquent hatred as Sarah's green eyes possessed before she whirled away and ran toward the house. But there had been more than hatred in those eyes, he realized. There had been pain.

For some reason, that knowledge pierced his gut like a well-aimed shot from his father's Manton.

Chapter Ten

Cruelty had been his father's coin, but Justin had never fallen prey to that brutal madness. Now, however, a horrible thought seized him: was cruelty his blood legacy, his father's final joke on his hated offspring? Even in his brandy-induced haze, such a conclusion was inescapable.

Sarah had done nothing to earn his enmity, yet he had lashed out at her with words deliberately designed to wound. He had not meant merely to put her in her place. No, for one awful moment he had meant to destroy her.

What was it about her he found so threatening? She was just an actress, a woman who had put herself beyond the pale by taking to the stage. She belonged to a debauched world where women had their price, and it was nowhere near a thousand pounds. How did he know he could hurt her by simply acknowledging that fact?

To be sure, she had put on a performance tonight at dinner he would not soon forget. Dressed in a demure gown cut from a pink fabric that lent a rosy innocence to her features, Sarah had orchestrated her every move to proclaim her virtue. The single strand of pearls around her neck looked as delicate and pure as the pearls seeded in a baby's christening dress. She was solicitous to Aunt Clarissa, amiable to Harriet Simms, complimentary to Cook. Toward him she displayed a deferential manner that might have disarmed him, had he not seen the militant spark that the actress in her could not entirely suppress.

Sarah was a survivor. Her bravado performance at dinner had thrown the matter firmly back into his face. He owed her an apology.

Again.

How had he come to such a pass? He had been at great pains to appear to be everything his father had been, knowing it was that uncanny resemblance that would help wring a confession from Lady Greywood's tormented conscience. Yet he had tried to separate the man from the role, to be scrupulous in a way that his father was not. He had seduced no innocents, nor trifled with any woman who wished for more than a spirited time in bed. He wanted no woman's tears on his conscience. His father's careless debauchery had spawned grief and broken hearts, but Justin had harmed no one.

Until now. The disbelief and pain in Sarah's eyes provided all the proof he needed.

Taking a deep swallow of brandy, Justin surveyed the contents of his bookshelves. His grim eyes lit upon *Faustus*. Had he indeed sold his soul to the devil? Had the prospect of revenge driven all sensibility from him? Had it turned him into . . . his father?

Perhaps the masquerade had become more than a role. Perhaps he had played the cynical rake too long. How long could one live an illusion before it became all too real?

Anh had spoken of changes. Justin had laughed at the divining rods. He was not laughing now.

"Oh, my dear, a letter! It could only be news about your family!" Aunt Clarissa clapped her hands eagerly, while Miss Simms looked up with a suspicious frown.

Sarah stared at the missive on Anh's silver salver. It was addressed to her, in care of Lady Justine Linton. She met the butler's eyes. They gave no sign that there was anything unusual about correspondence coming to her in care of a fictitious person; nor did they hint at why Anh had brought the letter directly to her instead of his employer.

"Thank you," she said politely, hoping her expression did not betray her alarm at receiving a communiqué from her brother. Sarah had always kept William apprised of her whereabouts, inventing a number of genteel employers as she moved around the circuit. With her move to Lintonwood Sarah had invented Lady Justine to replace her last employer, who—she had written William—had gone to meet her maker. All of Sarah's "employers" had gone on to their final reward. It made matters much less complicated.

Filled with foreboding about what William would deem so important as to break his longstanding abhorrence of writing,

Sarah tucked the letter into the pocket of her dress. The two ladies stared at her expectantly.

"Do not stand on ceremony, Sarah," Aunt Clarissa said. "You will not slight us by reading your letter now, as I am certain you must be eager to do. We are not in the least offended, are we, Harriet?"

"No, indeed," Miss Simms agreed, and Sarah did not miss the keen light of curiosity in her pale eyes.

"Who knows, but this is communication from your long-lost relatives?" Aunt Clarissa trilled happily.

"Indeed," echoed Miss Simms, focusing her beady eyes on Sarah. "You must read it now."

Sarah cleared her throat. "Very well, then." She broke the sealing wax and opened the envelope. Straining over her brother's uneven scrawl, Sarah was aware that the two women watched her closely. It seemed that William had had some dispute at school with a fellow student who had heretofore been his best friend. The result was that, rather than traveling to Yorkshire with his friend for next month's holiday, he had decided to visit her at Lintonwood.

"Oh, my!" Sarah exclaimed in dismay.

"What is it, dear?" Aunt Clarissa's violet eyes brightened with concern. "Perhaps we can help."

By next month, Sarah and Lord Linton would be in London. She could write William that her employer was traveling to town, but that news would likely make him even more eager to visit, for he had longed to explore the delights of London. Sarah would have to think of something else, but for now there was a pressing need to answer Aunt Clarissa's question. Her usually agile mind went blank.

Aunt Clarissa waited expectantly. Miss Simms's eyes sharpened with suspicion. Sarah opened her mouth to speak, but not a word came out. Where was Lord Linton's glib tongue when it was needed? Sarah clutched the letter, but to her dismay it slipped her fingers and fluttered to the floor. Miss Simms rose speedily to pick it up. Just as her long, bony fingers plucked at the pages, a decidedly masculine hand snatched the letter away.

"Ah, the communiqué from your father's solicitors," drawled a familiar baritone. "I have been expecting it for some time." Lord Linton scanned the contents. When he finished, he gave no hint that anything was amiss. Instead, he smiled in satisfaction as he turned to the ladies.

"The solicitors believe they have several leads on the whereabouts of Miss Armistead's relatives." Sarah marveled at the ease with which the lie tripped off his tongue. Not for the first time she thought Lord Linton had missed his true calling. His acting abilities would have given Mr. Kean pause. "There are some confidential matters we must discuss," he added, turning to her. "If it is convenient, Miss Armistead, perhaps you will be so kind as to come to my study later."

Such polite words for an imperial order, Sarah thought wryly, knowing she had not misjudged the note of command in his voice. She dreaded the coming confrontation. On the other hand, there was something satisfying about the prospect of clearing the air. Lord Linton had canceled this morning's shooting practice, and she knew it was because of the angry words they exchanged yesterday. Her own anger had carried her through dinner last night, but by today it was spent. Sarah was weary of the uneasy tension, weary of trying to maintain her pride behind a mask of indifference. Anything, even another angry confrontation, was preferable to the strained silence between them.

"I will be happy to do so, my lord," Sarah said with such deference that his gaze shot to hers. There was a message in those gray depths, but Sarah could not read it.

Aunt Clarissa looked crestfallen. Miss Simms smirked. Lord Linton merely bowed and left the room, taking William's letter with him.

Sarah found him absently shuffling a deck of cards, studying some strange symbols in a book whose binding bore the title *Magus.* He looked fatigued, as if he had been searching for something that still eluded him.

"Sit down, Miss Armistead."

"Once you called me Sarah," she said quietly. "I do not mind if you do so again."

Only a single lamp on his desk illuminated the room, but it was enough to reveal the surprise that chased some of the weariness from his gaze.

By evoking the memory of that scandalous kiss, the only occasion on which he had used her given name, she wanted to remind him that he had not always kept her at arm's length nor hidden behind that imposing desk. As the sudden spark in his eyes indicated he recalled the occasion quite well, Sarah decided that she had been too bold.

And perhaps unwise.

Making a tent of his hands, he studied her silently for what seemed like an eternity. The moment in which he might have accepted her invitation came and went. Unnerved by his wordless refusal, Sarah reddened in embarrassment.

Then he surprised her.

"My remarks of yesterday were unforgivable," he said, placing his palms on the desk and meeting her gaze squarely. "I meant no harm or disrespect." He paused, then took a deep breath. "No, that is not true. I intended to wound you, for reasons that are not entirely clear to me. For that, I do not deserve your consideration. Humbly do I beg of you to grant it, nevertheless."

What had happened? Had a man who resembled Lord Linton in form and appearance somehow invaded his mind and spoken to her in his voice? Sarah stared at him in wonder.

A familiar wry smile told her that Lord Linton was still very much in possession of himself. "Would I be more convincing if I couched my apology in shades of irony? For I assure you, I mean to persuade you of my sincerity."

Sarah shook her head. " 'Tis just that I am unaccustomed to hearing such sentiments from you."

"That is not true," he reminded her, a teasing glint in his eye. "Have I not been compelled three times previously to apologize to you for my various sins?"

"Not *compelled,* surely," she protested.

He sobered. "No. Not then, and not now." Abruptly he rose from behind his desk and crossed the room to her. "I am most sincere, Sarah. Will you forgive me?"

His sudden nearness almost robbed her of breath. "Of course," she murmured.

It was as if he had been holding his own breath, for he sighed heavily. Instantly, Sarah wanted to ease whatever troubled him. "I am as much to blame as you," she added. "I should never have called you a monster."

"Do not apologize for stating only the truth." His abrupt scowl reminded her that there were angry currents in this man that she could not begin to fathom. The subject was apparently closed, for he returned to his desk and picked up William's letter.

"Now," he said briskly, "who the devil is William and why does he wish to visit you and, er, 'Lady Justine'?"

"William is my brother," Sarah confessed. "He is away at Eton. I invented Lady Justine in order to explain my presence at Lintonwood."

"Eton?" His brows arched in surprise. "I take it that your brother does not know of our arrangement."

Sarah studied her hands. "My brother does not even know that I am an actress. He believes that I have been employed by various ladies as a companion. I send him money each quarter from my wages." She met his gaze. "William thinks me a respectable woman."

"I do not understand." He frowned. "Why create all these difficulties for yourself? Why did you turn to the stage instead of more genteel employment?"

Sarah walked over to the window. It was impossible to explain her reasons to a man of such wealth that he could afford to satisfy his every desire and dream.

"In the beginning, I was certain I would make money in the theater. My parents and friends had praised my talent. I wanted to believe that in a matter of weeks I could win acclaim as well as secure a lucrative wage."

Her eyes focused on the far horizon beyond Lord Linton's well-manicured lawn. "It was not like that, of course. The country is full of actresses seeking employment. At last I managed to get Mr. Stinson to hire me. The circuit provided steady work, but it is not precisely what I envisioned.

"I had seen Mr. Kemble, you see, and Mrs. Siddons as well, when my father took us all to London one year." So clear were the images, that joyous excursion might have happened yesterday. "Covent Garden was the most amazing theater I had ever seen. I remember the Greek portico, the ornamental friezes, the grand vestibule—I thought I had entered a foreign land."

Sarah shook her head. "But that was nothing to the stage itself. It was enormous, and the actors who stood under the arches amid those lofty pilasters and laurel wreaths commanded all eyes. They were grand figures, larger than life, with voices that could project to the stars. When the curtain came down, it was as if the door to some exciting, exotic world had closed. I wanted to open it again." She turned from the window, embarrassed at revealing such foolish childhood dreams.

The smoky gaze that locked with hers held no ridicule. Instead, it bore something very like understanding. "You are a fraud, Sarah," he said gently. "It was not the money at all, was it? Faced with the prospect of spending your days reading sermons to some deaf dowager, the theater was a much more attractive alternative."

"I have always loved acting," she confessed. "The notion of becoming someone else, if only for a moment, was vastly appealing. I love to immerse myself in a role, to leave behind everything else, to stop worrying for a while whether I will have enough money to send William this quarter, or whether our old house in Surrey has a tenant."

"You have taken much upon yourself," he said, studying her. "Is there no one else to share these burdens?"

"My parents grew sick and died five years ago. At first we lived off the kindness of neighbors and what little funds my father had remaining. But I wanted William to get a gentleman's education. It was his birthright. Squire Gibbons said he could get a tenant for the house. After we left I never heard from him again. He never replied to my letters."

"I see." He looked down at her brother's letter. "William's holiday begins soon. We cannot have him hying down here, nor would it be appropriate for him to join us in London."

Sarah eyed him apprehensively. "What are you going to do, my lord?"

"*I?* I shall not do anything, Miss Armistead." His eyes glinted mischievously. "My butler has a bit of time on his hands, however. I believe he would enjoy Eton. I expect Anh can occupy William most adequately."

Imagining the taciturn butler entertaining her spirited brother proved impossible. Sarah frowned.

"I can see that you doubt Anh's abilities. Many have made that mistake. You must not worry. Anh will take care of everything."

His tone told her he considered the matter settled. She knew he was not being kind—he simply wanted to make certain her brother did not jeopardize his plan. Yet there was nothing calculating or cold about those eyes, no evidence that mere expedience ruled him. If anything, the gray gaze held only a strange and dark vulnerability.

But then, Lord Linton was a master of illusion.

Chapter Eleven

Anh did not betray by so much as the blink of an eye his thoughts about playing nursemaid to a fifteen-year-old boy. Not that Justin would have noticed. He was too busy poring over Albert Magnus's medieval magic manual.

"I fear you search in vain, my lord. Mr. Magnus had no more possession of truth than the oracle of Delphi."

Justin looked up in irritation. "Who said anything about a search for truth?"

Anh shrugged. "Meaning and being are inextricably entwined."

"Do not speak to me of metaphysics, man," Justin snapped. "I am merely looking for items of interest."

The butler drew closer. "I see that you have marked the passage on the banishment of lust." Anh gave him a pitying look. "My lord, one can no more defeat the pull of yin and yang than one can ignore the five elements."

Wearily, Justin closed the tome. Debating such matters with Anh was about as rewarding as trying to turn stone into gold. Or trying to prevent his Aunt Clarissa from placing her colorful flower arrangements throughout his house. Justin glared at the vase of daisies on his desk.

"Magnus would have me carve out the heart of a turtle bird, encase it in wolf's skin, and wear it the rest of my days. I daresay that will remove most anything from a man's mind, but it is not precisely the cure I imagined."

"There is no 'cure' to what afflicts you, my lord. You must submit to the change. It is the only way."

Damned if he would get into that again. "Enough," Justin declared. "The only immediate change I have planned is in your duties. I want you to find out all you can about the young Lord

Armistead and his interests. You will meet him at Eton, and I expect you to keep him fully occupied while we are away."

"I shall consider it a privilege to meet Miss Armistead's brother," Anh said as he bowed his assent.

"There is one more thing." Justin said in a deliberately casual voice. Anh eyed him expectantly, an anticipatory gleam in his black eyes. "Look into the affairs of a Squire Gibbons of Surrey, most particularly whether he has rented out the late baron's property."

Anh's enigmatic smile as he left the room prompted Justin to toss Magnus's volume aside in disgust. He had never put much faith in the old magic manuals anyway. What some called magic, others called religion, still others science. As a youth, particularly in that terrible time surrounding his father's death, Justin had found magic a fascinating art, a way to manipulate small aspects of his world and gain a measure of power over it. In time, he decided that illusion held more power than fact. Between art and life, he vastly preferred the former.

Perhaps Magnus's spells and chants had worked for some, but they did not hold the secret to managing his warring impulses toward Sarah. Mixing potions and cutting out the hearts of birds would not curb his growing attraction to her. Anh's mystical wisdom held no answers, either, especially given his butler's limited experience of women. As for all that talk of yin and yang, Justin was sufficiently familiar with eastern thought to know that the female yin, for all its association with life, also connoted darkness, weakness, something to be feared.

Justin Trent—afraid of a female? It did not bear thinking.

But neither had he imagined that behind Sarah's bravado lay a story that would tug at his heartstrings. She had taken on too much for a woman so gently bred, entered a world that was not for the faint of heart. The least he could do was try to ease one or two of her burdens. It was nothing to him to look into the dealings of that squire of hers. As for her brother, well, he certainly could not allow William to interfere with his plan.

None of that meant that Sarah was anything more to him than a gifted actress in his employ. That she could also raise his pulse with a mere look was entirely beside the point. Lust was simply lust, nothing more. Baron's daughter or no, Sarah was steeped in a world in which a woman would take a man for all

he was worth. Succumbing to her charms could ruin his scheme
and destroy what he had worked for.

Justin needed no medieval alchemist to tell him that he was
playing with fire.

"It is very strange the way they go off like that, shooting at
targets all morning."

Aunt Clarissa looked up from her knitting. "I think it is very
kind of Justin to school Sarah in the handling of a weapon.
Times have changed, Harriet. Sarah is alone in England, without her family. Who knows but one day she may need such
skills to protect herself?"

Miss Simms's eyes narrowed above her long, pointed nose.
"Alone? How can you say that, Clarissa? She is with Linton
most of the day. If they are not shooting in the meadow, they
are huddled in his study examining mysterious papers. Any
chaperon worth her salt would not allow it. Miss Armistead
would be compromised beyond redemption if such a thing
should be known."

"I trust that it will *not* become known," Aunt Clarissa said
sharply, prompting a startled look from her companion. "At all
events, Justin has Sarah's best interests at heart, of that you may
be certain."

"The only thing of which I am certain is that the apple never
falls very far from the tree," Miss Simms retorted. "You have
only to recall the father to see that it would be prudent to fear
for Miss Armistead's fate."

Aunt Clarissa's knitting slipped to the floor. "Silvester does
not like to hear such talk about Justin's father," she said in a
strained voice. "It upsets him greatly."

"Silvester is the most thin-skinned spirit I have ever encountered," Miss Simms muttered.

"You can be remarkably cruel sometimes, Harriet." Aunt
Clarissa's eyes shimmered with moisture. "You ought not den-
igrate Silvester. You know how important he is to me." At that,
Aunt Clarissa buried her face in her handkerchief.

Quickly Miss Simms left her chair and sat on the divan next
to her employer. "I did not mean to hurt you, Clarissa." Somewhat awkwardly, she took the other woman's hand.

" 'Tis not me you have hurt"—Aunt Clarissa sniffed—"but
Silvester."

Miss Simms sighed. "I did not intend to hurt Silvester, either. Sometimes, though, Clarissa," she added gently, "I think you rely too much on his opinion."

"He is all I have to rely on," Aunt Clarissa said simply.

"That is not so," Miss Simms protested. "You have Linton. And Agatha, if you would ever speak to her." At Aunt Clarissa's sharp intake of breath, she hastened to add, "I know that you do not like to think of her, but one day things might change."

"Never," Aunt Clarissa pronounced.

"And," Miss Simms added gruffly, ignoring the interruption, "you have me, of course."

Brilliant light from those violet eyes bathed Miss Simms in their glow. "I know," Aunt Clarissa murmured. "Thank you, Harriet."

A speck of dust in her eye caused Miss Simms to reach for her own handkerchief and rub the offending particle so violently that it left her eyes quite red. With a small cough, she returned to her own chair.

"I have always been grateful to you for taking me in," she said stiffly. "I was but a governess, after all. You asked no questions, and for that I owe you much."

"You have long satisfied any obligation to me." Aunt Clarissa dabbed at her eyes. "You need not remain in this position out of a sense of duty."

"It is not against my wishes to continue as your companion, Clarissa. And now, let us have no more of that. Or we will both turn into watering pots."

"Silvester has always liked you, you know," Aunt Clarissa confided, an impish look in her eyes.

A heavy sigh was Miss Simms's only reply.

Sarah had dreaded this day, for they were to rehearse the shooting scene. In the last weeks, they had honed her shooting skills until she could manage the pistol. They had talked about how she would pull the weapon from her muff and fire it, and she had even practiced the move. Never had they actually played out the scene, however, or said the vengeful words he had written for them. Now it was time.

What frayed Sarah's nerves was not the knowledge that the final stage of Lord Linton's plan was about to begin, and that they would soon go to London. It was the prospect of facing

him alone in his study, playing the part of a woman so over-
come with angry passion for the man she loved that she killed
him in her rage.

No, she mentally corrected. Not love.

This is a relationship based on carnal instinct—not love.
Lord Linton had been very clear about that, and perhaps he had
a point, for a woman in love would not kill her lover. Only a
woman who hated, who had endured his humiliation and scorn,
would do such a thing. Perhaps Lord Linton's father had in-
spired such emotions, but it was difficult to imagine that any
mistress of Justin Trent's would come to hate him, or, indeed,
that he would treat any woman so basely as to earn her enmity.

No matter that he was reputed to be a hardened rake, no matter that he had insulted her that day in the meadow. Sarah did
not hate him, and it was difficult to pretend that she did. She
was now sure that the darkness that sat so heavily on his soul
did not stem from an evil nature. Oh, he was cunning and ma-
nipulative and spent a disconcerting amount of time immersed
in the study of the black arts. But he was no demon, only a man
pursued by them. Revenge had very nearly destroyed him.

But not yet.

Only a man who still possessed some redeeming nature
could have offered that heartfelt apology. Only a man with a
glimmer of light in his soul could have sent his butler to occupy
William rather than giving orders to turn her brother away from
Lintonwood. Only a man with good in him could have tolerated
Aunt Clarissa's addled wits with gentle affection, as Sarah had
seen him do.

Perhaps there was hope for Lord Linton yet. But not if he
carried out his plan to destroy Lady Greywood, not if he allowed his thirst for revenge to drive out all compassion for an
aging woman who must daily be filled with regret for her long-
ago actions.

Sadness overwhelmed Sarah as she pushed open the study
door. She did not know how to reach that sliver of goodness in
Lord Linton's heart. Since his apology, he had been as distant
as the far horizon.

Now she was to hurl accusation at this unreachable man with
the fury of a woman scorned. She was to pretend an intimacy
with him that she had never shared with any man. And while
her profession required her to exercise a great deal of imagina-

tion, Sarah found it impossible to imagine what it would be like to know Lord Linton intimately. That one kiss, that searing touch on her bare skin, had not been enough to allow her to imagine the rest. Not nearly enough.

And yet . . . Sarah's pulse quickened as she stood on the threshold. If ever there was a man who could tempt her virtue, it was Lord Linton. *Justin.* It was a strong name, a fitting name for such a fierce, implacable man. A man any woman would be proud to call her lover.

But not her love, Sarah reminded herself. Never that.

"Good afternoon." He looked up from his desk. Sarah clutched the pages of her script, although she knew her lines by heart now. "Are you ready?" She nodded, hoping he did not see the lie in her eyes.

Briskly, as if there were nothing out of the ordinary about his actions, he took the dueling pistol from its case and inserted it into the large muff she was to carry that night. Over the next minutes he proceeded to block out the scene, positioning himself near the study window that was to represent the one in the ballroom. Some bookshelves behind her were to be the dozens of onlookers before which the drama would unfold.

"How do you know that Lady Greywood will be in attendance?" Sarah asked, anxious to fill the silence.

"Lady Hogarth is one of the few who did not cut her following the shooting," he replied. "Largely due to Lady Hogarth's efforts, Lady Greywood's reputation was eventually rehabilitated. I suspect it is a combination of gratitude and bravado that keeps Lady Greywood returning each year to the site of her lover's demise."

Sarah paled. "I had not realized that it was Lady Hogarth's ball at which your father was killed."

An anticipatory gleam leapt to his eyes. "Our scene will take place exactly as it occurred fifteen years ago—just as everyone is gathering for the presentation of honors for best costume. You can be sure Lady Greywood will be among the witnesses."

Sarah turned away from that disquieting gaze. "I still do not understand how Lady Greywood and your father could flaunt their relationship so publicly. Were not their spouses in attendance that evening?"

"My mother was at home with the ague. Lord Greywood was about, but he and my father kept their distance after the duel.

Even so, an affair can be conducted under a spouse's nose—with circumspection."

"If circumspection was the goal, then I do not see why Lady Greywood would have a spat with your father and shoot him with the whole world looking on."

"Rage will cause almost anyone to forget their society manners." He continued to mark off their positions. "I imagine Lady Greywood was enraged that my father had the temerity to refuse to marry her."

If I cannot have you no other woman can. But a woman who uttered those words would not have hated her lover. She would have been desperately in love with him. Sarah frowned. Nothing made sense.

"Lady Greywood hoped your father would divorce Lady Linton?"

He shrugged. "It was quite impossible, of course. My father would never have troubled to leave my mother, although he held her in no great affection. He was incapable of fidelity to any one woman."

"Then why would Lady Greywood hope for a divorce?" Sarah persisted.

"My father was not above twisting the truth. He may have made her promises."

"That does not sound very honorable."

"My father was not an honorable man." The bitter twist of his mouth told her it was best to leave this subject.

"You must have been a youth at the time," she said. "How do you know enough about what happened that night to duplicate it?"

"No one in the family was particularly eager to share the details with me," he admitted. "Agatha had her hands full trying to console my mother, and Clarissa has never been much use in a crisis. When my mother killed herself the next day, Clarissa fell apart. She has not been the same since."

"It must have been very difficult for you."

Straightening a pile of papers, he avoided her gaze. "I tried to find out all I could. It was not easy, given my family's silence on the subject. Fortunately, the event was deemed sufficiently scandalous to have been written up in the newspaper." He pulled something from a desk drawer. "Here," he said, handing it to her.

It was a yellowed clipping from *The Times*. The account was obviously incomplete, although the writer had done his best to fill in as many details as possible.

A shocking event occurred at Lady Hogarth's masquerade ball on Thursday night that resulted in the unfortunate demise of Lord Linton. His lordship, attired in a black domino, was noted by several of those at the ball to be engaged in heated words with a Lady costumed as the infamous Marie Antoinette. The Lady's true identity was impossible to discern, as she was wearing a wig and mask that effectively obscured her features. Witnesses who had gathered for the midnight unmasking and awarding of prizes for most successful costume reported that the Lady was overwrought, to the point of throwing her corsage at his feet and declaring that his lordship had misled her as to his intentions. It was after that declaration, which various witnesses reported as stating that the Lady would not allow his lordship to bestow his affections upon any woman other than herself, that the shooting occurred.

The Lady was reported to have pulled a pistol from her muff, although the witnesses were not certain at first whether the weapon might not have been a stiletto. The shot that followed provided further illumination, however, and Lord Linton immediately collapsed in a pool of blood, mortally wounded. The Lady fled through the terrace and has not been located, the onlookers being so occupied with tending to Lord Linton's wounds that no one thought to restrain his Assailant. One of Lord Linton's dueling pistols, later determined to be the work of noted gunsmith Joseph Manton, was later discovered in some bushes. It seems that his lordship was felled by his own weapon.

Stunned, Sarah looked up from the clipping. "It is exactly as you have written in your script," she said softly.

"Yes." Swiftly, he replaced the clipping in the drawer, his eyes glittering with some dark, demonic force.

Revenge.

I am interested in many things, Miss Armistead. I am consumed, however, by only one. It went deep in him, Sarah realized, deeper than she had thought. There, on that yellowed page, the crime was laid out from start to finish. He kept the clipping in his desk, where it could be read and reread at will. He had inscribed the words in his script, immortalized them in his soul.

"Now," he said, an unsettling undercurrent in his words, "I do believe it is time to get on with our scene."

Chapter Twelve

Looking down the barrel of a gun wielded by a furious female had a way of riveting a man's attention. Fortunately the pistol held no bullet, and Sarah's rage was only pretense. Justin was pleased to see that she gripped the weapon easily and that her aim did not waver.

He had trained her well. She would be ready .

How easily she inhabited the role of a woman scorned. Intrigued, Justin stared at the blazing emerald eyes. What color were Lady Greywood's eyes? he wondered idly. His father must have known their color. He had had time enough to study them from the business end of the pistol before his jealous mistress sent him to his maker.

Justin never understood how a worthless rake like his father could drive a woman to commit such a desperate act. What prompted a woman to give herself to a debauched scapegrace to begin with? Hope of bringing the scoundrel to heel, if only for a time? The urge to reform him, to tame him with her feminine power? Whatever her motive, it was a dangerous game. Even Persephone, who had captured the heart of the devil himself, had had to spend her time in hell.

Any woman who thought to tame his father was wrong in the upper story, for Oscar Trent cared only for cards, a willing woman, and a bottle of spirits. Indifference was the kindest emotion he ever expressed, and Justin had always sensed that his father felt something much more akin to hate for him. Never had he seen a father's proud smile upon his lips; never had he known a father's affection or delight. Well, almost never.

More than once over the years a childhood memory had intruded, giving him the image of a father whose face bore no lines of dissipation, no scowl of cynicism, no bloodshot eyes narrowed in scorn. Long ago, he had taught Justin to swim, to

ride, to shoot. In those days his father was merely distant, not
the jaded and scornful man he would become. What had happened to turn his father against him?

Perhaps he would never know. He supposed the real question
was why he felt it necessary to avenge the death of a man who
left no real mourners. His mother, God rest her weak soul, had
shed tears aplenty, but Justin could not imagine why. The long
nights when sounds of the beatings and her muffled cries
floated through the house had left him no doubt that she was
better off without her husband.

An eye for an eye . . . See that justice is done. It is your duty.

Yes, it was his duty to avenge his father. But there was more
to it—something drifting just beyond the vision of his mind's
eye, something lurking offstage waiting for the proper moment
to make its entrance. Something dark and forbidden, as elusive
as that magic bird of Magnus's, as compelling as the pull of yin
and yang.

Justin closed his eyes, letting the sensation take him into that
dark corner of his mind where a pistol lay facing him across the
table and the devil himself smiled his encouragement from
within his father's deep blue eyes.

Pull the trigger. The jeering command, the wild laughter as
Justin ran for the door, dropping the pistol like a hot coal.

Pull the trigger. His father's whispered taunt as he left for
Lady Hogarth's masquerade, the black domino a mantle of demonic splendor over his shoulders.

Pull the trigger. The battle cry echoing in Justin's brain hours
after that mock duel, for deep down he had wanted to use that
weapon.

But, God help him, not on himself.

"My goodness! Have you no sense of the theatrical? This
will never work if you simply stand there staring straight ahead
like a statue."

"What?" Justin rubbed his forehead and tried to bring himself back to the present. Sarah eyed him in irritation. "What?"
he repeated.

"I shall say it again, my lord. When do you wish me to pull
the trigger?"

Justin frowned. "As you are finishing your speech, of
course."

Sarah sighed impatiently. "It is not that simple. If I fire as I speak the final words, the report of the gun will drown them out. I could wait a second or two after the speech for effect, but that might allow an onlooker time to seize the pistol and prevent me from firing."

"Er, I see what you mean. I believe it is best not to let it go too long. Let us try it the first way."

"The only problem with that is the timing must be perfect. I am not certain my nerves will stand it."

Justin shot her a wry look. "*Your* nerves? Think of mine, standing there wondering whether you will remember to avert your aim at the last."

"That is not the sort of thing I am likely to forget, my lord," Sarah insisted, clearly appalled.

"Good. Shall we try it again?"

"Only if you promise to pay attention this time."

As she pointed the pistol at his chest, Justin smiled. "You have my undivided attention."

"Good. Now where was I?" Carefully, Sarah placed the gun back into her muff. "Oh, yes. There is something else. What shall I use for the corsage?

"I am having a precise duplicate made by my father's old florist. You can use this for now." He plucked one of the infernal daisies from the vase on his desk.

Sarah accepted the flower, cleared her throat, and drew herself up like some avenging angel. "You dare to trifle with my affections, sir. Well, I shall tell you something that is no trifling matter." She took a step forward, eyes flashing as she uttered the angry words. Then she hurled the daisy at him.

Justin could not suppress a grin. He had chosen well. Sarah would take on Satan himself. She was a fireball, a blinding ray of light chasing demons from her path.

Devil take it. Had he once again likened her to a sunbeam?

"You take too much upon yourself, madam," he said sternly, repeating the words he had written. "You read too much into a casual flirtation."

"A casual flirtation?" Seemingly incredulous, Sarah stared at him. Then a look of cunning crept over her features. Justin was mesmerized as slowly she pulled the pistol from her muff. Pointing it at his heart, she moved the hammer to full cock.

"I will give you *this,* my lord, for your casual flirtation, and bid you take it to your grave so that no other woman may be similarly misled." She paused for a heartbeat. "For if I cannot have you, I vow that no other woman can."

As she spoke the final words, Sarah shifted the pistol almost imperceptibly to the right. Justin saw the movement of the trigger and heard the click of the hammer as it met the flashpan. Instantly, he dropped to the floor.

A sudden giggle assaulted his ears. He opened one eye indignantly. "What, pray, is so amusing?"

"I am afraid you do not look the least bit convincing, my lord. Especially when you take care to fall so that your head does not crash into the desk."

"I will manage to die credibly, never you fear. If I were you, I would occupy myself with fleeing. Otherwise, you will soon find yourself clapped in irons. And do not forget to drop the pistol in the bushes as you leave."

Instantly, she sobered. With nimble grace she raced to the wall that served as Lady Hogarth's terrace door and carefully placed the pistol at the base of a lamp that was meant to represent a bush. Then she turned, waiting for his reaction. "Well? Did we manage it?"

Justin picked himself up from the floor. "Yes. I believe we did. Well done, Sarah."

Flushed from his praise and her exertions, Sarah's cheeks glowed like new pink blossoms. Her hair fell about her face in delightful disarray, like the petals of some rare, exotic flower. She made an appealing picture, a portrait of spring coming into full bloom.

Persephone, Justin thought in irritation. Why the devil did Sarah suddenly remind him of Persephone?

"We leave for London tomorrow to meet with Miss Armistead's solicitors. They have assured us that they can provide information about her relatives."

Justin's declaration following dinner sent an excited Aunt Clarissa into a whirl of chatter about packing and the like. Miss Simms merely arched a brow.

"You are taking her to London without a chaperon?" Her eyes were censorious.

"I have hired one of the village girls to serve as Miss Armistead's maid," Justin replied.

"I do not think a serving girl . . ."

"Oh, Harriet, do leave off," Aunt Clarissa directed. "Justin will take good care of Sarah. Let us not waste time on trivialities."

"Trivialities!" Miss Simms echoed, incredulous. "I hardly think this falls into that category."

Impatiently, Justin waved a dismissive hand. "It is little more than two hours to London. The presence of a maid is sufficient to protect Miss Armistead's reputation for such a short time."

"But where will she stay?" Miss Simms demanded. "Surely you do not mean to keep her at your house?"

"Certainly not," Justin replied easily. "Miss Armistead will have her own, er, establishment. It has all been arranged. Her reputation is of prime consideration, you may be sure."

How easily he manipulates the truth, Sarah thought in grudging half-admiration. She would indeed have her own establishment—as mistress of a wealthy and powerful peer—to help establish her "reputation" beyond Aunt Clarissa's wildest imaginings.

Aunt Clarissa smiled. "Are you sure you do not wish us to come? Silvester does not mind London in the least."

Justin deposited a kiss on his aunt's cheek. "Thank you, but that will not be necessary. I deeply appreciate your coming to Lintonwood on such short notice. You will be wishing to return to your own home."

Miss Simms looked as though she had much more to say on this subject, but Justin quickly strode from the room, depriving her of her desired audience. Instead, she was forced to turn her attention to Sarah.

"Do not say I did not warn you, missy," Miss Simms said, a fateful expression on her face. "Men like that one have only one thing on their minds—and it has nothing to do with finding your relatives, mind you."

Aunt Clarissa pursed her lips but did not speak, and the remainder of the evening passed without incident.

Later, Sarah stared at the walls of her chamber for what she supposed was the last time. It was hard to believe that tomorrow she would be in London, playing the part of Lord Linton's mistress in earnest. Never had she thought to find herself ensconced in a love nest and paraded before the *ton* in a most public declaration of the fact that he was her protector and lover.

With a sigh, Sarah began readying herself for bed. She was

used to managing for herself and did not know what she would do with the maid and dresser he had hired to turn her out in the style expected of one of his women. All of these changes were unsettling, but Sarah reminded herself that this was just a role like any other. There was no shame in her actions, for she would not really be Lord Linton's mistress. Still, everyone would think otherwise. Perhaps there was shame enough in that.

For the first time she would be *living* a role. Acting and real life would mingle in a dizzying complexity. Could she separate the two?

Did she wish to?

A tap at her door ended her disturbing reverie. Aunt Clarissa poked her head in the room and smiled.

"I wanted to wish you good fortune, my dear," she said as she took the chair near Sarah's bed. "And to give you this." She opened her hand to reveal a small, round locket.

"It is beautiful," Sarah exclaimed as Aunt Clarissa pressed the necklace into her hand. "Thank you."

"Arabella—Justin's mother—gave it to me a long time ago. Shortly after she married, in fact. It was a token of her affection." A troubled look shaded the violet eyes. "I was a disappointment to her, I am afraid."

Sarah opened the locket to reveal miniatures of the two sisters. Though time had faded the portraits, the young Clarissa's eyes still bore their startling hue. Justin's mother was a pretty woman who, like her son, possessed somber gray eyes that appeared to hold secrets. The murky currents in this family obviously ran deep.

Sarah suspected that the locket meant a great deal to Aunt Clarissa, especially since Justin's mother was long dead and she was at odds with her only remaining sister, Aunt Agatha. "I could not take a family keepsake," Sarah protested. "You will wish to keep it, surely."

"Not at all." Aunt Clarissa smiled through the sheen of moisture in her eyes. "Silvester agrees with me. It is time to let it go." She fastened the locket around Sarah's neck. "It is meant for you, I think. Since you have no immediate family, perhaps you can think of this as one sister's token of affection. Mine for you."

Sarah swallowed hard, thinking that Aunt Clarissa would

never give her such a treasure if she knew Sarah was about to take up the scandalous role of her nephew's mistress. "I do not deserve this, ma'am."

Shaking her head, the woman brought her fingertips to Sarah's lips. "None of us deserves what we get in life, dear, but we cannot control our fate. When we try, we muddle it terribly." Her eyes took on a faraway look. "There was a time, before Silvester, that I thought otherwise."

Aunt Clarissa was still greatly affected by her sister's suicide, Sarah realized, feeling doubly guilty for accepting the locket. "Ma'am, are you certain you do not wish to keep this? I would not deprive you of your only memento of your departed sister."

"Oh, I have others," Aunt Clarissa said, patting Sarah's shoulder. "I have the best of all, in fact." She leaned forward with a conspiratorial grin. "She left me Silvester, you see."

Smiling happily, Aunt Clarissa left the room.

The sedate little house on Brook Street exuded respectability. Sarah wondered about the other women who had lived here as Lord Linton's mistress. Had they clapped their hands in glee at the sight of the gray stone and brick house, its windows sparkling clean, its masonry in top repair, its brass fittings in gleaming splendor? Had they nodded regally to the respectful servant at the door, who betrayed no sign that there was anything sordid about a woman accepting her living from a peer of the realm? Had they trilled in delight at the inviting bedchamber, decorated in warmest peach and melon?

None of them, Sarah was certain, had quailed in trepidation at this tangible evidence of the enormity of the step they had taken. None had viewed those sparkling windows and gleaming brass as bars on a prison of her own foolish making. None had taken two steps back from the enormous bed, scarlet with thoughts of what activities took place in this chamber of delights.

"Is everything satisfactory?" Lord Linton asked as Sarah studied the tasteful furnishings in what was now her bedchamber. That Sarah had allowed him to show her even the most private parts of the house proved her internal compass had spun drastically awry. Her mother would have been shocked beyond speech.

"Yes," Sarah said, her voice not entirely steady as he took her arm and walked them out of the room.

Although Sarah had told herself repeatedly in the carriage that this was merely a role, that when it ended she would have the means to a respectable and perfectly ordinary life, seeing the house provided a sobering antidote to her optimism. Before her respectability could begin, she would have to live and breathe the part of Lord Linton's mistress, even in the present of the servants. Servants gossiped, he had reminded her, and it would not do to raise their suspicions.

Sarah had blithely agreed.

Thus, when Lord Linton stood in the foyer prepared to take his leave, he pulled her into his arms within view of the servants scurrying past with her trunks. He made the embrace seem natural, as if they had been lovers for a long time, rather than strangers whose only previous intimate encounter had horrified them both. Undoubtedly he had welcomed other women to this house in similar fashion.

"I will see you tonight," he said, promise in his eyes and passion in his voice. The kiss he deposited on her lips was designed to leave observers no doubt as to what activities were planned for the evening.

Remembering that she was supposed to welcome the intimacy, Sarah leaned into him, placing her arms around his neck. At first the position seemed strained, but she soon discovered that she liked being enclosed by that solid, masculine warmth. She was sorry when the kiss ended, although grateful he had not turned it into a torrid clench in front of the servants. His kiss bore warmth enough to make the point, restraint enough to remind the viewer that further activities of this nature would be continued in a more private time and place.

It was a very practiced, *professional* kiss, Sarah decided.

As he took the steps down into the street, Sarah touched her lips, tasting bitter disappointment.

Chapter Thirteen

Lady Devon's ball proved to be the perfect place to introduce Sarah to society. A bit of a hellion in her day, the countess delighted in lively entertainment and a scintillating mix of guests. To be sure, the usual stiff-necked dowagers and prim society matrons were present, but Lady Devon herself was no high stickler. The waltzes were plentiful, the ratafia flowed freely, and a merry round-game table for both sexes had been set up in a parlor adjacent to the ballroom.

All the *ton* was in attendance. Sarah had quickly taken their measure and played to it with such ease that Justin was again forced to congratulate himself on his brilliance in hiring her. The role of mistress fit her to perfection. He was the envy of every man at the ball.

Glittering gold combs held back her auburn hair, which cascaded in classic coils from the crown of her head. She radiated fiery elegance, her salmon pink gown easily eclipsing the insipid pastels of the debutante set. Its neckline seemed to defy gravity as it skimmed the rise of her breasts with a breathtaking dip over the seductive space between them. The product of one of London's most fashionable modistes, the gown stopped short of being truly scandalous; many of the women exposed far more of their charms. Still, irritation shot through Justin each time Sarah fluttered her ivory fan and drew attention to that tantalizing neckline.

Compliments fell around her shoulders like rain. She accepted them gracefully, her flushed cheeks and sparkling eyes a cornucopia of riches in themselves. Justin could not decide whether it was the actress in her or the woman herself who bloomed like some exotic flower. As mistress of a man whose appetite for pleasure was notorious, Sarah evoked images of unfettered carnal delight; yet something in the way she conducted herself commanded respect. Although it was not difficult to guess what was on the minds of the men, their frankly admiring looks bore no outright lechery. Her manner was beguiling, but subtly so.

Sarah had insisted that his mistress would display no hint of coarseness, and her instincts had proven true. Many of the dowagers kept a censorious distance, of course, along with watchful mamas and their muslin-clad chicks. Still, Sarah shone like the brightest candle in the room. Men hovered around her, especially when they saw that Justin meant to offer no objection. With an air of supreme insouciance, he had danced with her only once, handed her over to a tulip in a parrot yellow waistcoat, and disappeared into the card room.

Now, eyeing Sarah's court, Justin smiled in satisfaction. Abandoning the field for a time had allowed Sarah's admirers to move in. It had also drawn attention to the fact that he did not intend to sit in her pocket. Most importantly, it signaled that while he was perfectly willing to keep Sarah in style, he was not about to change his rakish ways. On his way to the card room, Justin had openly flirted with several women, including a voluptuous countess with whom he had once enjoyed a brief liaison.

Most mistresses would be irritated by his conduct, and Justin and Sarah had agreed that she would publicly show her displeasure at the first opportunity. They had only a fortnight before Lady Hogarth's masquerade; the seeds of discord had to be sown rapidly. That would not be difficult, Justin decided, frowning as Sarah's bubbling laughter floated across the room to him. It was hardly necessary for her to flirt so blatantly or to enjoy herself so thoroughly in his absence.

With a casual air that owed much to his own acting ability, Justin sauntered toward her, stopping to speak to Amanda Tremaine, a duke's daughter whose late husband had possessed neither title nor breeding but managed to squirrel away a fortune from his India investments. The exceedingly wealthy widow collected lovers like snuffboxes. She had shown more than a passing interest in him in recent months, but Justin had been preoccupied with finding the actress vital to his plan. Once Lady Greywood was brought to justice, perhaps a dalliance with Amanda might be just the thing, however. A man could do worse than while away nights with the lovely creature now clinging to his arm and fluttering her lashes at him. In the meantime, she was an excellent prop for the next part of this scene.

Approaching the circle of Sarah's admirers, Justin saw by the sparks in her eyes that Sarah had noticed his attention to Amanda and was ready to follow his lead. Almost as magic, the crowd parted for them.

"Lady Amanda, may I present Mrs. Manwaring?" Justin said, using the name Sarah had adopted. Although Armistead was not an especially common name, they had not wanted to risk exposure from anyone who might make a connection to the baron or his daughter.

"What a charming creature she is—a veritable bird of paradise," Amanda trilled, allowing her gaze to rove condescendingly over Sarah. "I believe you are the envy of every gentleman in attendance, Justin."

His "mistress" arched one elegant brow. "Perhaps the viscount does not realize his good fortune, Lady Amanda," Sarah said sweetly, fluttering her fan, "else he would not squander it on cards and other *vulgar* follies."

Her barb brought an offended gasp from Amanda and titters from those around them. Well done, Justin thought as Sarah's chin rose in triumphant defiance. Her every gesture and expression conveyed her anger at being neglected for a pack of cards and another woman. A man of his repute would never allow his mistress to criticize his conduct, however. Justin forced a scowl to his face.

"I need not remind you, madam, that *anything* of mine is also mine to squander," he said pointedly, a dangerous edge to his voice.

Around them the crowd fell silent. Some of the men bore predatory looks—especially Lord Pembroke, who was probably already calculating how long it would take him to get Justin's spurned mistress in his bed. That unsettling thought sparked Justin's temper in earnest, even as he told himself there was no reason to become upset. This was but a charade; Sarah was nothing to him. Yet the image of her cavorting with Pembroke was sufficient to cause his hands to ball into tight fists at his side.

Lady Amanda took one look at Justin's steely features and abruptly released his arm. "Perhaps we will talk later, Justin," she purred. "But at the moment it appears you must endeavor to get back in Mrs. Manwaring's good graces or risk having your *fortune* stolen from under your very nose."

"Such wisdom," Sarah commented dryly, turning a blinding smile on the nearest member of her court. The poor idiot looked confused but soon was staring at Sarah with a worshipful expression.

Amanda was no novice at this game, but Justin doubted whether the others followed all the undercurrents. For that matter he himself did not understand why, when Sarah turned her simmering gaze on him, his pulse suddenly thundered in his ears like a wildly rushing tempest.

Pools of restless fire swirled in her eyes, holding him in their sway and igniting an answering flame deep within him. As the heat roiled his gut, Justin realized in shock that something very real had supplanted pretense—something that must not gain even the hope of rooting in the barren earth of his soul. With one stride, he closed the distance between them.

"Do not think to play games with me, madam," he growled, clasping her wrist roughly, "for you will undoubtedly lose."

Her knowing smile held a feminine mystique as old as ancient prophesy, and it stirred the caldron of heat bubbling inside him. Justin gritted his teeth. Whatever the source of her strange power, it would bend to his will. Had he not created her? She could gain no hold on him that he did not allow.

Pulling Sarah toward him, Justin was conscious only of the need to claim her, to remove her from that bright firmament in which she had been suspended for all to see. Whirling her around, he brought their bodies together, perversely enjoying her defiance even as he tamed it. Let Pembroke and others of his ilk salivate: *this* woman was his, on his terms, whenever he wished her to be.

Music and laughter faded from his awareness as he stared into her face, feeling the pull of her as deeply as he had felt anything in his life.

It was some time before Sarah's stricken expression finally intruded on his senses. Slowly, with the heaviness of a man drugged, Justin looked around. They were alone, twinkling lanterns and shrubbery their only audience. The strange force that held him in its grip began to dissipate, like a heady potion that peaks too quickly and leaves its victim with a dry mouth and pounding head.

When had he dragged her out to the courtyard? How long had he been holding her arms like a vise? Glaring red marks on her skin provided the answer.

Instantly, Justin took a step backward, freeing her from the circle of his arms.

"Forgive me," he rasped.

Smoothing her gown, Sarah did not quite meet his gaze. "I have no quarrel with your performance, my lord," she said in a low voice that seemed unnaturally husky. "I imagine that everyone now understands just how . . . tempestuous is our liaison. You have set the stage admirably for the latter part of our drama."

Good God. He must have behaved like a ruffian, dragging her from the ballroom, mauling her in the process—and now she was commending his performance. Justin exhaled slowly. "I believe I may have forgotten myself."

"Undoubtedly the fault was mine." She tilted her head as if considering the matter. "I have not played such a role before. I imagine I was too provoking."

"Damnation, Sarah," he snapped, "you are *supposed* to be provoking."

"Then you find no fault with my acting?" She pursed her lips in concern.

Justin studied that inviting mouth, plumped into a question mark that ought to be answered with a kiss. He willed himself to control. "None at all," he replied uneasily.

"In that case," she said, gathering her skirts about her, "I believe you ought to escort me inside for this waltz. Everyone will wish to know the outcome of our quarrel, and it will suit your purpose to have them think that we have made it up. Do you not agree?"

"Perfectly," he muttered, extending his arm with all of the charity of a man on the way to the gallows.

As she moved, the salmon-colored fabric caressed the curves of her body like a triumphant lover. Justin stared, riveted by the image. How, he wondered, would he endure the frustration of having Sarah as his mistress without claiming any of the rewards.

* * *

"You must invite me inside."

At his terse whisper, Sarah's satin slipper poised in midstride on the stone steps.

"Of course," she acknowledged with what she hoped was a confident smile. They must appear to be lovers to the servants as well as any passersby who might recognize the viscount and his new mistress.

As the expressionless butler admitted them, Sarah wondered how any evening could be so endless. She had flirted with more gentlemen tonight than in her entire life, endured their transparent flattery, and stood forever in a scandalously cut gown trying to protect her modesty behind a fan that was woefully inadequate for that purpose.

Now the man who had given her goose bumps all night was accompanying her into the privacy of her temporary home, where she longed only to remove her borrowed finery, stretch out on the plump featherbed, and forget she had spent all evening pretending to be his fancy piece.

Sarah stood awkwardly in the middle of the parlor while the butler poured Lord Linton a brandy and discreetly pulled the door closed as he left the room. He would not wait up, Sarah knew, the viscount having given him a pointed look that communicated everything that needed to be said.

Tossing off the brandy in one impatient gulp, Lord Linton immediately refilled the glass and sat in the enormous leather chair that previous mistresses had undoubtedly placed there for his own comfort.

"You need not act as though you are waiting for the executioner," he growled. "Sit somewhere and remove that wary expression from your face. I have no intention of doing any harm to your person, much as you have sorely tempted me to this evening."

Sarah stared at him. "What have I done to earn your displeasure, my lord? I thought you were happy with my performance."

Stormy eyes looked out from a visage as dark as night. "Your performance was adequate. I have no complaint. Other than the fact you were coming it too strong."

"Strong? I do not understand."

Disbelief leapt to his eyes. "Come, now," he said, arching one brow. "Pembroke will command all ears for a week with the story of how closely you allowed him to hold you during the waltz, how sweetly you pulled on his sleeve while assuring him our quarrel was insignificant, how willingly you allowed him to view the charming display provided by the front of your gown."

"My *gown*!" Outraged, Sarah put her hands on her hips. "If it is not to your liking, you have only yourself to blame, for you had it made for me, along with every stitch of clothing I now possess."

"I did not say it was not to my liking."

Sarah blinked. "I do not understand you in the least, my lord. You wished me to attract attention as your mistress, and I have. What have I done to anger you?"

"Everything. Nothing." He drained his glass a second time.

Bewildered, Sarah walked over to the brandy decanter and poured a small amount of liquid for herself. She sipped it cautiously, then sat stiffly on the divan near his chair. He did not say a word, but stared into his glass as if it contained some strange substance he had never seen.

When at last he met her gaze, there was a pained look in his eyes. "You have done nothing wrong," he conceded. " 'Tis merely that I have discovered my part is a bit difficult to play."

"Rehearsals are not like a performance," she agreed carefully, sipping the amber liquid. Tonight had certainly illustrated that point. The inviting smile he had bestowed on Lady Amanda had ripped through her like a knife. Being called a "charming creature" by that brazen woman had set her teeth on edge. But when he had the audacity to claim that Sarah was merely one of his assets to be squandered according to his will, fury had seized her—a fury that suddenly became something quite different when he grabbed her like a brutish, possessive lover. . . .

"Indeed," he observed, scowling. "A performance *is* vastly different." With a black look, he resumed the study of his brandy glass.

Silence settled over the room like a mantle of gloom. The viscount's forbidding countenance did not encourage speech, and for some time Sarah sipped her brandy and perched awkwardly on the edge of the divan. Once, she rose and poured herself some more of the stuff, thinking that indulging in spirits could be no worse than enduring his brooding company for the rest of the evening.

"How long are we obliged to sit here?" she ventured at last.

He started as if he had forgotten she was in the room. "What?"

"I simply wondered how long is it necessary to sit here," she explained, blushing. "How long must you remain in the house so that people think . . . what they must think?"

From those unreadable eyes came a very odd expression. He studied her for some time over the rim of his glass.

"Lord Linton?" she prompted.

"I am contemplating the matter."

Sarah sighed. Finding out what was on his mind was like trying to squeeze juice from a dried orange. "I do not see what is so difficult about my question," she prodded.

"On the contrary," he drawled, his gaze speculative. "It requires extensive contemplation to imagine how long I should wish to enjoy your charms, were we spending our time in the manner of most people in our situation."

Sarah blushed deep scarlet as she caught his meaning.

"I think," he continued, holding his glass aloft and studying the droplets as they ran down the side, "that at the moment there is simply no adequate way of answering the question."

Quickly gulping her own brandy, Sarah savored the bracing burning sensation against the back of her throat. "Then what shall we do?" she asked, fearful of the answer but determined not to spend the rest of the evening in this uncomfortable situation.

Opening a drawer in the table next to his chair, he pulled out a deck of cards. "Piquet," he declared in a resigned tone. "That should pass the time. Four hands and I will take my leave."

"I am afraid I never learned to play." Apparently he had not anticipated this deficiency in her education. Sighing heavily, he absently shuffled the deck. Though he scarcely paid the cards any heed, they moved like lightning over his palm and through his fingers. "I could teach you," he said in a flat voice that eloquently conveyed his lack of enthusiasm for such a task.

"I have no wish to learn," she replied. "But you may teach me some of those card tricks of yours."

Amusement flared in his eyes. "Card tricks? Whatever should you do with such knowledge?"

"I do not know," Sarah conceded, "but it is ever so much more interesting than trying to build a quart or a quint."

His gaze narrowed. "I thought you did not play piquet."

"I do not, but I have watched many dull games. I should vastly enjoy learning tricks instead. Will you teach me?"

Before the words were even out of her mouth, he fanned the cards and placed them face up on the table between them. Sarah stared in amazement. Despite the extensive shuffling they had endured, the cards were arranged in suits and perfectly ordered, from ace down to two.

At least they seemed to be, until Sarah studied them more closely. "One card appears to be missing," she said. "The two of clubs."

Leaning forward, he regarded the display. "So it is."

With a fluid motion, he reached over and plucked something from behind her ear. Sarah did not need to see the card to know that it was the club two.

"I do not see how you manage that. I have been watching your hands all this time. Nothing was hidden in them as far as I could see. How did you do it?"

In answer, he merely gathered up the cards, divided them into three piles and effortlessly shuffled them with blinding speed. When he was done, he fanned them out again.

Dumbfounded, Sarah saw that the cards were still in perfect descending order, from ace to two, spades to clubs. The two of clubs was once again missing.

"It is a false deck," she declared. "You have done something in the cards."

Shaking his head, he smiled. "It is what I have *not* done."

Pure glee danced in his eyes. Sarah stared at the shimmering silver gaze that had moments ago seemed flat as gunmetal. The cards had accomplished an alchemy she could hope for only in her dreams.

"We will begin," he announced, flourishing his hands like a seasoned performer as he once again plucked the club two from behind her ear, "with the India shuffle."

Chapter Fourteen

Holding her head high like the respectable woman she was inside required all of Sarah's acting skills. Sometimes, like tonight, she retreated for a time to shore up her courage. Here in the ladies' withdrawing room, where one's manners were not on public display, few women acknowledged her and she gained a moment of peace. But it was a fleeting calm, for staring into the cheval glass forced her to confront her own disturbing reflection.

Although no one could fault her gown—Lord Linton saw fit to costume her in creations as refined and elegant as any duchess's—Sarah looked every inch his fancy piece. Her high color owed as much to her paint box as to her feverish spirits. Her eyes were a shade too knowing, her laugh too provocative.

No matter that the man who purported to be a jaded rake had taken no liberties beyond those intended for public consumption. No matter that he left Brook Street each night without so much as touching her once the servants had gone to bed. The fact remained that he had provided her with a house, clothing, carriage, and generous living allowance. No one knew that Sarah was not what she seemed. She could pretend to herself that she still had her self-respect, but she was not entirely certain of that. How long could one play at a part before it became real?

Moreover, she thoroughly enjoyed her protector's company. Not now, at these society parties where they performed the combative roles he had created for them. But afterward, in the confines of her drawing room, as the evening stretched into morning and he became the magician, the sorcerer who truly could control fate with a deck of cards and a pair of clever hands.

Each night Sarah sat spellbound, watching his dazzling

tricks, deceptive dealing, sleights of hand. No matter how hard she tried, she could not master the techniques; her attempts sent them both into laughing fits. And in those magic hours before dawn, as they sat bleary-eyed and weary from the long evening behind them, a kinship formed.

It was the kinship of any two performers, whiling away the time backstage between acts, waiting for the last line of the night to be spoken and the audience to make its boisterous way home. It was a kinship Sarah had experienced many times in the theater, never in her private life. Yet somehow this new bond between them was not just a bond between two actors. It was more personal, more intimate in a way that eroded some of the barriers between them.

On stage, they played battling lovers before a rapt audience eager for the next explosive scene. In public, Lord Linton grew more peremptory with his "mistress," relishing Lady Amanda's attentions and often setting the two women against each other. Yet there was a strange possessiveness in his manner toward Sarah, a tension in him that she could not explain. For her part, Sarah grew more and more brittle as Lady Amanda's slyly assessing gaze said it was only a matter of time before she had him in her bed. Lady Greywood must have faced similar trials, Sarah decided. Caring for a libertine who cared only for his own pleasure left a woman with a raw, festering wound.

But within the privacy of the house on Brook Street, she and Lord Linton were not those people who played out their private turmoils in such a public fashion. In that house there was no jealousy, no possessiveness, no brittle anger. There were only the two of them, a deck of cards, and the occasional glass of brandy. The masquerade required that he remain long into the night for appearances' sake, but in all other respects they were offstage, freed from the enslavement of their roles.

With that freedom, the tension left her. Similarly, Lord Linton seemed almost carefree, taking a boyish delight in her amazement at his skill. In this manner they had passed a week, and it now seemed as natural as breathing to walk him to the door as dawn filtered through the fog and to feel a genuine pang of regret that was very close to longing. The more time she spent with him, the more Sarah realized that he was an enigma and the more she yearned to know the man behind the mask.

In those magical hours before dawn, perhaps she came as close as anyone could.

Now as she stared in the cheval glass in the ladies' withdrawing room, the wistful sigh that escaped her lips was not worldly or wise, as one would expect from the celebrated mistress of the *ton*'s most scandalous rake. It was pure Sarah Armistead, confused and uncertain. She looked around quickly to ascertain whether anyone had witnessed her lapse.

One woman had. She sat on a chair near the doorway. Sarah had not heard her enter.

"You are Mrs. Manwaring." The voice betrayed no warmth, only pointed curiosity.

"Yes." Sarah forced a smile, but the woman's stoic expression did not alter.

"I am Evangeline Greywood. You will have heard of me from Lord Linton. But perhaps he does not confide in you?"

Lady Greywood. The woman they would bring to justice. Despite herself, Sarah stared. Fatigue was etched in the lines of the woman's face, and something in her brown eyes reminded Sarah of a hunted animal. The drab biscuit gown did nothing for her complexion, which bore the mottled tones of age. Her frame was bent slightly, as if with untold burdens, and her hair had long since gone to gray. Frail and small, she bore no resemblance to a woman who might have murdered her lover in a spirited rage.

"If you have any influence over him at all, you must make him stop this madness. It will end badly, I assure you."

Summoning all her professional artistry, Sarah schooled her expression to innocent curiosity. "I do not know what you mean."

Lady Greywood studied her. "No, perhaps you do not. I am not sure myself what he is about. I only know that Linton is a dangerous man, like his father, but perhaps even more ruthless. You must stop him."

"I am afraid I have little influence over the viscount."

The dull gaze sharpened. "I have seen him look at you. You possess more influence than you think."

Was that true? Sarah shook her head to deny the hope that rose inside her. It would not do to confuse pretense with reality.

"I do not know what Linton is planning," Lady Greywood

continued, "but already it has gone too far. Innocent lives have been damaged."

The countess referred to the duel, Sarah surmised. Poor woman. She must have feared Lord Linton would force Lord Greywood to pay for his mother's sins with his life.

A thousand questions came to mind. Had Lady Greywood truly loved Lord Linton's father or hated him? How had she borne the fact that she had caused his death? What of her own husband? How had she endured his fury?

Feeling sorry for Lady Greywood was a mistake, Sarah told herself. The woman had gotten away with murder. But somehow, looking at her frail form and sorrowful eyes, Sarah felt nothing but pity. Oddly, the woman was looking at her with something akin to the same emotion.

"I can see that you do not know what Linton is," Lady Greywood said. "You are blinded by his cleverness. He uses women, as his father did before him. The Trents are incapable of love. And that is what you truly want, is it not—love? Your eyes give you away, poor child."

With an almost painful dignity, the woman rose and slipped out of the room, leaving Sarah reeling in shock. *The Trents are incapable of love. And that is what you truly want, is it not— love?*

Lady Greywood was wrong. Not in a hundred years would Sarah expect Lord Linton to feel anything other than that special kinship that had sprung up between them—if he felt even that. She was simply an actress he had hired. He was beyond the touch of a woman like her. Even if she deluded herself into thinking otherwise, Sarah knew that he was incapable of delicate feelings for any woman.

Sometimes, though, Sarah allowed herself to wonder how it might be to climb the stairs with him to her chamber at night rather than remain in the drawing room with cards and brandy. Remembering the kiss that had fired that fierce passion between them at Lintonwood, Sarah thought perhaps he would be willing.

But the kisses he now bestowed on her for the servants' benefit were restrained, practiced gestures devoid of passion. Clearly, he saw her only as a means to an end. She was in his employ, as much as his butler or her maid. If he seemed overly possessive and tense at these parties, it had nothing to do with his feelings for her.

Preparing to rejoin the party, Sarah practiced her smile in the mirror. Lady Greywood had misread what was in her eyes. Obviously, her acting still needed work.

"If you tire of her, I trust you will let me know."

Justin held Pembroke in no great charity, but he could not explain the sudden urge to rearrange the man's features. "I assume you are speaking of Mrs. Manwaring?" he replied evenly.

Pembroke did not conceal the admiring gaze in his eyes as Sarah crossed the ballroom toward them. "You surprise me, Linton. Your previous mistresses have been rather bland creatures, without an independent thought in their heads. Not that I like a woman who is overly interfering, but Mrs. Manwaring has spunk. She leads you a merry dance, does she not? I warrant it is never dull."

Dull? No, that was not a word that applied to Sarah. The more time he spent in her company, the more he wondered what he had done without her. Indeed, her very absence from the room provoked a strange uneasiness within him. It would not do to confess such a thing to Pembroke. As far as all London was concerned, Sarah Manwaring was merely his latest mistress, with whom he was rapidly becoming disenchanted.

"I prefer a more complacent woman," Justin said in a bored voice. "Mrs. Manwaring's temperament is too volatile for my tastes. She is the sort who takes a man's attentions too seriously. I believe she has expectations beyond her station."

Pembroke nodded sympathetically but added, "I have more patience than you, perhaps. Putting up with a few female hysterics is not an especially burdensome price for having a woman like that in one's bed."

The image of Sarah in Pembroke's bed jarred him, especially since Justin had been imagining her in a rather different situation. As she moved toward them, he marveled at how perfectly she resembled the fantasy that had beset him weeks ago at Lintonwood. Describing the emerald gown to the modiste had been awkward, but the seamstress had dutifully concocted a dress that exactly matched the one Sarah had worn in his mind's eye when she reclined provocatively for him on a satin comforter. On his order, a Bond Street jeweler had crafted the diamond ornament in her hair to precisely resemble the one of his imagination.

Sarah would not end up in Pembroke's bed if he had anything to say about it. Perhaps when this business was over he would pay her a little extra to ensure that she need never seek a man's protection again. It would be worth it to banish the image of Pembroke rutting over her like a sweating pig. For now, however, Justin had to play the part he had written for himself.

"I am not yet weary of Mrs. Manwaring's charms," he said in a warning tone.

Pembroke laughed. "That is high praise indeed, Linton, for I have never known you to stay with a woman who tried your temper. But I am a patient man. I can wait."

Until hell freezes over, Justin thought darkly as Sarah rejoined them. The dazzling smile she bestowed on Pembroke would have blinded most men. It lost a bit of its luster, however, when she turned to him.

"Come," Justin ordered. "It is time to leave."

"But we only arrived an hour ago," she replied, puzzled.

Pembroke arched a brow, but the telltale gleam in his eyes betrayed him. Undoubtedly the man thought his interest in Sarah had kindled Justin's jealousy and provoked him into canceling an evening of dancing and cards in favor of more private activities.

"Do not quibble, madam," Justin commanded, irritated at Pembroke's assumption that he would succumb to such a ridiculous emotion as jealousy. "I have decided to depart."

"But I wish to stay. Have you no concern for *my* pleasure, sir?" Sarah retorted.

They had planned to create yet another tempestuous scene in the ballroom, and Justin knew that Sarah was merely improvising now so that the opportunity would not be entirely lost. Nevertheless, the arch gaze she shot Pembroke made his blood boil. With a look that would have caused most females to quail in their dancing slippers, Justin gripped her shoulders.

"You seem to have forgotten that your pleasure is to see to mine," he drawled. "I see that I must spend the next hours refreshing your memory." With that, he propelled her out of the room as Pembroke's laughter followed them.

"That was very bold, my lord," Sarah whispered, her face

scarlet. "I hardly think it necessary to hold me up to such ridicule."

"Ridicule?" he echoed, no longer certain as they swept out into the night air whether either of them was playing a part. "I do not know what you mean."

Sarah gave him a fulminating look. "You might as well have announced to all that we were going to spend the rest of the night in . . . in lascivious pursuits. Would a man treat his mistress so?"

"A man may treat his mistress any way he pleases."

"A ruffian might," she retorted. "But a gentleman would . . ."

"Do not mistake me for that miserable breed."

Glaring, Sarah wrenched her arm away and stepped into the carriage. "Perhaps you are right. A gentleman would hardly devise a scheme to destroy a frail old lady who is clearly more miserable than you could ever make her."

Justin stilled. "You will explain yourself."

"I have met Lady Greywood," Sarah said. "She does not seem anything like the horrible creature you have made her out to be."

"You know nothing of her."

"I know that she is tired and afraid."

"She is a venal woman who has escaped being called to account for her considerable crimes," Justin said coldly. "She killed my father. Her actions were responsible for the death of my mother."

Wearily, Sarah leaned against the squabs. "One cannot excuse your father's murder, or course. But it seems harsh to blame her for your mother's suicide. Who really knows what drives people to take their own lives? You were a youth at the time. Perhaps you do not know the whole truth. Can you not reconsider this madness?"

Cold steel wrapped around his heart, keeping him impervious to her pleas, feeding the anger that had driven him to pull her with him out into the night. "The only thing I am reconsidering," he said coolly, "is whether I made a mistake in hiring you."

Sarah flinched, almost as if she had been hit, and Justin immediately wanted to withdraw the words. But he did not. She wrapped her arms around herself and sat stiffly on the seat until they reached the town house.

* * *

Justin had performed the trick so often he no longer thought of the motions required. Instead, he simply watched Sarah as she studied the cards. She said very little, although for the butler's benefit she had touched his arm lightly and managed a flirtatious smile. This had such an instant effect on Justin that it put him in mind of that day at Lintonwood, when Sarah had shown him with the merest touch the feminine power she possessed.

The cold fury she tried to restrain gave her touch a painful intensity even more mesmerizing than that day in his study. Anger lent her cheeks a flush akin to the warmth desire had provided then. Rage brought the same feverish gleam to her eyes, the same trembling to her mouth.

Anger, Justin decided, was a powerful aphrodisiac.

How else to explain the answering desire that shot through him as he sat across from her, seething at her temerity to challenge his judgment of Lady Greywood?

When the butler had seen to their comfort and closed the door behind him, her provocative smile dissolved. Unhappiness swept her features, but a look of such determination followed that Justin knew she had resolved to endure the next hour or so in his presence. The knowledge that this time between them was no more to her than a chore sent a wave of angry disappointment rippling through him.

Sighing, Sarah plucked a card, studied it, then carefully inserted it elsewhere in the deck. She did not say a word, but her wounded air projected her thoughts clearly enough. Damned if he would apologize again. The fault was hers. She had no right to criticize his plan. He had purchased her cooperation and he would have it.

Surreptitiously, he used his left little finger to create a slight break between the card she had chosen and the rest of the deck. Though she stared intently at his hands, Justin knew she detected nothing amiss in the triple cut that brought her card to the bottom of the pile. When he turned the deck over and displayed her card, she blinked in amazement.

"I still do not understand how you do it," she said in grudging admiration.

Justin did not want her admiration. He did not want to sit here and perform like a trained animal. Those first few nights the cards had helped pass the time and somehow drawn them together. But tonight the cards made him restless and uneasy, for they underscored the barriers between them. Between his skill and her scant understanding of what art lay behind the tricks was a vast gulf, very like that which separated a master from his servant and a man from his mistress.

Sarah was not his mistress, Justin reminded himself. Nor did he wish to make her his in that way. His plan was too precious, his goals too vital. He would not let any woman distract him from the thing that drove him. He would not listen to her criticism, nor give her arguments weight. If she became his mistress in truth, he would not be able to keep her at bay. For he was not a rake who cared for no one but himself. He was not his father.

Perhaps greed was behind her efforts to discredit his scheme. Perhaps she did not wish to relinquish the house, the gowns, the servants. As long as she made herself amiable, as long as she applauded his card tricks and refilled his brandy glass, they could continue indefinitely. A sudden blinding anger shot through him. If he was paying for her keep, he would damn well have her.

Ruefully Justin realized where his thoughts had taken him. Anger was indeed a powerful aphrodisiac. But not for him, not tonight. He was wiser than that. Abruptly he rose.

"You are leaving?" Surprise lent her voice a breathless, husky note.

"Yes."

"But you have not stayed long enough to . . . that is, to keep up appearances." Flushed, she bit her lip, and Justin wondered why it was that a woman of her worldly experience found it difficult to speak of such a topic.

"A man who has quarreled with his mistress might not be inclined to remain overlong in her presence." Justin marveled at the effort it took to restrain the impulse to crush her in an embrace that would put her in her place once and for all. "I am certain the servants will not expect our every night to be one of carnal bliss."

"No. I suppose not." She searched his face.

Justin made to brush by her. A gentle touch on his sleeve stopped him cold.

"I am sorry for my harsh words," she said. "I know you believe your cause is just. But when I saw Lady Greywood, I realized how much the past can destroy the present and the future, if one allows it. I did not wish that for you."

Against his better judgment, Justin allowed the cold vise around his heart to loosen somewhat. "That is the first time *you* have apologized to me," he said stiffly.

A shy smile brightened her face like a ray of sunlight. "You will stay a bit longer then?" she asked hesitantly, a pleading vulnerability in her eyes. "I should like another chance to plumb the mysteries of that trick."

Surely there was enough of his father in him to give him the strength to turn a blind eye to one woman's charms. Surely there was enough of his father's ruthlessness to banish the need that threatened his scheme. If he succumbed to that need, Justin knew he would never be the same.

What had Anh said? That Sarah would destroy him? Was that what he meant?

Summoning all of the power within his command, Justin shook his head. "It is late. I must go."

Disappointment shadowed her face. She removed her arm from his. "Good night, then."

But this was not their usual parting. Tension unsettled the air between them, and the power he had summoned ebbed to nothing before it. Indecision wedged its way into his will, and Justin found himself standing awkwardly before her like some tongue-tied youth. No woman had ever made him feel so unsure.

What if he gave in to the force that was drawing him to her? What if he swept her up the stairs to that peach-colored chamber of delights? What would it be like to share that plump featherbed with Sarah?

In his fantasy she had been in that bed, wearing the same gown, the same diamond ornament she wore now. Had his vision foretold the future? Did he possess a sorcerer's skill to see his own fate?

With his heart pounding like a thousand exploding cannons, Justin pulled her into his arms, knowing that only she could calm the restlessness inside him.

A man would be a fool to believe in magic. And a fool not to.

Chapter Fifteen

This kiss was not intended for an audience.

That was Sarah's fleeting thought as Justin put to shame those other, practiced kisses he had bestowed on her for the servants' benefit. This caress was both intimate and new, as if they were strangers who had found in each other a deeply resonant chord of recognition.

No dark angel could lurk behind this heavenly kiss, Sarah thought giddily as his teeth nibbled at her bottom lip and his arm steadied her against the strange force erupting within her. Even when he tilted her head back to look deep into her eyes, nothing sinister stared out from that gray gaze. Indeed, there was something almost tentative there, a hint of uncertainty.

Within the circle of his arms, Sarah's own confusion melted away like ice before a roaring fire. Simmering anger at his senseless revenge faded in a surge of passion that defied the small, embedded voice of propriety that had guided her for so long. Her mother would not approve, Sarah thought weakly as Justin trailed kisses over her shoulder, summoning goose bumps from her flesh. But something silenced that internal voice, something mystical and masculine, and it kindled a heat deep within her that would not be denied. Her fingers itched to touch him. As he rained kisses over the rise of her breasts she captured that glossy chestnut hair and pulled him closer, so that the delicious heat warmed her nipples as the bodice of her gown opened to the insistence of his probing caress.

Her small moan stilled him. He raised his head to look at her, his eyes dark with need and a question. It was a lover's gaze, Sarah realized in sudden recognition.

That knowledge loosed within her an emotion so new and so tenuous that it seemed to settle over her like gossamer, giving hazy form to the passion surging within her and stirring her restless soul to joyous life.

He was hers. Her lover. Her love.

Waiting, he watched her silently. Sarah understood that he waited for her decision but would not wait much longer. As she stared into those smoldering eyes, she realized that she belonged to this man with the devil's thirst for revenge and a sorcerer's skill with illusion.

Was this certainty she felt about him but an illusion? To be sure, there was nothing false about the intense need in that gaze. Her own need was almost blinding in its power. But, as she was learning, the line between illusion and truth sometimes blurred.

Sarah closed her eyes, denying him for the moment the answer he sought. He was a man any woman would ache to call her lover. *But not her love. Never that.*

Justin Trent could not love. Revenge owned him. There was no room for anything else. Except perhaps lust.

I would settle for that, Sarah realized to her amazement. Sometimes a woman had to make compromises. Justin stirred within her a need that banished all else, even the need for respectability. If there was meaning to her struggle to hold herself up to some righteous standard of behavior, Sarah could no longer recall it.

In a man incapable of love, lust would have to do.

Opening her eyes, Sarah met his gaze, knowing that there was nothing to save her from her fate.

The moment their gazes locked, Justin knew he would have her. Sweeping her into his arms, he carried her out into the hall. He would not have her on the small divan in the room where they had spent so many hours keeping each other at arm's length. He would have her in that upstairs chamber filled with peach and amber and the plump featherbed of his fantasies.

She would lie on the bed for him in that emerald gown. He would undress her slowly, peeling away the fabric as if it hid a treasure beyond price. She would be his, the woman of his dreams.

No, not that. Sarah was merely an actress, a woman who used the art of illusion to capture a man's imagination.

Illusion or no, he was about to discover her secrets.

Carrying her in his arms seemed effortless, as if he were floating on air. They did not speak. There was no need. Both of them knew what came next. It would be a relief to exchange fantasy for flesh and blood. He would know her in all the ways a man could know a woman, and that knowledge would disarm her power. Familiarity would mute its force. Those green eyes would command him no more.

Like a magician taking charge of an art that had momentarily escaped him, he would once again control his fate.

Clouds of peach satin surrounded her as he laid her on the lush comforter. A brace of candles cast the room in tones of amber that lent her complexion a sensual, beguiling warmth. The restless flames reflected in her eyes as she watched him silently from the bed.

As he removed his shirt, Justin thought fleetingly of the other women he had brought here, the women for whom he had paid as surely as he had paid for Sarah. He could not recall their names, their faces. They had meant nothing to him, except as cover to further his reputation as a libertine. They had, however, been wise in the way of such women. Sarah had never displayed that sort of wisdom. Even now she projected a charming innocence, even though the games between them had finally ceased.

Lowering himself to the bed, Justin plucked the diamond ornament from her hair and loosened her hairpins. Running his hands through those auburn tresses, he savored their silky feel against his fingertips and drank in their beauty as they fanned over the pillow.

Sarah merely regarded him with disconcerting somberness. A woman ought to know her art better than that, he thought uneasily. A man took no pleasure in being stared at as if he were a catch of fish left in the sun too long. Frowning, Justin traced the curve of her shoulders. As his fingers slipped beneath the fabric of her gown and touched the satiny smoothness of her skin, desire ripped a shudder from him. Despite her faint, answering tremble, she lay still and silent, her unflinching gaze probing his for something he did not understand.

"You are mine," he whispered defiantly against her lips, daring her to disagree.

"Yes," she answered without an instant's hesitation.

With shimmering sensuality, the emerald gown submitted to

his will. It slid off her shoulders and away from her breasts, pooling around her waist as it granted him access to Sarah's lush secrets. The comforter slithered to the floor as he drew her into his embrace and cradled her against his bare chest. She seemed small and delicate, and Justin felt oddly protective as he held her.

"Sarah," he rasped.

Again she trembled, and he wrapped his arms around her more tightly for warmth. When her tremors did not cease, he pulled back to study her. Her eyes widened, and though they were glazed with passion, they held uncertainty.

"Are you cold?" he asked gently.

Sarah shook her head. "I suppose I am a bit frightened," she confessed.

"Do you take me for a monster? I promise I will not hurt you."

"No. Of course not." She colored, and in the amber light her cheeks took on an ethereal, almost cherubic rosiness.

Bemused, Justin tried to banish the distracting image. In his fantasy Sarah had displayed neither maidenly fear nor cherubic innocence. He ran his hands over her hips, impatient at the barrier of her gown, desperate for the joining to come.

She gave him a timid smile. He frowned. Something was not right. Sarah was not a timid woman.

"Damnation," he growled. "Will you stop this game of cat and mouse?"

"What game?"

An exasperated sigh escaped his lips. "I will tolerate no more of your antics. Tonight you dance to *my* tune."

"Oh." She stared at him. Then her brow furrowed. "You might be a bit more considerate," she admonished.

This evidence of her spunk pleased him. How many times had he wondered how that spirited nature would manifest itself in a moment of passion?

"No woman has ever accused me of being an inconsiderate lover," Justin said, half amused despite his pique.

She lowered her gaze. "I am certain those . . . other women had no cause for complaint."

"Come, Sarah," he said impatiently. "This is no time to play the jealous mistress. I know you want me. There are some things that a woman cannot hide."

Slowly, he traced the tip of her breast with his finger. Her small breathless moan betrayed her desire, but his smug satisfaction at this victory was lost in the sudden jolt of passion that claimed him as her nipple hardened in response to his touch. He felt like a volcano waiting to explode. He must have this woman, and soon.

With a primitive growl, he covered her with his body, bracing himself on his elbows as he let her feel the effect of his own desire. Sarah stared up at him with wide eyes.

"I imagine that all of your . . . women have been rather more experienced," she ventured breathlessly. "I am afraid that I am new at this."

Her statement hit him like a bucket of cold water.

"What did you say?" Every muscle in his body tensed.

Sarah bit her lip. "I know you think that a woman in my profession is experienced in such matters. The truth is, I have never done this before. I was hoping you would be . . . understanding."

"Good God." Justin stared incredulously, then abruptly rolled away from her. Rage tore through him. "This is too much."

"I am sorry you are disappointed," she said, tears welling in her eyes. "It is just that . . ."

"Spare me the tears," Justin commanded, snatching up his shirt. "You are a conniving wench, are you not? I suppose you have a vial of sheep's blood stashed somewhere to scatter upon the sheets after I fall asleep." He shook his head in disbelief. "A *virgin*, by God! You must think me an idiot. You did not mean to settle for the thousand pounds, did you? You wanted more— much more."

Her wounded gasp simply inflamed him further.

"The privileges of being my mistress are vastly superior to those enjoyed by a circuit actress, are they not?" he demanded sardonically. "You did not intend to relinquish them, did you? You meant to bind me in the most effective way possible—by pretending an innocence you must have known only in your dreams. Did you think to cajole from me a proposal of marriage? Or merely to wrangle another year or so of my protection?"

Dazed, she stared at him. "You are mad."

Justin flung open the door and turned to eye her scornfully.

"It is you who have lost your wits for thinking to fool me. You are not that good an actress. Once you made me believe you were Harry's wife, but this time you attempted the impossible. There is nothing I do not know about illusion. Do you understand that?"

But Sarah had finally found her tongue. Grabbing the comforter to cover herself, she rose with a surprising dignity. "I understand only that revenge has destroyed you, my lord," she said, her voice shaking as she wrapped herself in peach satin. "It has swallowed you like some carnivorous bird and eaten away at your soul until it is as black and empty as the night. You think you are wise. You think you see everything. But you see nothing!"

Striding into the hall, Justin slammed the door, cutting off her scathing accusations. The words followed him, however, echoing in his brain like a ghostly chant that would not let him be. *You see nothing.*

He would wring Anh's neck.

"Well, my dear. I suppose it is not every day that Justin loses you in a card game." Lady Devon eyed her sympathetically. "I am certain he is not himself. I have never seen Justin fail in a game of chance."

Sarah smiled, but it was nearly impossible to hide her mortification. Putting her up as the stakes in his game with Lord Pembroke said more eloquently than anything else what she was to him: a commodity, a thing to be bought and sold as much as his matched bays or carriage. And even though the game took place in the home of one of the *ton*'s most respected hostesses, it was still a lowering and disgraceful event. No real lady would be put on public display like this, forced to watch as her protector handed her over with nary a blink of the eye.

With Sarah Manwaring's insouciance, she smiled carelessly at those who had gathered to watch the card play. But the role did not sit well on her shoulders tonight. Truth be told, Sarah no longer knew where the boundaries of the part left off and she began. Nothing had been the same since that disastrous night. The contempt he publicly displayed for her was no longer pretense. The message that he had tired of her was all too genuine.

To be sure, he still needed her; she was essential to his plan, which was why Sarah knew he was but toying with her now. He might have lost her to Lord Pembroke, but it was only for show, to put her in her place.

Lord Pembroke seemed delighted with his fortune, but Sarah could see that he was also troubled by the notion of winning a woman in such a way. When he offered Justin a chance to win her back, Justin merely shrugged.

"If you wish, Pembroke, although I am perfectly satisfied with the results." He yawned. "There is a new deck on the table. You may have the first cut."

Lord Pembroke cut the cards. Justin shuffled rapidly, cut them twice more, and began to deal.

Vingt-et-un was one of the few games Sarah understood. Each player was dealt one card facedown and one face up. The object was to get as many total points without going over twenty-one. Lord Pembroke greeted the arrival of a ten with glee, especially when Justin's face-up card was a lowly two of clubs. Lord Pembroke took a peek at his hidden card and spent the next moments deciding whether to take another card.

"Buy," he said at last.

Justin, who as dealer was not allowed to look at his hidden card, seemed heedless of the tension in the room as he tossed the two of hearts on Lord Pembroke's ten. He arched a brow to query whether, with twelve points showing, Lord Pembroke wished additional cards.

"Not on your life, Linton." Lord Pembroke grinned with the confidence of one who holds a winning hand. "I feel exceedingly lucky. And if you lose this one, I shall not feel obliged to give you another chance to win the return of your lovely lady."

Raising a glass, Lord Pembroke saluted Sarah. Although she nodded politely, Sarah quaked inside. What if Justin did not win her back?

All that kept her from racing out of the room in a panic was the certain knowledge that nothing Justin did was the product of random thought. Everything was calculated according to his plan, and while the card game was a last-minute wrinkle that undoubtedly stemmed from his anger at her, Sarah could see that it fit admirably into the overall scheme of things. What better way to set up that final stormy public scene than by disgracing her so publicly? He might as well have announced that he was about to give her her congé. When she erupted in rage at Lady Hogarth's masquerade two nights hence, everyone would shake their heads and say that it was perfectly understandable.

Justin turned over his hidden card. It was the two of diamonds. He dealt himself another—seven of diamonds. Then another—eight of clubs. Now he had nineteen points. Surely he would not risk going over by dealing himself another card. Only if his next card were a two would she be saved—and the odds of that were slim, since three twos already were showing.

Sarah closed her eyes. He really *did* mean to lose her. Perhaps he had devised some other plan for eliciting Lady Greywood's confession. Perhaps something had snapped in him and he simply did not care anymore.

No. That could not be. Revenge meant everything to him.

All those nights in her drawing room suddenly appeared in her mind's eye. He had shown her how it was done—the shuffle that did not truly shuffle, the cut that did not disturb the careful order of the deck, the sleight of hand that sent her card to the bottom of the pile.

Hope shot through her. If he could manipulate her card to the bottom, he could send others to the top where they could be dealt from a seemingly random arrangement.

The crowd inhaled audibly. Sarah's eyes flew open just as Justin casually dealt himself a final card. The two of spades.

Twenty-one points.

Grimacing, Lord Pembroke turned over his hidden card. Eight of spades. Twenty points.

Loud gasps and a few cheers rippled through the room. Pembroke looked crestfallen. Justin merely sighed.

"I suppose you will be coming home with me tonight, my dear." Justin rose, nodded blandly to Lord Pembroke and casually met her gaze.

Lucifer himself looked out from those smoldering eyes with unholy glee.

Chapter Sixteen

"How did you know that Lord Pembroke would offer you a chance to win me back?"

Justin kept his eyes fixed on the view out the carriage window, even though the blur of night whirling past barely registered in his mind. He did not need to look at Sarah to sense her fury.

"I did not know," he replied calmly. She had no reason to be angry, he told himself. The money he was paying her was sufficient to cover any slights to her dignity.

"And you did not care, did you?"

Despite himself, Justin turned to Sarah. Her ashen complexion and trembling lips sent a spasm of guilt spiraling through him.

"That is not accurate," he said, careful to keep any hint of emotion from his voice. "I would not have allowed anything to jeopardize my plan. You are essential to that plan. Therefore, I did not intend to leave you in Pembroke's protection."

"Yes. That is what I thought," she replied in a flat voice. "That you would wish to save your plan."

"Pembroke is not like me," he drawled. "He has an elevated moral sensibility. I guessed that he would not feel comfortable with the arrangement and would offer me a chance to recoup my loss."

One chance. He had allowed fate to ride on that one chance. He must have been mad.

"I see," she said slowly. "You made a simple prediction based on your excellent understanding of human nature." She paused to look at him. "I believe that was how you once explained your perceptiveness, was it not?"

"Yes." Justin was not sure why hearing his own words repeated should embarrass him.

She fiddled with her fan. "And yet, you could not have been absolutely certain that Lord Pembroke would play the gentleman. Or that you would win the second hand."

"There is risk in everything. My prospects of winning the hand were never in doubt, however."

That was not really a lie. He had been all but certain that Pembroke would not risk accepting another card. He had counted on that fact when he had arranged the deck beforehand. If Pembroke had decided otherwise, of course, all would have been lost.

"You cheated." Her solemn, unblinking eyes held his.

"I simply manipulated the sequence of events," he corrected. "I would never have done so in a money game. But this was a lark. No one took it seriously."

"I did. Lord Pembroke did. And so did you." She paused. "You wanted to punish me, did you not? You intended to humiliate me in front of the entire *ton,* to show that I was beneath them. That was the real purpose of your game."

The game that was not a game. Justin closed his eyes as that long-ago scene in his father's study came to mind, a scene of cruelty and humiliation—his blood legacy.

"Sarah," he said softly.

Fury darkened her eyes to the color of stormy seas. "I am nobody to you, merely a woman who bartered her talent for a thousand pounds and in the process lost any hope of gaining respectability in your eyes."

Wearily, Justin shook his head. "We have a business arrangement. Your respectability—or lack of it—has nothing to do with anything."

"It has everything to do with it."

The trembling in her voice filled him with yearning for the impossible—to be better than he was. Why did she always affect him this way?

"If you traded in your self-respect in the process of posing as my mistress," he declared coolly, "the consequences are yours to bear. You sold yourself to me. That is what women like you do."

"And you traded me to Lord Pembroke. That is what men like you do. I am a thing to be bought and sold, am I not?"

"There was never any chance of your ending up with Pembroke," he protested, wondering how he would have lived with himself if fate had played him false.

"Tell me, my lord," she said, studying his face intently. "Did you do this because you think I tried to trick you in my chamber the other night? Because you did not believe in my innocence? Because I did not play the part of your whore?"

Such a word did not belong on her lips, he thought incongruously, then chided himself for his charity. An actress might not sell her body in Covent Garden, but she was little better than the women who did. Unlike them, however, Sarah would not be content to leave her lover with merely an empty purse and the devil's head in the morning. She would have it all, if he let her.

Thank God Lady Hogarth's masquerade was tomorrow. The sooner he was done with Sarah the better. She threatened everything, from his carefully laid plans to his very sanity. If she had simply allowed him to enjoy her body, to wrap himself around her as he had yearned to do when he first laid eyes on her, he could have dispensed with this restless obsession for her. But she had pretended innocence—something absurd in a woman of her history. Her audacity had enraged him. That is why he had put her in her place tonight. She had dared too much. The woman of his fantasy wore an emerald gown and reclined for him on a peach satin comforter. She demanded nothing. She gave herself to him and took what he had to give her. She did not threaten his world with hints of impossible possibilities.

Sarah would not stay within the boundaries of her role. And he was not his father, who would have lost his mistress in a card game and shrugged it off. The distinction between father and son had blurred. Humiliating Sarah had been unworthy of him, yet it fit perfectly with the dissolute, cynical rake he played. It fit his plan, the plan that now left a taste in his mouth as bitter as loss.

As the carriage pulled up to the house in Brook Street, Sarah folded her arms protectively around herself and bit her lip until Justin thought she would draw blood. She barely looked at him as he helped her down. The butler admitted them but vanished after one glance at Sarah's tremulous features. Standing stiffly in the foyer, Justin was uncertain whether to leave or stay.

Sarah decided for him. Walking to the front door, she threw it open like a queen banishing a wayward courtier.

"I would have been your mistress," she said with a fierce sob. "*Never* your whore."

Lady Greywood studied the Chinese wallpaper for so long Sarah was afraid the woman had forgotten where she was. When the butler had announced the countess, Sarah nearly jumped out of her chair. Since Sarah's arrival in Brook Street, no one had come to call except Justin. That her caller should be the very woman whose downfall they would bring about tonight made her heart race wildly.

"You would appear to be very comfortable here," Lady Greywood said, her tone betraying neither censure nor approval. She perched stiffly on an overstuffed blue chair as if it were made of nails.

"The house is to my liking," Sarah replied warily, wondering whether the countess would soon make the purpose of her visit clear. She did not have to wonder long.

"I come to make a final appeal to you," Lady Greywood said in a voice devoid of emotion. "When we spoke earlier, I begged you to make Lord Linton stop this madness. I realize now that it was an impossible request. A man like Linton is too ruthless to alter his plans, even at the request of a woman he holds in affection."

Sarah stiffened. "I believe you overestimate the extent to which I occupy Lord Linton's affections."

Lady Greywood studied her. "With Linton, we shall never know, of course. The point, Mrs. Manwaring, is that you hold the fate of others in your hands."

"I do not understand."

From a small box, Lady Greywood pulled a yellow iris banded about the edges in purple and nestled in a bunch of violets. "This corsage was delivered to my house today. It is identical to one that was worn fifteen years ago to Lady Hogarth's masquerade."

Sarah drew in her breath sharply. He had said his father's florist would make a precise duplicate for her to wear tonight. She did not realize he also meant to send one to Lady Greywood. It was another of his diabolical touches.

"I suspect Linton wishes to punish me for his father's death," Lady Greywood said with a heavy sigh. "I have thought for some time that he is trying to drive me out of my mind. He has very nearly succeeded."

"I am sorry," Sarah said simply. There was so much more she wished to say, but despite her differences with Justin, she could not betray his plan.

Sharp brown eyes held hers. "You need not worry that I will try to pry it out of you, girl. I know that Linton sent those flowers, just as I know that he orchestrated that duel with my son and has made himself into a pattern card of his father—all to torment me."

Sarah chewed on her lip.

"I do not know what else he has planned," Lady Greywood continued, "but I know that Linton is not a man to leave it at that. If you cannot sway him, I implore you to look to yourself. Do not be a party to this, Mrs. Manwaring. It will destroy lives."

Helplessly, Sarah shook her head. "I cannot do what you wish, ma'am."

Lady Greywood rose abruptly. Her gaze softened. "Let me give you some advice, Mrs. Manwaring. A man like Linton will only take and give nothing back."

Sarah was surprised at the strength in her voice.

"Some women are up to the task," the countess added quietly. "Others are not. For them, being used by such a man is tantamount to destruction. They can never let go of their hopes, you see. They are seduced by his charm, by his ability to manipulate a woman into betraying every principle she holds dear. Some women think that love can change a man like that. It never does."

Lady Greywood's gaze narrowed. "Something tells me you possess such illusions, Mrs. Manwaring. I warn you, it is a fatal mistake. If one's life is built around hope, and hope fails, one has nothing left. It is the woman who is destroyed in the end."

Long after Lady Greywood left, Sarah was still contemplating her remarks. It was not until hours later, when Sarah sat in Justin's carriage costumed as Marie Antoinette—wearing a corsage of iris and violets identical to the one Lady Greywood had received—that she forced herself to face the truth of the countess's words.

Justin was everything Lady Greywood had said, and more. She *had* allowed herself to hope that he could change, that he would abandon his quest for revenge, that she would be the source of his redemption.

Some women think that love can change a man like that. Did she love him? Might as well love the devil himself as a man whose soul was filled with the desire for revenge.

A man like Linton will only take and give nothing back. There was no corner of his soul that the darkness had not touched.

They are seduced by his charm, by his ability to manipulate a woman into betraying every principle she holds dear. She had sold herself to him, as much as any prostitute. She had been willing to become his mistress in truth. Now she was about to help him destroy a frail woman and stir up wounds that ought to be allowed to heal.

How clear it all seemed now: he had been the puppeteer, she the marionette. Whatever hope she cherished that he would come to care for her had proven as groundless as the wind. She could never get beyond the mask to the real man, whoever he was. Meanwhile, she had become the very role she played: a woman paid to serve his demonic passions.

"Dr. Quincy will be wearing the shepherd's costume. He will be the first to reach me and to declare that I am in mortal danger. You may depend on him to arrange for me to be transported from the house forthwith."

His words pierced her dismal reverie. "You have paid him well for his services, I suppose," she said bitterly, fingering the corsage.

"Quincy is a good man," Justin said coldly. "He attended my father that night and always regretted that the killer was not brought to justice."

"I see."

"Afterwards, he will send word of my death. I do not expect the countess to confess immediately, although she might, of course. When I present myself to her two days hence, I fully expect that she will be so distraught as to thoroughly unburden herself of her crimes."

"She will no doubt have endured two sleepless nights since the ball," Sarah commented in a dull voice.

"Precisely," he agreed. "She will be more than ready to confess."

Sarah stared miserably at the large muff on the carriage seat.

The dueling pistol was inside, primed and in the half-cocked position. Although she did not look up, Sarah felt the force of his gaze.

"If you are even considering not going through with this," he warned, a dangerous edge to his voice, "you are being most unwise."

"I am afraid that wisdom has always eluded me, my lord," Sarah replied with a reckless laugh.

Large hands grasped her firmly about the shoulders. He forced her chin up so that she had to look at him. What Sarah saw in his eyes made her recoil. There was blackness through and through, the devil's own fury.

"You made a bargain," he snarled, "and you will keep it."

Sarah cringed, half expecting a blow. But words were his weapons—for now.

"If you do not, I will make you pay. If you flee, I will find you. I will hunt you down like a hound hunts the fox and I will show you no mercy. I have waited too long for this to allow you to jeopardize my plan."

"Your plan is unworthy of you, my lord," she said as tears welled in her eyes. "It is unworthy of both of us."

He stared at her for what seemed like an eternity. As the carriage rolled to a stop at Lady Hogarth's mansion, he touched her face. To her surprise, his touch was gentle.

"I never claimed to be worthy, Sarah."

She looked into the sorrowful gray mist of his eyes and cried.

Everything was perfect, just as Justin knew it would be. Sarah had given him a few moments' doubt in the carriage, and she had barely pulled herself together before it was time to greet their hostess. He should have known, however, that the actress in her would triumph.

She was a perfect Marie Antoinette. That blond wig she wore was an enormous construction of pomaded curls and ostrich feathers. Her elaborate claret and lace gown plunged from a dramatic décolleté into a cinched waist before flaring out again into a panniered skirt adorned with rich brocade and voluminous lace. It was a duplicate of the gown his father's assailant had worn fifteen years ago. It was also heavy and difficult to maneuver. What had possessed Lady Greywood to think she could shoot a man and flee unscathed in such a gown? Justin wondered. She had been exceedingly fortunate, in that she did not have far to run—her home was but two houses from Lady Hogarth's.

A nagging doubt plagued him. His coachman had been instructed to wait discreetly for Sarah at the next corner, ready to spirit her to a respectable inn miles away with a change of clothes and the balance of her money. She would have to run a full block, however. Justin had not thought of the difficulties the gown would pose. What if she were caught before she reached the carriage?

Justin took a calming breath. Nothing would go wrong. Lady Greywood was in attendance, as he had known she would be. He had seen the countess gasp in horror at Sarah's costume and he wanted to rub his hands together in glee. Soon his father's killer would be brought to justice. Revenge would be his. He could taste it. It was sweet.

Why, then, this bitterness in his mouth? Why the sudden pang when he looked at Sarah gamely managing her voluminous gown, muff, and wig like the skilled actress she was? Why the sorrow inside him at the knowledge that after tonight, he would never see her again?

The answers, if they existed, lay in some recess of his brain that he could not afford to explore. Not tonight, anyway. The curtain was going up.

It was Lord Pembroke who made the evening bearable. Had he not flirted with her and been kind enough to fetch her punch, Sarah would have collapsed under the weight of her gown and the burden of the task ahead. Every time she looked at Justin, the brooding gray eyes impaled her with a raw intensity that fairly took her breath away. Lady Amanda was often at Justin's side, flirting outrageously, and once gaily wrapping herself in the folds of his black domino.

Like a badly written play, the evening plodded along. Then, abruptly, it picked up steam and rushed headlong toward the disastrous climax. Suddenly it was time for the unmasking. Guests packed the area near the windows that sent cool breezes in from the terrace. Lady Hogarth prepared to announce the costume awards. Lady Greywood stood nearby, a haunted look in her somber eyes.

Justin moved toward one of the windows, positioning him-

self near the thick, velvet curtains. The terrace door was to
Sarah's left. It would be a simple matter to fire the weapon and
run outside, dropping the pistol in one of the bushes as they had
practiced dozens of times. It wanted only his sign that he was
ready to begin. At the moment, however, Justin had his hands
full with Lady Amanda, who had had too much to drink and
was draping herself over him like a second skin. He would have
to get her out of the way, for Sarah needed a clear shot at the
curtain.

Not that she would mind nicking Lady Amanda instead,
Sarah thought wryly, as the woman lifted her face to Justin's.
When she formed her lips into an inviting pucker, Sarah froze.
The encroaching creature expected him to kiss her—here, in
front of his mistress and everyone at Lady Hogarth's ball! Had
the woman no sense of propriety?

Justin caught Sarah's eye and shrugged. Already Lady Hogarth had signaled the orchestra to quiet. They were not going to
get a better moment, his eyes said. It was time to proceed, Lady
Amanda or no. He had obviously decided to turn the situation
to their advantage.

As the woman's arms snaked around his neck, Justin allowed
her to pull him toward her. In the next moment, his lips were on
Lady Amanda's, kissing her quite thoroughly and publicly as
Sarah stood not fifteen feet away.

Around her, people stopped their conversations to watch the
scandalous embrace. When at last Justin ended the kiss, Lady
Amanda gave a breathless sigh and then a tiny giggle that shattered the awkward silence.

Fire roiled Sarah's veins. He had set the stage, all right. All
eyes were on them. Putting her hand into the muff, she allowed
the pistol's cool metal to sooth her feverish temper. Bestowing
her haughtiest gaze on the couple, she took a step forward.

"How dare you?" she demanded in a voice so tightly controlled, it might have come from someone else.

All remaining activity in the room ceased. Lady Amanda
giggled again, but her eyes widened a bit as Sarah took another
step forward.

"You dare to trifle with my affections, sir. Well, I shall tell
you something that is no trifling matter." Sarah struggled to remember her lines amid the turmoil inside her. She stroked the
hammer of the pistol and found the sensation calming. Her

other hand touched the corsage. She could no longer recall when she was supposed to throw it.

Justin arched one contemptuous eyebrow at Sarah, then firmly set Lady Amanda from him. The inebriated woman was forced to steady herself on a nearby potted plant. She reeled slightly before regaining her balance.

"You take too much upon yourself, madam," Justin drawled. "You read too much into a casual flirtation."

"I beg your pardon?" Lady Amanda said indignantly, but Lord Pembroke stepped forward to grasp her about the waist and propel her resolutely to a nearby chair.

Now there were only two players.

"A casual flirtation?" Sarah's voice dripped with scorn as she pulled the pistol from her muff and moved the hammer to the full-cock position. "I will give you *this,* my lord, for your casual flirtation."

Gasps went up from the crowd, but no one dared move. Sarah thought she recognized Lady Greywood's shocked cry among the others, but there was no way to be certain. The moment seemed suspended in time. Locked in the pages of Justin's script, Sarah was powerless to do anything but continue this nightmarish drama. Between the actress and the woman, there was no longer any distinction. She had somehow become her part, the spurned mistress in love with a ruthless cad.

Who said anything about love, Miss Armistead? This is a relationship based on carnal instinct, not love. You must not make the mistake of confusing one with the other.

Subtly, Justin touched the curtain, indicating his readiness for the climax of their scene.

Not love. Never love. He had been quite clear about that. But he had been wrong. She loved Justin Trent. And she could not let him do this to his mortal soul.

Her lines vanished from her memory as surely as if someone had blotted them out. Sarah stood center stage in her climactic moment with no recollection of the words she was to speak. The audience waited breathlessly. Her fellow actor stared expectantly, waiting for her to continue. But the lines were gone.

All that remained were the words in her heart.

"Let it go, my lord," she said softly. "Give up this disastrous plan before it paints your soul as black as the night, before you fall into an abyss from which there is no escape."

Justin frowned, commanding her with his eyes to get on with it, to pick up the threads of the scene. A cramp shot through Sarah's fingers as she clutched the pistol, heavy and immobile, like the unbearable weight it was.

"Do not do this," she pleaded. "It will not restore your father's life. It will only destroy yours and the lives of others. If there is any compassion in you, let it save you."

But those gray eyes were implacable. Again he touched the curtain, a director's impatient cue to the actress who stumbled out of control.

Sarah shook her head, and he stared at her in angry disbelief as he realized the import of her rejection. His eyes darkened with smoldering rage.

"God's blood, Sarah," he cried with all the fury of an enraged bull. "I will kill you for this!"

A mighty trembling began inside her. Tears welled deep in her heart and sprang to her eyes with the force of a frozen river finally unleashed by the spring thaw. They streamed down her face, blinding her to all but that enraged cry. A sob ripped from her throat.

And in that pivotal moment, Justin's answering cry of denial was abruptly silenced, for the cramp that had frozen Sarah's fingers suddenly relaxed against the trigger of his father's Manton pistol.

Chapter Seventeen

Things were proceeding precisely as he had planned. Even Amanda had played into his hands, her giggling tipsiness the perfect spark for the ugly scene.

People were motionless, their faces frozen in shock and horror as Sarah pointed the pistol at him. They were staring at her, so they did not notice him surreptitiously pat the bag of pig's blood under his waistcoat and edge a bit closer to the heavy drapery. Inhaling the cool night air that wafted through the window, Justin waited calmly, making no move to escape his fate.

He had not expected such a riveting performance. Twin blotches of angry passion rose on Sarah's cheeks, visible even through the dusting of talc that covered her luminous skin. Through the mask, her eyes blazed emerald fire. Emotion pulsed like a fiery aura around her. Even that perfectly styled wig she wore had begun to curl erratically, as if it, too, were permeated with passion.

Justin congratulated himself. He had chosen her. He had choreographed her every move, put every word in her mouth, lifted her from the obscurity of the circuit to the central role in a drama no one would soon forget.

Their arduous rehearsals had paid off, although for some reason she had not yet thrown the corsage. Her delivery was brilliant, her timing otherwise so impeccable that he would not hold that lapse against her. He smiled to himself. Now she would shift the pistol imperceptibly to her right, training the barrel on the curtain. The bullet would bury itself behind the thick, forgiving velvet like a rock hurled impotently against a cloud.

She was speaking again. Justin frowned. The words were not those he had given her. Something about an abyss and his soul.

Why was she improvising, the little minx? Did she hope to pry another guinea from him for her trouble?

He might have known that a woman would take it upon herself to try to improve upon what was already a perfect plan. But in the art of illusion, there was no room for error. She would ruin everything.

Watching her with a mixture of irritation and awe, Justin could not tell whether her theatrics were genuine or contrived. She had better not get carried away, he thought grimly. Her aim had to be sure and true. He caught her gaze and pointedly directed his own toward the curtain. He hoped she was not too far gone to read his silent message.

Her mouth curved upward in an expression that was anything but mirthful. Justin eyed her lips in fascination, recalling the last time he had claimed them. He would regret not having the opportunity to do so again. But there would be other women.

Thank God this one could shoot straight.

She said something else, something about compassion, about his father. What the hell did she know about his father? Her finger hovered on the trigger. He hoped she remembered his warning not to apply pressure prematurely.

Inhaling deeply, Justin tried to control his anger. Again he touched the curtain, signaling her. To his utter amazement, she shook her head. Disbelief shot through him. She was not going to go through with it. She was going to sabotage his plan, to kill everything he had worked for.

Rage erupted within him as he shouted his fury.

As if from afar, he registered the sound of gunfire and the force of the shot that sent her reeling backward. A plume of smoke spiraled upward from the pistol in her hand. There was a strange ringing in his head, an odd warmth stealing over him. He felt unaccountably weak as he clutched the curtain for support.

It occurred to him that she had not shifted her aim.

Something warm trickled over his skin. Not pig's blood. His blood. That was his last thought as he fell to the floor.

Justin was dead, as far as anyone in London knew. Dr. Quincy had done his part and trumpeted the doleful news although, as he told Sarah, he had deep reservations about jinxing his patient's recovery. He had hesitated when Sarah said she wished to remove Justin to Lintonwood, but then conceded that the country air could hardly do him more harm than she had.

In the three days since the shooting, Justin had not come around. Sarah could draw no satisfactory explanation for that fact from Dr. Quincy, who insisted that the wounds did not appear to be life-threatening. Fever, of course, was always a possibility, and the doctor warned her of the grievous consequences should the move provoke an increase in the viscount's bodily temperature.

"You must keep him warm and bathe the wound thrice daily. There is an elixir I have found useful for fever, but I cannot guarantee it. There is the devil to pay, madam, when people like you and Linton take fate into their own hands. I cannot answer for the consequences."

With this dire condemnation ringing in her ears, Sarah decided to take Justin home, for that is how she had always thought of the welcoming house at Lintonwood. And so, under the cover of night, she had commandeered Justin's sturdy traveling coach, his burliest footmen, and a coachman who gave no sign that there was anything out of the ordinary in sneaking a man who was supposed to be dead past the watchful eyes of London and Bow Street, which was greatly occupied in trying to locate one Sarah Manwaring.

Now, as Anh stood by Justin's bedside, murmuring strange, incomprehensible words and forcing an exotic potion through his lips, Sarah knew she had made the correct decision. If anyone could bring him about, it was this mysterious little man. He did not seem to be surprised that Justin had not yet awakened, even though Dr. Quincy had long ago removed the ball from his shoulder.

"His body is healing, but his soul is locked in disharmony," Anh said. "I have prescribed a diet according to the five tastes. The *shên* potion must be drunk every five hours. If he is unable to drink, a small piece of *shên* must be placed under the tongue and allowed to dissolve. But I cannot say whether that will bring him about."

"I see." Sarah bit her lip.

Anh studied her closely. "I will tend his lordship. I urge you to see your own rest."

"It was I who shot him. I cannot leave."

Anh nodded, as if that explained everything. "I will go and

prepare some *shên* tea for you, Miss Armistead. Perhaps it will help."

As Anh closed the door behind him, Sarah doubted anything would ease the torrent of guilt and sorrow that had washed over her since her finger tripped the trigger of Justin's pistol. It had been a horrible accident, but that did not help Justin, who had laid as still as death since that awful night. A nightmare of repeating images besieged her: Dr. Quincy's stunned expression as he worked over Justin, the shocked faces of Lady Hogarth's guests, Lord Pembroke's softly urgent tone as he slipped her out the door and into his carriage.

Had it not been for Lord Pembroke, Sarah knew she would have been behind bars. He had shaken his head but otherwise offered no objection when she tearfully insisted that he take her to Justin's house so that she could be present when Dr. Quincy arrived bearing his lifeless form.

All had been a blur since then, save the stark knowledge that she may have killed the man who had come to mean everything to her. She had failed him miserably, and perhaps he would pay the ultimate price.

Now that lean, strong body lay still and immobile in the enormous bed, surrounded by soft pillows and bedding. Those mesmerizing eyes were closed, their power to captivate robbed by a single bullet. Lips that had summoned from her a need so great it had no name remained pale and motionless, unable to speak even the sardonic words that had maddened her so. Fingers that had handled cards with nimble grace and breathtaking ease now lay inert on the covers, their magic defeated by her carelessness.

Sarah wanted to pray, but the only words that came to mind sprung from Ophelia's lips:

"O heavenly powers, restore him!"

"Sarah?"

At the familiar voice, she turned. "William!"

Her brother stood uncertainly in the doorway but stepped forward as Sarah flung herself at him. Brother and sister embraced as tears coursed down Sarah's face. Finally, William put her gently from him. "What has happened?"

"Oh, William, it is so awful," Sarah cried. "I have accidentally shot Lord Linton. I was supposed to shoot him, you see, or pretend to. But my hand got a cramp and I did not shift my aim before the pistol went off. If he dies it will be all my fault."

William's eyes widened. "I do not understand, exactly, but I am sure that whatever happens, it is not your fault."

Sarah smiled through her tears. "Oh, William, you will ever believe the best of me. But you do not know the truth. I have deceived you. You will not wish to claim me as your sister when you hear it all."

William listened carefully to Sarah's tearful confession— how she had not been in the employ of various genteel ladies all these months, how she had taken to the stage and accepted Lord Linton's offer of an extremely unusual job, how she had posed as his mistress in London and finally, shot him in a scandalous scene before all the *ton*. He said very little until she had finished. Then he eyed her somberly.

"While I was away at school, blissfully unaware of your sacrifices, you were humiliating yourself to keep me in the style you imagined a baron should enjoy. You never even hinted at our grave financial circumstances."

"You were too young, William. There was nothing you could do."

"I am fifteen now. That is old enough to earn my keep, and yours, too." His chin rose defiantly. "You were wrong to keep this from me. Did you think I would dodge my responsibilities?"

"No, but . . ."

"It was not your decision to make, Sarah. I know you tried to protect me, but I am a man now. It is my job to protect you from such a horrible fate as you have had to endure. You did not even give me a chance."

Sarah studied the solemn figure before her. He had grown, somehow, in the months away from her. His reddish hair was tousled in the style of the day, but his green eyes, mirrors of her own, bore a somberness that removed any impression of boyishness. William had indeed grown up.

"I am sorry, William. It seems I have much to apologize for on all counts."

He smiled gently. "You have done nothing but that which your heart dictated. But you must let me take over now. I shall quit school. I will see about the house in Surrey. Squire Gibbons has much to answer for. Anh told me he has been pocket-ing the rent. I will force him to pay us our due."

"Anh?" Sarah frowned. How had Anh come to be involved in their financial affairs? She eyed the deathly still figure in bed. William answered her unspoken question.

"Anh told me that Lord Linton had him look into our affairs. We have become great friends—that is why he brought me here. Did you know that he knows magic? Or at least all sorts of mysterious things I have never heard of. He has promised to teach me."

In spite of her dejection, Sarah smiled. For a moment William's enthusiasm for Anh's tantalizing secrets transformed him into the boy she remembered. Something told her that Anh could teach William far more than a few magic tricks. It would be good for him to learn from such a man. Her gaze returned to the bed. Justin was a man of many secrets, too. Beyond that black revenge in his heart lay compassion and wisdom and strength.

Was Anh right? Did war wage within his soul even now?

This time his father drew the ace of spades. Thin lips smiled mirthlessly at Justin's paltry king. Bloodshot eyes glowed with the triumph of victory.

"Alas, you are dead," the ravaged voice said.

The pistol pointed at him, its gleaming barrel the maw of death.

"I have been watching you, my boy, waiting for the chance that has come at last."

A bony finger hovered over the trigger, and Justin shivered as something cold and unearthly passed over his skin. It was too cold, but before he could wonder at that fact, something ex-ploded in his chest. White-hot heat seared his shoulder, but it was not that which hurt him so unbearably. He looked at the smoking pistol and the finger that rested on the trigger. Not bony. Soft, feminine. His gaze shot to the face of the person who held the weapon. The deep blue eyes that had been his father's transformed to the color of precious emeralds.

Sarah. His mouth tried to form itself around the name, cry-ing out her betrayal. But all that he heard was his father's un-godly laughter, and the words that were branded on his soul for all eternity.

Revenge . . . An eye for an eye . . .

Cold. It was so cold. And hot. The heat in his shoulder burned him even as he shivered.

Emerald eyes. Betrayal worse than any his father could have devised. Or had he plotted this poetic justice from the grave? *I shall find a comfortable grave and watch the lot of you make fools of yourselves for all eternity.*

Justin knew he had been a fool. If only he could fight off the cold, he might find her and exact revenge.

No. Not revenge. Not against Sarah. It hurt to think about it. Almost as much as his shoulder hurt. Something else, then. He must think of something else. Sarah in his arms, holding him, wrapping herself around him. Warming him. Chasing the cold. Pleading with him.

Yes, he would think of that. He would think about it so hard that he could almost touch her, hear her whispered words in his ears, feel her salty tears on his face.

Sarah.

In his arms. In his heart.

Chapter Eighteen

The bat returned Sarah's gaze with glowing jade eyes that did nothing to settle the growing turmoil inside her. The unfamiliar smoky sweetness of incense burning at the base of the statuette contributed to her uneasiness, which was heightened by Anh's incomprehensible chanting as he sat cross-legged before a diagram of broken and unbroken lines.

If magic could cure Justin, then so be it. But none of the strange artifacts, chants, and smells that filled the chamber had changed that cold, pale form on the bed into anything resembling the vibrant man who had once occupied it.

It was as if Justin's spirit had vacated his body.

Only once, in the impossibly lonely hours just before dawn, had there been any sign that he was still among them. He had begun shivering, and Sarah had covered him with blankets and quilts. When that did not stop his teeth from chattering, she lay in the bed and wrapped her arms around him, not caring whether Anh or anyone else might discover her there. That quieted him, and she lay there for several hours, holding him tightly, willing her strength into him. Once, she thought she heard her name on his lips, but it faded as quickly as a sigh taken by the wind.

Anh's chanting abruptly ceased. Sarah looked up to see him watching her steadily.

"Are you finished?" she asked, her voice groggy from lack of sleep.

"It is never finished," Anh replied calmly. "The end is also the beginning. The cycle renews itself with each sunset and sunrise, each ebb and flow of the tide. Life never stops. It only changes form."

Sarah fought back an impatient sigh. Anh's cryptic axioms were setting her teeth on edge. "What happens next?"

"What will."

With that, Anh rolled up a piece of parchment on which had been painted a series of symbols and held it to the tiny flame in the statue's base. When only charred ashes remained, he murmured some words she did not understand and slipped from the room.

Sarah stared dejectedly at the bat. For all the mystic power with which Anh's rituals had invested the jade figure, it still looked rather repulsive. As she eyed it wearily, its death's head grin seemed to take on an eerie life of its own. Sarah blinked. Was it her imagination, or was there movement about its unsightly snout, a barely perceptible fluttering of its revolting wings? She rubbed her temples. The lack of sleep had obviously distorted her senses.

"Ugly, is it not?"

With a little shriek, Sarah whirled. From the bed, Justin's haunted eyes held hers. There was life in his gaze, but her relief and delight stilled as she identified the cold shard of bitterness there as well.

"How do you feel?" she whispered.

Ignoring the question, he condemned her with a look as hard as stone. "You betrayed me."

Sarah did not have to ask what he meant. "I failed you," she conceded. Her eyes filled with regret, yet willed him to understand. "But I did not mean to shoot you. My finger cramped, and the gun went off. I cannot tell you how deeply I regret what happened."

Did he believe her? His closed expression revealed nothing. His gaze flicked to the statuette. "A bat," he observed. "Symbol of happiness and long life. Anh is ever the optimist."

His mouth quirked into a bitter smile, and Sarah knew another surge of relief even as he emitted a dry cough. Whatever he thought of her, at least his wits were intact. She poured a glass of water from the pitcher at the bedside table and held it to his lips. "Drink this."

Silently he accepted her assistance. "I am as weak as a kitten," he muttered.

"That will soon change, now that you are awake," Sarah assured him. "We have only been able to give you water and Anh's special tea, but now that you can eat, you will regain your strength."

"You have attended me?" Uncertainty crossed his bleak features.

Sarah nodded. "Along with Anh. You are a remarkably complacent patient when you are senseless, my lord." She gave him a tentative smile. It would not do to confess how desperately she had urged those precious drops of liquid past his lips, how fearfully she had thought never to see that familiar sardonic smirk again.

"And you are remarkably docile at the moment." His eyes bored into hers. "Does a guilty conscience plague you, Sarah? Is that why you tended me so diligently? Tell me: Is Bow Street on your heels? Or did you escape the masquerade with your identity still a secret?"

Sarah bristled. "I am told that an officer appeared at Brook Street the day after the shooting, my lord, so my identity is no great mystery. I may have worn a mask, but the entire *ton* knew of our bickering. And only your mistress would have taken such umbrage at your scandalous attention to Lady Amanda. Indeed, I believe I am the object of a most diligent search."

Impassively he considered her words. "How is it, then, that you have not been taken into custody?"

"Lord Pembroke was kind enough to help me to your town house," she explained irritably, irked at his lowering opinion of her motives. "Later, I had you brought here under cover of darkness. By the time Bow Street discovers my whereabouts, you will have recovered sufficiently to make it impossible for me to be tried for your murder."

"Then all of London believes me dead? My plan is still intact?" His eyes gleamed feverishly.

Illness had done nothing to modify his twisted craving for revenge, Sarah realized forlornly. "I believe that everything is indeed as you wish it. Except, of course, for your injuries."

"You expect some remuneration, some tangible evidence of my thanks, I suppose." He watched her carefully.

With a hard thump, Sarah set the water glass on the table. "I expect nothing from you, my lord. Nothing at all." She rose. "I shall send your valet to you now. You will be wishing to bathe."

When Justin awoke from his afternoon nap, a pair of impossibly green eyes was watching him with unnerving intensity. They were so precisely the shade of Sarah's that Justin stared back in amazement. Freckles dotted his observer's nose and cheeks in far more profusion, but the resemblance was uncanny.

"You must be William," he observed. At the sudden flare of hostility in that green gaze, Justin quickly added, "Forgive my familiarity. Lord Armistead, of course."

William nodded silently, and Justin fought to suppress his amusement at the mixture of pride and reserve that warred with the youth's natural curiosity. Unlike Sarah, the brother was as transparent as glass. For a long while they stared at each other, and Justin was surprised to feel a twinge of recognition at the vulnerability he read in William's steady gaze. At times, he recalled, the cusp of manhood was a frightening place to be.

"I am indebted to you for your hospitality and your attention to my financial affairs," the young baron said at last. "I assume that your relationship with my sister is the reason for your efforts."

William held himself stiffly, and Justin could see the question in his eyes. The lad was loath to broach such an awkward subject, but the burdens of manhood were upon him. Justin knew what would come next, just as he knew how intimidated William must be by a man such as himself.

"Your sister informed me of certain financial difficulties arising from the administration of your affairs in Surrey," Justin said easily. "Likewise, she told me of your decision to seek her out during your school holiday. It was not convenient for me to have her distracted by either situation, so I took it upon myself to send Anh to you and to investigate the Surrey matter." Justin frowned. Anh was supposed to have kept William occupied at Eton, but the man was ever his own master. For some reason he had decided to bring the boy here. The divining sticks had been at work again, no doubt.

"I see." The youth looked troubled. "I do not understand the nature of your relationship with my sister, sir. Perhaps you would be so good as to explain."

If he could explain *that*, Justin thought wryly, he could as easily fly to the moon. "I employed Miss Armistead to play the role of my mistress in order to bring my father's killer to justice," he said in a matter-of-fact tone. "I imagine that sounds rather strange to you, but it is a plan I have been formulating for some time. I have hopes that the result I seek will soon come to pass, thanks due to your sister's excellent performance."

Angry currents swirled within those green depths. "Sarah is excellent at all she undertakes, sir, but I would not have her stoop to ruination. I can provide for her well enough."

Justin met the youth's gaze. "My relationship with your sister was a pretense only, Lord Armistead."

William frowned. "Do you mean to say that she is not . . . ?" Flushing, he broke off.

"Miss Armistead is not my mistress," Justin said quietly, wondering why the admission brought such a sour taste to his mouth.

William absorbed this information in obvious relief, until another thought intruded. "But if she was presented as such before all the *ton,* she was compromised just the same."

"You may be certain that no one knew her," Justin assured him. "She used another name and altered her usual appearance. At all events, Armisteads have not moved in London circles for years. There was little chance of her being recognized."

"Whether or not she was recognized, it seems to me that she was compromised nevertheless," William insisted. "And she is here, is she not, alone in your home? How much time has she spent thus?"

Justin did not think that William wished to hear the truth stated so baldly—that one could hardly compromise an actress in such a manner. The lad was only trying to do his duty and seemed genuinely troubled by the potential wrong done his sister. But Justin was not about to let a green youth force him into the parson's noose.

"Your sister freely accepted the conditions of her employment," Justin said gently, not without sympathy for the boy. "Earlier at Lintonwood she was in the company of my aunt and her companion. There was nothing improper about her visit. In London, she was but playing the role she had agreed to perform. No wrong was done to her."

"Lord Linton is correct, William."

William's face turned scarlet as he saw his sister standing in the doorway. Sarah smiled. "Do not play the avenging brother, William. If there is damage to my reputation, it is my doing for taking to the stage in the first place. You must not hold Lord Linton responsible."

"I hold myself responsible," William said morosely. "I should never have gone away to school and forced you to sell yourself for our daily bread."

"I did not 'sell' myself, William," Sarah said in exasperation. "What an unflattering notion you have of my character."

William's eyes gleamed fiercely. "I have the highest estimation of your character, Sarah," he declared. Then he rounded on Justin. "My sister is an honorable woman, Lord Linton. I would urge you never to forget that fact."

Touched by the youth's passionate defense of his sister, Justin nodded somberly. "Miss Armistead has my deepest respect."

His words seemed to satisfy William, who flung one last fulminating look in his direction and quickly left the room. Sarah stared at Justin in disbelief.

"You might have reassured him without telling a bold-faced lie," she said, flushing. "You mock me by such an obvious falsehood."

Justin shook his head. Truth and lies had somehow gotten all mixed up in his mind, for despite all that Sarah was, despite all that he surmised of her past, it stunned him to realize that he had told no more than the truth. She had courage, spunk, and compassion, and whether or not she had meant to shoot him, she had not consigned him to the devil but had stayed to nurse him back to health. Most women in her position would have long since vanished, but Sarah had remained to face him and the consequences of her actions. He should despise her for putting a bullet in him, but strangely, his feelings bore no resemblance to hatred.

There was, he realized, no one he respected more.

"I am not an invalid, woman. A ball in the shoulder does not render one incapable of managing the simple task of taking tea."

Sarah arched a brow. Justin had been impossible, a sure sign that he was improving. She watched silently as he maneuvered the teacup awkwardly to his lips. It had been a day since he had regained his senses, and though she knew his shoulder still pained him, he was determined not to show it. When the tea

sloshed onto his sleeve, he let out a curse. Sarah bit her lip to
avoid smiling. His thunderous gaze met hers, and she braced
herself for a sharp rebuke.

Instead, his mouth curved in a rueful smile. "I have been in-
sufferable, I suppose."

Carefully, she nodded.

He sighed. "It is galling to lie here weak as a babe."

"You were six days without food."

"And seven days beyond Lady Hogarth's ball," came his instant rejoinder. "The time to confront Lady Greywood is slipping through my fingers. I ought to leave for London
tomorrow." His brow furrowed in dark determination.

Sarah studied her teacup. "You still mean to proceed with
your plan, then? I thought perhaps your injury might have
changed your thinking."

He made no immediate reply. When Sarah looked up, enigmatic currents churning in his eyes set her pulse to racing.
There was a searching alertness about him that caused her to
tremble from head to toe.

"Did you shoot me so that I would reconsider my scheme?"
he asked finally. Despite the harsh accusation, his tone was
light, almost amused.

"N-no," she stammered, taken aback. "You must believe me
when I tell you it was an accident, my lord. I did not mean . . ."

"Why do you never call me Justin? It is my given name, you
know."

Sarah's eyes widened. "You have never given me leave."

"But *you* gave me leave long ago, Sarah," he said softly.
"Does it not seem unjust that you deny me the privilege of hearing my name on your lips?" Keen eyes watched her like a
hawk.

Years of wary habit caused Sarah to stiffen at honeyed
phrases that were the tools of theater Lotharios—and practiced
rakes. "What are you about, my lord?" she demanded suspiciously.

His wistful smile nearly took her breath away. "I do not
know," he acknowledged. "But you are correct about one
thing."

"What is that?"

"Being wounded does seem to have altered my mind," he

said in a bemused voice. "I seem to have traveled a great distance from Lady Hogarth's ballroom."

"From London to Lintonwood, my lord. It cannot be above thirty miles."

Justin fell silent. "It feels like ten thousand," he said at last.

Chapter Nineteen

Young Lord Armistead had a wretched sense of duty, Justin thought glumly. Cook's picnic luncheon included ample food for three, but Justin had hoped that William would find it more entertaining to remain behind and prevail upon Anh to pull out his divining rods. The desire to protect his sister's honor proved the stronger call, however, which is why the three of them were sitting so cozily on a horsehair blanket this fine afternoon.

With William shadowing them like a watchful puppy, finding a moment alone with Sarah had proven nearly impossible—to Justin's great frustration, for nothing preoccupied him more. Apparently he had misjudged Sarah's character. If he had underestimated her sense of honor, what else had he been wrong about? He yearned to find out, but not in William's presence.

"I have been poring over some of the magic books in your library, Lord Linton," the youth said, making a game attempt at conversation despite his host's glowering countenance. "They are exceedingly fascinating."

Justin saw no need to reply to such a banal observation and continued to recline pensively on the blanket they had placed at the meadow's edge. His fingers toyed with a colorful rock that had caught his eye.

Sarah rushed to fill the silence. "They are, indeed, William." She smiled. "I thought at first Lord Linton must be some sort of sorcerer, so filled were his shelves with mysterious lore and strange spells."

"Have you ever tried any of the spells, sir?" William asked earnestly.

The two of them were chattering like magpies. Justin rubbed his aching shoulder. The only spell he wished to try at the moment was one to make an interfering young chaperon disappear.

That thought gave him a sudden idea. Carefully, he pocketed the small rock.

"I have had some success with Mr. Magnus's invisibility charm," he said idly.

William's eyes grew wide, but he schooled his voice to a worldly tone. "Invisibility? Surely that is a lot of poppycock. I know of nothing that would make a man disappear."

Justin pulled the rock from his pocket. "Ophethalminus," he said gravely.

William stared at the stone.

"When wrapped in a bay leaf," Justin explained with the air of one disclosing a carefully guarded secret, "it is widely rumored to possess the qualities to make one invisible. Constantinus, the Roman emperor, swore by its powers."

"Truly?" William asked dubiously, in awe despite himself. Justin hid a smile of satisfaction. The youth was old enough to disdain fairy tales, but still enough of a boy to be seduced by a clever yarn.

"So I understand," he said in a casual tone. "Do you wish to try it?" He handed William the stone. "There is a cove of bay trees just beyond the second turn in the stream."

William held the rock as if it were a rare treasure. "I suppose it is a silly notion," he said, somewhat abashed. "Still . . ."

"You need feel no embarrassment," Justin said smoothly. "One never knows how things will turn out. Experimentation is the tool of great minds."

"Beyond the second turn, you say?"

Justin nodded, and in the next moment he was alone on the blanket with Sarah.

"That was poorly done, my lord." Sarah's eyes sparkled with amusement.

"William needs to spend more time in his own company," he said blandly.

"He has decided that his duty is to protect me, and he takes it very seriously." Sarah sighed. "Poor William. It is harsh to have to grow up so soon."

"Sometimes events force responsibilities on us. William is not too young to handle them. You must let him be the man he is becoming."

She studied him. "You were young when your father was killed. That must have been very hard."

"Hard enough." Justin made a dismissive gesture. "I do not wish to talk about that." He paused. "I would like to ask you something."

"Yes?"

Justin shifted awkwardly on the blanket, suddenly feeling like the merest youth himself. "I wish us to be . . . friends."

She looked puzzled. "We are friends, my lord."

A wave of impatience gripped him. "Is my given name repulsive to you? Can you not say it?"

Sarah flushed. "Of course—Justin."

Never had his name sounded so pleasant to his ears. Justin knew he would have to hear it a few thousand times before he could decide what about her saying it made it so special. But that was for later. William would be back at any moment—doubtless as visible as before.

The wound had indeed addled his wits, he reflected, but befuddlement was a rather pleasurable state that seemed to generate a desperate need to look into those green eyes and touch the woman who possessed them. Justin took Sarah's hand. Her flush deepened, but she did not draw away. Her skin felt warm and vibrant. This small physical connection with her was something, but it was not enough. Yet he did not want to frighten her. For one who purported to be a seasoned rake, he felt woefully at sea.

"I do not suppose I could persuade you to drink a potion made from the hairs of a wolf," Justin muttered.

Sarah laughed, and he marveled at the musical, captivating sound. "Certainly not," she replied, smiling.

"I did not think so." Justin inhaled a long, deep breath, like a man about to jump off a cliff blindfolded. "Then I have no means to persuade you, I am afraid, other than this."

Closing the space between them, he brought their lips together. Her mouth opened slightly in surprise, such that he could taste the wine she had sipped. Although he had kissed her before, the act had never held such reverence for him. It seemed ages ago since he had let his passions run amok upon the occasion of that first kiss in his study. Eternity had passed since he had put himself through the torture of those spurious kisses for the benefit of the servants in Brook Street. A lifetime had fled since he had too briefly lain with her in that chamber once occupied by women whose faces he could not now recall.

Only one face, one smile, one pair of green eyes called him from the precarious precipice on which he had been perched for most of his adult life. One name remained on his lips, summoning him from the void in which his soul had lost its way.

Sarah.

Warming like the sun, banishing the chill of night, radiating light like a sunbeam. How had he ever thought that comparison absurd? She was a ray of sun in the shadows of his heart.

Like delicate buds, her lips blossomed under his. Her pliant body pressed against his chest. He felt the pounding of her heart and the answering echo of his own. Dare he hope that she, too, sensed this inexorable force pulling them into some mysterious place he had never dreamed existed, not in all his travels or congress with the mystical and exotic?

Sarah was the most exotic mystery of all. He wanted to discover all of her secrets, and yet the prospect was as frightening as it was tantalizing. With gentle fierceness, he wrapped her in his arms. His very soul took flight when he heard his name on her lips.

"Justin. Justin." She murmured it over and over again as he stroked the back of her neck and ran his hands through the silky mass of her hair.

"I have never wanted anything as much as I want you," he whispered, desperation lending his voice a pleading note. "Say you will be mine. Say it, Sarah."

"Yes." Her answer held no doubt. Justin could hardly comprehend his good fortune. She, too, felt the magic.

"Lord Linton? I do not have the hang of it, I am afraid." William's words jolted him into sudden awareness. "I found the trees and wrapped the stone in bay leaves, but nothing happened."

With supreme effort, Justin turned toward the sound of William's voice. "Perhaps," he called in a pained tone, "I forgot to provide you with the magic chant."

As William's approaching footsteps drew him further into the present, Justin's lips brushed Sarah's ear. "Let me come to you tonight," he whispered as he released her.

Her dazed smile as William bounded into the clearing told him more than any words.

*   *   *

The clamoring at the front door shattered the placid mood in the dining room, where Sarah found herself staring at Justin as if he were some wondrous treasure placed before her eyes. Her mouth grew dry at the thought of what would happen when he came to her tonight. This time there would be no turning back. Justin Trent was not a man to be denied—especially not with that new vulnerability in his eyes that made her heart turn somersaults.

Whatever worlds were about to open to her, Sarah knew she was ready. There would be no second-guessing this time. She did not delude herself into thinking that Justin loved her. Yet his injury had softened him, somehow, and given her reason to hope—however foolishly.

Of one thing Sarah was certain: Her fate was inexorably entwined with his. No matter what the consequences, she would embrace that fate. It would be frightening, but breathtaking—like stepping onstage for the first time.

A footman appeared in the dining room to whisper something urgently into Anh's ear, and the butler left to attend to the matter. Soon a loud voice in the foyer drew their attention. With a muttered oath, Justin threw down his napkin and strode into the hall. Sarah followed, but pulled up short as she saw the figure of sartorial elegance studying Anh disdainfully through a quizzing glass.

"I expect you can do better, man, than to leave me standing here these many minutes," he drawled.

Anh bowed. "My apologies, Mr. Trent."

" 'Viscount Linton,' if you please," Harry said haughtily. "I am your new master, and you had best be quicker off the mark if you wish your employment to continue."

The butler merely eyed him impassively.

"I think you will find that Anh prefers to move at his own pace," Justin offered.

Harry whirled. "Justin!" he gasped in astonishment. "But—I thought you were dead!"

"Sorry to disappoint you." Justin's gaze narrowed. "Not to mention your tailor, of course. I see that you have already commissioned a new wardrobe based on your anticipated wealth."

Harry blinked rapidly, as if to assure himself that the sudden appearance of his cousin was but an illusion. "I do not understand," he said slowly. Then he spotted Sarah, and his face broke into an expression of relief.

"Sarah! I have searched half of England for you! Now that I have come into the title, Aunt Agatha has summoned me to Cheshire. Naturally, she wishes to see my 'wife' again, so I, ah, thought you might consider . . ." His voice trailed off. "I suppose that will not be necessary," he finished, red-faced, "now that Justin is still . . . with us."

"It appears that my resurrection provokes more grief than my demise," Justin observed dryly.

"Not at all," Harry quickly responded. "Happy to learn that you ain't dead. Aunt Agatha will be overjoyed. Word of your death put her in a green melancholy."

Justin's composed expression faltered, and Sarah wondered whether he had second thoughts about the fact that his plan had caused his iron-willed aunt to suffer.

"Though perhaps she is feeling better," Harry added, "now that Lady Greywood has come to comfort her."

Justin stilled. "Lady Greywood has joined my aunt?"

Harry nodded. "Always were the best of friends." He eyed Justin uncertainly. "I suppose I should continue on to Cheshire and spread the, ah, joyous news."

Justin's thoughtful gaze gave Sarah a moment of dread that was not in the least eased by his next words. "Oh, you will continue on to Cheshire, cousin. But as far as anyone there is concerned, I am still dead."

"What?" Harry was appalled. "I cannot keep a secret like that!"

Justin's slow smile was nothing short of diabolical. "Yes, you will, Harry. Upon peril of having all of your considerable and pressing debts instantly recalled."

Harry swallowed hard. "All of them, you say?"

The steely gaze never left Harry's stricken features. "Come and join us for dinner, Harry," Justin said softly. "Anh, please take Lord Linton's hat."

Like a man who has awakened to find his nightmare all too real, a stunned Harry allowed himself to be led away. Sarah remained motionless as the burgeoning hope and happiness within her died. When she did not immediately follow, Justin paused, a question in his eyes. There was nothing remotely vulnerable in his gaze now.

"You are not going to give it up, are you?" Sarah whispered. "You mean to hunt Lady Greywood down, to finish it."

No facile denial sprang to his lips. For a long moment he simply stared at her, and in that mute exchange lay a volume of meaning. "I have breathed revenge for half a lifetime, Sarah," he said at last. "I cannot let it go."

I am interested in many things. I am consumed, however, by only one.

Revenge, revenge, revenge.

It was too late, Sarah realized.

She had not been able to save him.

He rode outside the carriage on horseback, a solitary figure of vengeance silhouetted against the horizon. Sarah watched him through the window. Did his shoulder pain him? Or was he, like a dark angel of the night, beyond pain?

Beside her, snoring blissfully despite everything, sat Harry, who for all his flaws could never be accused of bargaining with the devil. Only Justin played that game. Only Justin meant to master his fate. Only Justin would never relent until he thoroughly destroyed the woman who had killed his father. Was it justice that drove him? Perhaps. Madness? More likely.

" 'O what a noble mind is here o'erthrown'," Sarah murmured.

"What's that?" Harry opened one eye and frowned. "Let a man rest, Sarah. I expect it will be hard enough to pull this off without being fagged out. I did not sleep a wink last night for thinking about it."

Sarah doubted that was the case, but she kept silent. Her own sleep had been horribly fitful—and uninterrupted, for Justin had not come to her after all. Perhaps he sensed that things had changed between them. Or perhaps he was simply consumed by thoughts of what lay ahead. Whatever the reason, Sarah had never felt more lonely in her life.

Her loneliness only deepened with the knowledge that they were barreling down the road toward Aunt Agatha's and some tragic conclusion that Justin alone had orchestrated. Indeed, he had quickly adapted his plan to this latest development. Harry was to continue as the viscount. Justin had disguised himself as Harry's new valet. Even her brother had acceded to Justin's will. Told only that Justin was taking Sarah to visit his aunt,

William quickly deemed Harry a suitable chaperon and elected to remain behind with Anh. He had not even risen early to see them off.

Even though Sarah had vowed never again to pose as Harry's wife, she knew she had no choice. For better or worse, she meant to be with Justin at the conclusion of his devil-driven scheme.

As the carriage rounded a particularly sharp corner, Sarah held on for dear life. Straightening her bonnet as the vehicle regained its balance, she sighed wearily. Only heaven could help them now.

Unfortunately, heaven had never been partial to dark angels.

Chapter Twenty

"My dear child. Welcome." Aunt Agatha's voice was tinged with sadness. "Harry, your bride is lovelier than ever." She placed a kiss on Sarah's cheek.

Sarah managed a game smile, but she knew herself unworthy of this grand lady's affection. Eventually Aunt Agatha would learn the shameful truth about her. For now, Sarah could only hope that her friend Lady Greywood would not recognize Harry's fresh-faced, freckled bride as the elaborately coiffed creature who had graced Justin's arm at those magnificent London parties.

Indeed, Lady Greywood wore a sad, distracted air as she greeted them, and Sarah breathed a sigh of relief when the countess displayed no sign of recognition. Now they had only to wait until Justin staged his confrontation with the dowager. His disguise as Harry's portly valet—complete with ample padding, graying wig and mustache—had raised no suspicions as he slipped upstairs, no doubt to discover which chamber the countess occupied.

"I am so sorry, ma'am," Sarah replied to Aunt Agatha, ashamed of offering condolences for what was merely a cruel hoax perpetrated by the very nephew she mourned. No help came from Harry, who stared guiltily at the floor. The man was an abysmal actor. He would give everything away if he did not absent himself soon.

Aunt Agatha squeezed her hand. "I suppose it was to be expected that he would come to such a terrible end," she said in an unsteady voice. "Poor Justin! He tried so hard to emulate his father. If he had only known the truth . . . but that was my fault. I am to blame."

"Now, Agatha," Lady Greywood protested.

"There is no use in pretending, Evangeline." Sorrowfully,

Aunt Agatha shook her head. "At first, I wished to protect him. Later, I did not want to dredge up all those tears and recriminations. And now, look what has happened. History has repeated itself. I will go to my grave thinking I could have prevented this."

Aunt Agatha's words made little sense, but perhaps that was to be expected. Clearly the lady was not herself, for Sarah had never seen those steely eyes filled with tears or that regal carriage marred by slumping shoulders. Her heart cried out to end this sham, to confess that Justin was alive after all. Anger surged within her. How could Justin be so callous, so heedless of the grief he was inflicting on those he loved?

There could be no stronger proof that he was incapable of love than this proud woman before her, broken by a sorrow that did not need to be.

"Come, Harry." Sarah pulled Harry away from the two women. "I believe your aunt needs time to compose herself."

Glumly, Harry nodded, and for the first time Sarah felt a glimmer of respect for him. If even Harry could see the wrong in this charade, why could not Justin?

It was at dinner that disaster fell.

A commotion of voices at the door heralded visitors of the female gender. A moment later, Clarissa Porter's sudden appearance in the dining room of the sister she had not seen or spoken to in years threw everyone into complete and profound silence.

The two sisters stared at each other. Harriet Simms stood stiffly behind Aunt Clarissa, watching intently. Sarah nearly slid under the table in horrified panic. Her luck could not hold. Eventually they must recognize her as the American "orphan" whom they had chaperoned and Justin had taken to London. Lady Greywood would make the inevitable association with Sarah Manwaring. Aunt Agatha would see that she was not Harry's wife. Harry himself would probably confess all, including the fact that Justin was not really dead. Sarah held her breath, waiting.

But all eyes were on the sisters. Aunt Clarissa took a tremulous step forward. Slowly and with great effort, Aunt Agatha rose.

"Clarissa," she said, her voice breaking.

With a heartrending sob, Aunt Clarissa walked straight into her sister's arms.

"Our poor boy," she cried. "Our poor, poor boy. It is all our fault, Agatha. Silvester tried to tell me it was not, but it is. Truly it is."

Gently, Aunt Agatha stroked her sister's back. Her gnarled hand moved uncertainly, as if unaccustomed to offering such comfort. But gradually the stroking turned into an iron embrace as she held her sister to her breast. "There, there, Clarissa," she murmured. "Do not cry. You will bring on one of your attacks."

Lady Greywood rose unsteadily and joined the sisters. Soon all three of them were sobbing their guilt like a trio of Fates mourning their handiwork. Amid tumultuous embraces, hairpins tumbled from graying locks onto the floor.

In the commotion, Harry slunk out of the room, no doubt seeking the comfort of his aunt's best brandy. Left alone at the table, Sarah stared at the women in confusion. Why did they blame themselves for Justin's death?

Even Miss Simms's eyes were moist with tears. Fumbling for her handkerchief, she averted her gaze from Aunt Clarissa and, in that moment, spotted Sarah. Instantly the dewy softness in her eyes was supplanted by hard suspicion.

Would Miss Simms accuse her here and now? Would she unmask her for the raw opportunist she believed Sarah to be and the liar she obviously was? The sharp gaze moved quickly to the three women locked in each other's arms. When Miss Simms again looked at Sarah, there was defeat in her eyes. Even Harriet Simms would not intervene in the tearful reconciliation taking place before them.

For the moment, Sarah was safe. But only for the moment. Biting her lips, Sarah said a silent prayer that whatever Justin was plotting, it would be over soon.

It was important to feel nothing. Certainly not regret for his actions, nor guilt at the grief that permeated this house. His aunts were together for the first time in years, so apparently his "death" had had some beneficial effect. Justin had listened in amazement to Harry's account of the scene in the dining room. He had never known his Aunt Agatha to shed so much as a tear in anyone's presence, nor could he ever have imagined that Aunt Clarissa would take it upon herself to initiate a reconciliation.

That his aunts had been united in their sorrow at his death touched something deep inside him, however, no matter how hard he tried to bury the emotions that threatened his ability to carry his plan to conclusion. Revenge had never seemed so empty as it did now, as he crept along the hallway toward Lady Greywood's room.

Justin drew comfort in the knowledge that he would soon have her confession. The sudden midnight appearance of a man she believed to be dead would send her over the edge. If she took him for a ghost, all the better. Guilt would rip the words from her, for guilt was a burden that could not be borne forever. It ate away at the soul until there was nothing left but the burning need to break free from that weight.

Tonight it would all end.

At his touch, the door opened soundlessly on its hinges, which Justin had oiled earlier so as not to give himself away. The stillness of sleep permeated Lady Greywood's chamber. A slight breeze from the open window ruffled the bed canopy. A ray of moonlight painted eerie patterns on the floor.

Drawing closer to the countess's sleeping form, Justin allowed his black domino to billow around him like a dark cloud. She would recognize the costume. He had worn it at Lady Hogarth's ball. His father had worn it the night of his death.

"Awake, lady, and confront the spirit who walks the night."

Abruptly, Lady Greywood sat upright in bed. He glared at her with all the righteous anger of the spirit wronged, but instead of the hysterical shriek he had expected, she studied him through narrowed eyes.

"Who the devil are you?" she demanded.

Taken aback, Justin drew his cloak around him and in his best ghostly tone replied: "I am a spirit doomed for a certain term to walk the night and for the day confined to fast in fires, till the foul crimes done in my days of nature are burnt and purged away." He had thought this speech by the Ghost of Hamlet's father well suited to his purpose, but oddly, the words now struck him as silly.

From the bed came a prolonged silence, then a heavy sigh. "I thought so," she said.

Justin frowned. He had not expected such a phlegmatic response. "It is well that you know me, lady," he persisted with an unearthly growl. "I seek your confession to crimes that have plagued your conscience these many nights."

"Clarissa was right," Lady Greywood muttered. "This *is* all our doing."

He stared. She should have been crying out her sins by now, and yet she simply watched him, measuring him with that shrewd gaze. He had the strangest feeling that *he* was the one expected to make a confession.

"Come, lady," he urged, twirling his cape malevolently. "Free yourself from the chains of guilt."

"I think it is *you* who had best free yourself from this masquerade—before you destroy your aunts."

Justin blinked. "What?"

"I tried to persuade that high flyer of yours, but I suppose she was part of your plan." Lady Greywood shook her head. "I had hoped otherwise. She seemed like a nice young woman."

"My plan?" he echoed, wondering whether he had heard correctly.

Reaching for her dressing gown, Lady Greywood eased herself from the bed. "Your plan, Justin Trent," she repeated sternly. "Your miserable, misguided plan."

Taking the candlestick from the bedside table, she advanced on him. Her eyes gleamed fiercely. "I think," she said softly, "it is time to pay the piper."

Sarah rubbed her eyes. Something had pulled her from the restless dreams that had plagued her since she retired to her chamber following the sisters' emotional reunion. She half expected to awaken with Harriet Simms in her chamber, playing the accusing angel.

But it was not Miss Simms who sat on the edge of her bed, staring at her with dazed eyes.

"Justin!" she cried. "What has happened?"

"I am not certain," he said in a bemused voice. "I just left Lady Greywood's chamber. Fled, to be precise."

Sarah's eyes widened, but before she could speak, he pulled her into his arms. His kiss bore a touch of desperation, as if he sought to reassure himself she was real. Closing her eyes, Sarah reveled in his touch and the realization that—for the moment, at least—he still needed her. To be needed by the man she loved with all her being sent her heart reeling in joy. With a sigh, she savored the tender strength of his caress.

But this was not how she had imagined Justin coming to her.

There was something else at work here, something else that had sent him fleeing to her arms.

Reluctantly, Sarah pushed herself away. His haunted gaze held hers. "What is it, Justin?" she whispered.

"Lady Greywood," he began haltingly. "She is not at all what I thought. She . . ." But when he would have continued, the door crashed open.

"Dear God!" Aunt Agatha stood in the doorway, flanked by Lady Greywood and Aunt Clarissa. Aunt Agatha took a step but then stopped and leaned weakly against the door frame. Lady Greywood put an arm around her friend for support. Aunt Clarissa slipped past them into the room.

"I am not the least surprised," Aunt Clarissa said cheerfully. "I always knew that Justin was fond of Miss Armistead. It is only logical that he would visit her from the Beyond. Silvester says that one's emotions are capable of living long after the body ceases to exist. That is why ghosts return to haunt a place, you know. They are simply following the dictates of their hearts."

"That is no ghost," Lady Greywood snapped. "I think you will find that Lord Linton is very much of the flesh."

Bewildered, Aunt Agatha stared at her sister. "Did you say 'Miss Armistead'? But this is Harry's wife—Sarah Trent."

For the first time, Lady Greywood studied Sarah. Her gaze narrowed thoughtfully. "With a dashing gown and a bit of paint on her face," the countess mused, "she might pass for Sarah Manwaring."

"I ought to know her," Aunt Clarissa retorted petulantly. "I was her chaperon." Abruptly, she laughed. "Can you imagine *me* as a chaperon?"

"Not in the least," muttered Lady Greywood.

Hurried footsteps in the hall signaled the arrival of Miss Simms, who at the sounds of commotion had apparently run the entire distance from her chamber. "I *told* you she was no orphan from America, Clarissa," Miss Simms began heatedly, before she was forced to stop and gasp for air.

Rubbing her temples, Aunt Agatha stared from Justin to Sarah and back again. "Justin?" she whispered hoarsely. "Is that really you?"

"I am deeply sorry, Aunt," Justin said, moving toward his aunt. "Allow me to explain."

With a great sigh, Aunt Agatha toppled backward into the outstretched arms of the breathless Miss Simms.

Chapter Twenty-one

"It is not a pleasant story, Justin."

Fully revived, Aunt Agatha sipped the French brandy hastily retrieved from a locked cabinet for the group assembled in her sitting room. With grim determination, she regarded her nephew. "I was determined to protect you from the truth, and I bent everyone else to my will. In so doing, I seem to have spawned a monstrous chain of events."

Justin glanced uneasily at the others: Aunt Clarissa, huddled in a rocking chair and talking quietly to herself—or, as he suspected, to "Silvester"; Lady Greywood, Harriet Simms, Sarah. He could not read their thoughts, but he sensed that Aunt Agatha's words would somehow affect them all.

"Your father had a wild streak," Aunt Agatha began. "He would leave Arabella for weeks at a time. She could not accept his waywardness, and I suppose it ate away at her, bit by bit."

A faraway look clouded her gaze. "She did not know how to manage Oscar. I was newly widowed, and I thought I knew a bit about men. I advised her to make him jealous."

Justin suspected that she was about to forever alter his perception of his parents. "Aunt," he began, but his protest died at the answering pain in her eyes. Whatever this might cost him, it had cost her more.

"Arabella had an ethereal, untouched beauty," she continued. "She never realized the power she could have wielded over men. Even my Henry, before he died—I could see that familiar yearning in his eyes." She cleared her throat. "But that is neither here nor there, I suppose."

Aunt Agatha took another sip of brandy. "Oscar never appreciated Arabella. He was too much in search of greener pastures.

I thought a harmless flirtation would put him in his place. That is when Greywood entered the picture."

Lady Greywood nodded. "There was something otherworldly about Arabella—almost magical, as if she were in touch with spirits that floated on the undercurrents of life. My husband and I often quarreled in those days. At first Arabella's innocent flirting provided a welcome diversion for him. Soon he was powerless to resist her spell." A wave of sadness swept her features.

"Arabella had not the skill to manage a flirtation, harmless or otherwise," Aunt Agatha said. "She had no idea Frederick was besotted, although everyone else could see it. When Oscar confronted her, Arabella confessed that the flirtation had merely been a ruse. He might have believed her, had she not found herself increasing."

From the haze of words, a picture had begun to emerge. Justin's senses stood at full alert, waiting for a truth one corner of his brain had always suspected.

"Arabella had not conceived after several years of marriage," Aunt Agatha explained. "When her delicate condition came on the heels of the flirtation with Frederick, Oscar assumed that . . ." She broke off, her gnarled hands tightly clutching the brandy glass.

"That I was Greywood's bastard," Justin finished. The answer hit him with blinding intensity, illuminating the shouting, the drinking, the cries in the night, the ugly hatred in his father's eyes when he regarded his only son.

His father thought Justin was another man's get.

"Oscar would never believe otherwise, no matter that Arabella pleaded and swore to the stars that no other man had touched her," Aunt Agatha said quietly. "I think he tried to accept you at first, even tried to be a good father. But as the years passed, the belief that she had played him false tormented him. He began to drink more heavily. Eventually, he decided to get even."

Aunt Agatha glanced at her sister, rocking and talking to her imaginary lover in a corner of the room that might as well have been a world away. Justin followed her gaze.

"He went after Aunt Clarissa." Horrible certainty gave his voice a raw edge. Oscar Trent had repaid his wife by seducing her sister.

Aunt Agatha nodded. "Clarissa has always been . . . suscep-
tible to flights of fancy. I am afraid she has never possessed the
level head that has plagued me."

Pain and anger radiated in her steely gaze. "Oscar knew how
to seduce a woman," she continued bitterly. "He called her 'Violet'—for her eyes, you know—sent her flowers and all that
nonsense. Clarissa fell in love. I told her he was only toying
with her, that it was all a bitter game to him. I only meant to
save her, but I suppose I was too harsh. That is when she
stopped speaking to me."

"And that is when my shameful part in this came about,"
Lady Greywood said, meeting Justin's gaze evenly. "When
Clarissa pleaded for my help, I allowed her and Linton to meet
in my house. I was angry at Frederick for making a fool of himself over Arabella. I wanted to make him believe *I* was seeing
Linton. And he did—everyone did." For the first time, her gaze
faltered. "My foolish pride nearly cost him his life."

"The duel," Justin murmured. Greywood had issued a challenge, despite Oscar Trent's reputation as a crack shot. Now
Justin understood why his father had deloped. Letting Greywood live with the disgrace of his wife's apparent unfaithful-
ness was a more effective means of destroying Greywood than
killing him outright.

"The ordeal took something out of Frederick," the countess
said, confirming his suspicions. "He was never the same after
that."

His father had hit upon the perfect revenge. In one stroke, he
had avenged himself on Arabella by seducing her sister and
sent them all down a dangerous road that would destroy Greywood and his marriage.

"We were all racing toward some awful conclusion." Aunt
Agatha shook her head. "It came the night of Lady Hogarth's
ball."

"Clarissa grew increasingly . . . unhinged," Lady Greywood
said quietly. "I suppose part of her suspected that Oscar was
using her. That night, the flamboyance of her costume persona
seemed to give her confidence. She called Oscar to account just
as Lady Hogarth was about to present the costume awards. You
should have heard her, railing about his other flirtations, cursing him for making her suffer, threatening to prevent him from

ruining others—it was a performance worthy of Marie Antoinette."

Marie Antoinette. Justin gaped. "*Aunt Clarissa* was Marie Antoinette?"

Lady Greywood nodded sadly. "The way she pointed that muff at him and tossed her corsage in his face—it was, I think, her finest hour."

"Do you mean to say that *Aunt Clarissa* shot my father?" Justin demanded.

Lady Greywood stared at him. "I knew it was something like that," she said slowly. "That is why you had Mrs. Manwaring wear that costume. That is why you staged the shooting. You thought *I* was Marie Antoinette. You thought recreating the events of that night would force me to confess. Like everyone else, you thought I killed him."

"My father's blood was on the costume—the costume found in your bedchamber," Justin insisted. "That is why I thought it was you. I never dreamed that Aunt Clarissa . . ."

"His blood was on the costume because Clarissa embraced him after the shooting," Lady Greywood explained. "In the confusion, I was able to pull her away, although it was a near thing, what with her scrambling desperately to retrieve the corsage she had flung at him. No one recognized me, for I was in costume as well. I took her to my house, gave her one of my gowns, and sent her home. No one even knew she had been at the ball, just as no one ever found the mysterious Marie Antoinette."

The countess grimaced. "But everyone remembered that Marie Antoinette had pointed something at Oscar just as the fatal shot was fired. As Oscar's supposed mistress, I was the obvious suspect. The authorities searched my house and found the costume, but Frederick claimed someone had planted it there. He swore he had been with me all evening. There was nothing they could do."

"For a long time, Evangeline lived with that suspicion clouding her reputation," Aunt Agatha murmured sadly. "She went along with my decision to say nothing."

"You have never understood, Agatha." Lady Greywood shook her head. "It was the least I could do to atone for my part in all of this. When Frederick swore to my innocence—at the time, probably convinced of my guilt—I realized that he loved

me after all. When I told him the truth, he understood my reasons for keeping my own counsel. He agreed with me that no
more lives should be destroyed because of Oscar." She eyed
Aunt Clarissa, still rocking in the corner, but quiet now.

Dazed, Justin stared at the women. "I do not understand. Did
Clarissa shoot my father, or did she not?"

Aunt Agatha and Lady Greywood locked gazes. Aunt
Clarissa glanced up and smiled before resuming her soft croon-
ing.

"No," Aunt Agatha said softly.

"Then who did?" The question hung in the air, as deafening
as a shout, though Justin had spoken in a low, hushed tone.

"Arabella." Aunt Agatha's raw whisper held a note of disbelief that fifteen years still had not banished.

Justin stilled. "My *mother*?"

His aunt nodded. "Arabella pretended to be ill that night and
remained home. She took one of Oscar's dueling pistols from
his study, went to the ball, and lay in wait for him outside on
the terrace. As Oscar stood at a window quarreling with
Clarissa, Arabella crept up and shot him. Then she fled. No one
realized the shot came from outside."

His mother had murdered his father.

"I had never realized the extent of Oscar's abuse," Aunt
Agatha said, her voice breaking. "The years had left Arabella
bitter and angry—and perhaps a little mad. Clarissa thought her
relationship with Oscar was a secret, but Oscar made sure Arabella knew. I think the knowledge that he had gone after her sister finally drove Arabella wild." Aunt Agatha's sigh bore the
soft keening of a lament. "She confessed everything to me afterward and made me promise to take care of you—she knew I
had always wanted children. Then she went into her chamber
and hanged herself."

A searing pain tore through Justin's gut.

"You were but a boy at the time. I wanted to shield you from
the ugliness." Aunt Agatha clutched her glass. "We let you—
and the world—think that the mysterious Marie Antoinette
killed your father. I see now that our lies just made things
worse. I deprived you of the truth that was your right to know."

Tears trickled down her wrinkled cheeks. "I shut the door on
that time, when I should have opened it to let the demons out. I
have been a miserable woman for it. I watched you change over

the years into a pattern card of your father, wondering how I could stop you from bringing about your own destruction."

The roaring in Justin's ears was like a waterfall spewing forth great waves of truth dammed up by years of silence—and illusion.

"I was never like him," Justin said in a tight voice, wondering whether in fact he had been more like his father than he knew. "I was only playing at a role, biding my time until I could exact revenge for his death."

Aunt Agatha studied him. "We have all paid the price, it seems, for my secrecy. I am convinced the ordeal shortened poor Greywood's life. As for Clarissa—well, you see what became of Clarissa. She has never been the same."

"But I have had Silvester," Aunt Clarissa said softly from her rocking chair. "Arabella sent him to me. And he is ever so much nicer than Oscar."

"I do not know what is to become of you, Miss Armistead, but I wish you luck." Harriet Simms was actually smiling at her, Sarah realized.

That any of them were able to smile after the night they had endured was remarkable in itself. But there was actually an air of relief in the household today, as if the shedding of burdens had added years to everyone's life. All seemed eager to move on, perhaps to make up for time lost to the weight of lies, and by midmorning the company had begun dispersing. Justin and Harry had gone for an early-morning ride, but they, too, had plans to leave.

Lady Greywood had departed with an admonition that Sarah never allow herself to forget her principles—especially in the presence of a man like Lord Linton. For although Justin had explained the whole of his plan to the ladies, and had apologized to Lady Greywood for the wrong done her, the countess did not seem entirely convinced that Justin had not in fact become the rake he had pretended to be in his quest for vengeance.

Aunt Clarissa had turned the full force of her violet eyes on Sarah as she climbed into the carriage. "Silvester and I will miss you," she said gaily. "He always did enjoy your company."

Miss Simms hung back for a moment, and Sarah was surprised to see her holding out something. "Clarissa wished me to give this to you," she said.

Sarah recognized the dried bouquet of violets as the arrangement Aunt Clarissa had kept by her bedside at Lintonwood. Save for the yellow iris—which had apparently been lost in the fray that long-ago night—it was the exact duplicate of the corsage Justin had given her for Lady Hogarth's ball. It was no doubt the very corsage that Aunt Clarissa had flung at Justin's father fifteen years ago. No wonder she had been desperate to retrieve it as her lover lay dying. It was her only memento of the man who had called her Violet.

"You may not wish to keep it," Miss Simms said apologetically. "But Clarissa has decided she no longer needs this . . . souvenir and wishes to bestow it on someone who may understand its significance." Her eyes were misty as she regarded the woman in the carriage, who was chatting happily to some unseen presence. "If she is willing to let go of the past, then perhaps she will allow the present to come in a bit more."

Sarah was struck by the affection in the woman's gaze, and it occurred to her that Aunt Clarissa and Miss Simms had between them a very strong bond. "I am sure she will improve under your care, Miss Simms."

"I never told her the truth, you know," Miss Simms said quietly.

Sarah eyed her blankly.

"I was governess to Lady Greywood's daughter at the time the countess allowed Lord Linton and Clarissa to meet in the house. He would sometimes come to those assignations early. He was a relentless flirt. Foolishly, I imagined myself in love with him." Miss Simms sighed. "He had the most extraordinary blue eyes. He seduced me, you see."

Dear lord, Sarah thought. Was there no end to the secrets in this group?

"Like most of London, I also concluded that the mysterious Marie Antoinette killed him. But *I* knew that Clarissa had worn the costume—I overheard her talking about it the day before the ball—and was certain she was the murderer. Later, I asked Lady Greywood to recommend me to Clarissa as her companion. In my grief and anger, I meant to make her life miserable. I meant to destroy her."

Sarah's mouth fell open. "But you have stayed with her all these years."

Miss Simms nodded. "Clarissa has a beautiful soul, Miss Armistead. She could not have killed Linton, for she would never harm a fly. She gleaned that I had been hurt by some man, and she went out of her way to make me feel cared for. Eventually it ceased to matter who had caused Linton's death. Time taught me the truth about him. Clarissa taught me the truth about love and generosity."

"I see." Sarah was at a loss for words.

"Silvester has been with her since Linton's death," Miss Simms said with a wistful expression. "I gather he is everything that Linton was not. Perhaps one day she will send him back to the spirit world and seek her comfort among the living."

With that, Miss Simms walked to the carriage and settled herself in beside Aunt Clarissa. The two women waved as the carriage rolled down the drive.

"Well, that is settled." Sarah turned to see Aunt Agatha staring after her sister's carriage, an intrigued expression on her face. When she saw Sarah looking at her, however, she frowned as if suddenly recollecting something.

"Justin! Harry!" she called. Both men were walking toward the house from the stables. They quickly joined their aunt.

"Sarah's part in all of this has been deplorable, but I do not entirely blame her," she said, staring pointedly at the cousins. "She has had to make her own way in the world under difficult circumstances."

Harry was resolutely studying the ground. Sarah did not dare look at Justin, but she could feel his eyes burning into her.

"The girl has been woefully compromised," Aunt Agatha declared. "One of you must marry her, preferably within a fortnight."

No one spoke. Sarah wanted to sink into the ground in embarrassment. Just as she was about to plead a headache and depart, a clipped voice broke the tense silence.

"Miss Armistead will marry me."

Harry grinned in obvious relief. "Better this way," he informed Sarah in the silence following Justin's words. "Rich as Croesus, he is. Ain't going to quibble over every little bill from the modiste."

"Excellent," Aunt Agatha said, beaming. "I cannot pretend I

am not satisfied. Sarah will make you a fine wife, Justin. She may even be the making of you."

"Hear, Hear." Harry said, slapping his cousin on the back.

Sarah felt the heat of Justin's gaze. Hope surged in her breast, and she mustered the courage to search his eyes. What she saw there, however, dashed all hope. His were the eyes of a man who had lived his life in the pursuit of revenge and now had nothing to take its place. He had no rudder or compass to steer him clear of the rocky shoals of his own tempestuous emotions.

Confusion, regret, sorrow—all were mirrored in those gray depths. But not love.

Never love.

In a man consumed by revenge, there is no room for love. The fact that Justin's revenge lay around him in shambles did not mean that he was any more able to love.

Although Sarah had found it necessary sometimes to make compromises in life, she knew that this was not one of those times.

"I am deeply honored," she said in a clear, firm voice. "But I will not marry either of you. I have decided to resume my acting career."

In the stunned silence that followed her announcement, Sarah managed a polite curtsy before quickly crossing the drive to the carriage that had been provided for her. With all the dignity she could muster, Sarah signaled the coachman. As the carriage pulled away, Aunt Agatha, Harry, and Justin were still staring in speechless wonder.

It was an exit worthy of a great actress.

Chapter Twenty-two

Justin allowed the lavender-scented missive to float from his fingers to the desk. He had been home only a fortnight, but already Aunt Agatha had shocking news.

"Marrying Throckmorton?" He stared at the letter in bewilderment. "Has she lost her mind? The man will fawn all over her. Aunt Agatha always detested sentiment."

Anh lit the incense on the jade alter. "People often shun that which they fear most. Perhaps your aunt has decided that the rewards of love are worth the risks."

Justin eyed his butler suspiciously. "If that bit of philosophy is meant for me, you are wide of the mark."

"As you wish, my lord." Without expression, Anh handed him the hollow bamboo stick.

"I do not know why I put up with your rituals," Justin groused. "They never reveal anything useful." With a sigh of resignation, he shook the bamboo until one of the smaller sticks inside fell out onto the carpet.

With great ceremony, Anh tossed the wooden blocks to confirm that the choice was correct. "That is not true, my lord. The sticks foretold the change, did they not?"

It was the first time either of them had made even a veiled reference to what had occurred in Cheshire. Since Justin's return to Lintonwood, life had assumed its normal routine. Except that it was anything but normal. Sarah was gone.

Change. It was a perfectly ordinary word for the extraordinary transformation that had occurred in him since she had entered his life. When he reached for the anger he had carried around for so long, it was no longer there. Forgiveness, once unthinkable, had taken its place.

He could not hate Aunt Clarissa for what she had done, nor Aunt Agatha for keeping the painful truth from him. Lady

Greywood deserved only his deepest regret for the pain he had
caused her.

Most of all, Justin could not hate his mother for what she had
done out of weakness, desperation, and rage at the man who
had destroyed everything he touched.

What had Sarah said? *Women do not shoot their lovers.* But
they might shoot their oppressors, their tormentors, the instru-
ments of their degradation.

Memories washed over him, vivid as the bamboo sticks that
lay on the floor. Memories of his mother's tearstained face, her
cries in the night, the bruises that did not fade. Her gently
rounded stomach and its promise of new life, a life spawned
not by tender lovemaking but by Oscar Trent's relentless im-
position of his will upon a woman who could no longer fight
him.

No, he could not hate his mother, his aunts, or Lady Greywood. It was time he acknowledged the real target of his anger:
his father. Facing that pistol in his father's study so long ago,
Justin had truly wished him dead. Scant hours later, the wish
was fulfilled. Symbolically, at least, he had killed his father.
The twin burdens of guilt and anger had stalked him ever
since.

But those were empty emotions. One could not build of them
a life. Justin had tried, and it had very nearly destroyed him and
others besides. His father was doubtless laughing from the
grave at the legacy he had settled on his only son.

A great weariness filled him. Without the prism of revenge to
distort his vision, he saw how little he had to offer a woman like
Sarah. For all his wealth, his title, his cleverness, he had nothing. He had proven himself an empty, embittered man.

Anh was studying him as closely as he studied those
wretched bamboo sticks. Justin did not want to believe in their
power, yet recent experience had underscored his profound lack
of knowledge about some matters. And Anh looked as if a great
deal remained to be revealed.

"I still do not understand how you persuaded young William
to return to school," Justin said carefully, determined not to
broach the subject of Sarah directly.

Anh's face was impassive. "I simply told him that as Miss
Armistead's future husband you would pay his education ex-

penses and provide for his sister in the manner she deserved. He seemed quite satisfied."

Justin stilled. *"What?"*

The ghost of a smile flitted over Anh's features. "It was what the sticks foretold."

"You had best throw those sticks in the river," Justin snapped. "Miss Armistead refused my offer."

Not that it had been much of a proposal, he reflected ruefully. With Aunt Agatha and Harry looking on, he had been as tense as a fox surrounded by watchful hounds. The words had not come out the way he had intended.

Anh did not seem surprised. "When there is disharmony among the elements, balance is not easily restored."

Justin fought the urge to strangle his butler. "Come, man, I weary of this. You fortune-tellers find ways to justify your prophesies, no matter what occurs. Your facile art bears no resemblance to truth."

"If that is your position, my lord, then you will not wish to know what the sticks show." Anh reached for the solitary stick on the carpet.

"Wait."

Anh eyed him expectantly.

"Damn you, man. Go ahead." Justin sighed. There was no art so seductive as the promise of light to a man overwhelmed by darkness.

Silently Anh handed him the bamboo container. Justin shook it, and another stick fell onto the carpet. Its choice was confirmed in the usual manner, and the ritual continued until all of the sticks had been chosen. Anh studied them carefully, then eyed Justin in surprise.

"It seems, my lord, that you are destined to take to the stage."

Rose McIntosh had stolen her Venetian talc, along with the elderberry Sarah used to darken her eyelashes. Sarah had no doubt that Rose was also responsible for the mysterious disappearance of her wig. Fortunately, she still had in her possession the wig she had worn for Lady Hogarth's ball, which meant that her Ophelia now bore an uncanny resemblance to Marie Antoinette.

All because Mr. Stinson had seen fit to give Sarah the part of Ophelia when Rose had taken it into her head to run off with a Manchester swell who turned out to be nothing more than a conniving knave with a taste for women of Rose's ample proportions. When Rose had returned to the fold, chastened and without a feather to fly with, Mr. Stinson had made a heated speech about feckless actresses and had handed her the role of the Player Queen, a demeaning comedown for one of Rose's abilities. Further absences—by anyone in the company— would not be tolerated, he had warned, looking at both of the women.

Ever since, Sarah's possessions had been disappearing one by one. Transforming herself into Ophelia had become an exercise in suspense—she never knew whether she could scrounge the necessary paint and accessories. Fortunately, next week they moved on to another town and another play. A change of scenery would do them all good.

It was wearying to descend each night into the madness of a woman who had lost her prince to the blinding passion of revenge and whose love had saved neither Hamlet nor herself. Each time Sarah mustered the fortitude to plumb the depths of Ophelia's despair, she bolstered her resolve by telling herself that life must go on. Other roles, other places lay ahead. Someday she might even stop thinking of Justin Trent.

Even now, Sarah could almost imagine that the figure grappling with Mr. Stinson in the far wing bore more than a passing resemblance to Justin. Doubtless it was only the usual drunkard, trying to destroy the actors' concentration and wreck the performances. Forcing her gaze to Freddy Gilmore, who played Ophelia's brother Laertes, Sarah waited for her cue.

"How now! What noise is that?" Just as Freddy uttered his line and Sarah stepped before the audience, a crash resounded in the wing and a chair skidded onto the stage, evidently tossed by participants in the struggle taking place offstage. Titters rippled across the audience.

Freddy frowned. "O heat, dry up my brains!" he recited.

"Best dry up yer tongue, ye looby!" came a jeer from the pits. Hoots of laughter followed this sally.

Sarah closed her eyes as Freddy struggled with his lines. Usually it was possible to ignore the heckling from the pits, but the commotion in the wings had created a diversion that fueled the hecklers and left Freddy off balance. The performance was headed straight for perdition now. Fortunately, it was her last scene. From here on, the players would merely speak of her death in mournful tones.

"They bore him barefaced on the bier," she sang, trying to drown out the arguing offstage. She recognized Mr. Stinson's heated voice. It was a measure of her own madness that the other greatly resembled Justin's resonant baritone.

A sudden silence in the wing drew her attention, even as she prepared to launch into her final, poignant song. Against her will, Sarah risked a glance. A disheveled Mr. Stinson stood at the edge of the curtain, holding what appeared to be a large number of bank notes. At his side was Justin, arms crossed, glowering impatiently at the action on stage.

As Sarah met his gaze, her heart leapt to her throat, for in those stormy depths lay something she had never seen before.

"Thoughts and affliction, passion, hell itself, she turns to favor and to prettiness," Freddy declared.

Sarah simply stared at Justin.

"I *said*, 'She turns to favor and to prettiness,' " Freddy repeated loudly.

"Shut yer trap, clodpole!" came the cry from the audience. "Can ye not see she is sick of yer jabbering?" With that remark, a tomato sailed from the pits and hit Freddy in the chest.

Sarah's line suddenly popped into her head. "And will a' not come again?" she warbled unsteadily as another tomato barely missed her wig.

A growled oath erupted from the wings. In the next instant Justin was at her side. He slung her over his broad shoulders and carried her offstage as assorted fruit rained over them. In the narrow hallway near her dressing table, he set her on her feet.

"Justin!" she cried as he calmly took a cloth and began to wipe the talc from her face. "What has happened?"

"I believe Laertes and the rest of the company are presently engaged in rewriting the scene with certain members of the audience," he said dryly. "And your Mr. Stinson is counting the large sum I was forced to give him to release you from your obligation to the company."

"I do not understand. Why are you here?" Sarah stared. Though a tomato had caught his sleeve, Justin looked no worse for the daring rescue he had just carried out or the encounter with Mr. Stinson. He watched her with a mixture of amusement and something else that made her catch her breath.

"I am here to make you a proper proposal of marriage," he said, suddenly somber as he studied her intently. "I made a muddle of it at Aunt Agatha's."

Sarah shook her head. "You were a bit imperious, as is your way, but . . ."

"Humility is not my strong suit," he acknowledged, his tone a mixture of apology and defiance.

That endearing admission made her yearn to smooth his furrowed brow, yet touching him would only deepen her regret over what could not be. "That has nothing to do with why I cannot marry you." Her heart filled with sorrow as she spoke the words.

Justin seized her shoulders. "You will not persuade me that you do not care, Sarah," he growled, "for I know that you do."

Sarah did not ask how he knew. For all her acting abilities, she could never hide her feelings from him. "I love you, Justin," she confessed softly. "But I cannot marry a man who does not love me."

"How do you know what I feel?" he demanded. His gaze locked with hers.

"Once, perhaps, I thought you were capable of such feelings, but I know that was but an illusion."

Eyes as darkly compelling as any sorcerer's held hers. "Illusion is a pale substitute for reality." He paused, then added fiercely, "And for love."

Why did her heart suddenly soar with hope? Nothing had changed. And yet perhaps it had, for his eyes gleamed with the brilliance of fine silver.

"What are you saying, Justin?" Sarah whispered, trembling.

Gently, he folded her into his arms. "That I have been blind," he said roughly, "unable to see clearly into my own heart because of the ugliness there that I have spent a lifetime nurturing. That I have been a coward, afraid to risk love in order to gain it."

"Does that mean . . . ?"

"That I love you? That I wish to spend my life learning the love you teach so effortlessly? Indeed it does." Uncertainty shadowed his gaze. "If you will have me, that is."

Jubilant shouts from somewhere in the front of the theater signaled that the battle onstage had been resolved in favor of one of the parties. To Sarah's ears, it echoed the exultant cheer in her heart.

No fanciful dream, no playwright's fertile imagination could capture the joy that raced through her at Justin's declaration. "Yes," she cried. "Oh, yes!" Whatever else she might have said was silenced in the embrace that followed.

It was not until some moments later that Sarah was able to form a coherent thought. By then, her wig was askew and her face streaked with the elderberry that joyful tears had driven from her lashes. "What brought this about?" she whispered.

Justin considered the matter. "Vision," he said finally.

Sarah blinked. "I do not understand."

"I had an irresistible vision of somehow persuading you to undertake one final, lasting performance—as my wife. I had no right to hope that you would consent, but something drove me to pursue it." He shot her a bemused smile. "Perhaps it was that card trick."

"What?"

"Anh and I have a nightly ritual of cards. I employ various devious methods to hide the diamond queen. Despite my best efforts, he always finds it. Last night, however, he could not."

Having seen Justin's skill, Sarah could not imagine to what elaborate lengths he had gone to hide the card from his discerning butler. "Where did you put it?"

Carefully Justin removed Sarah's wig, took a brush from her dressing table, and began to smooth her hair. "Ah. Now *that* is a secret I will carry to my grave."

"Not fair," Sarah teased, although the rhythmic stroking of the brush was fast driving all curiosity from her mind.

"Very well." Justin wrapped a tendril of her hair around his fingers. "I simply placed the queen facedown on the top of the deck, in the most obvious position of all. He never guessed." Abruptly, he set the brush on the table. "Anh was unaccountably pleased at being bested."

Her heart leapt to her throat as she read the intent in his eyes. "I wonder why," she murmured.

"Because I confounded his expectations." Justin stroked her cheek. "A student who confounds his teacher has moved beyond his limitations to a different way of seeing. In so doing, he becomes his own teacher."

"Oh." Sarah barely heard his words, so intent was she on the sensation generated by his fingertip.

Justin smiled. "I suppose that sounds like nonsense. But it gave me hope that my vision could be yours."

As he brought their lips together, Sarah sighed in contentment. "Oh, yes," she whispered. "Yes, indeed."

Epilogue

"I hope I do not fall out of bed," Sarah said nervously as she eyed the peach comforter. "I do so wish to pass the test."

Justin, in the act of gently slipping his wife's night rail off her shoulders, froze. "What test?"

"Mr. Magnus's chastity test." Sarah hesitated, then pulled something from under her pillow. "In his book, Mr. Magnus states that if a lodestone is placed under a wife's pillow, she will embrace her husband if she is chaste. If she is not chaste, she will fall out of bed."

Aghast, Justin stared at the blue stone. "We have been married but a few hours. What makes you think you have to prove your faithfulness?"

"'Tis not my faithfulness at issue, my husband, but my past," she said, blushing. "I know you think actresses are a wayward breed."

His brows arched rakishly. "Wayward, is it?"

"Well, I *did* pose as your mistress, but I have never been a man's mistress in truth." Her eyes willed him to believe her.

"I know that."

Sarah stilled. "Because of the chastity test?"

"Because of what we are about to share." Reverently, he kissed her fingertips. "And because I know you better than I did when I first saw you posing as Harry's wife. If you are a wayward woman, Lady Linton, I am King George."

Sarah's eyes searched his. "Once, you scoffed at my claim to be a virgin."

Justin sighed. "Once, I was an idiot."

"Then Anh was right," she said in wonder. "He said you would not need Mr. Magnus to show you the truth."

A choking sound erupted from her husband. "You involved *Anh* in something as private as this?"

"Only after he cast the bamboo sticks for me. Did you know that we are destined to take a long trip?"

"Our wedding trip to the East is hardly a secret," Justin said sardonically, "especially from Anh."

"Of course not. But there is more. Do you wish to hear it?"

Wistfully, Justin eyed the featherbed. "Do I have a choice?"

"Did you know that Anh is betrothed?" she said, her eyes dancing as she ignored the question. "His bride is deceased, but he says they will be together in the afterlife. He means to accompany us as far as Malaya, where she is buried, so that the marriage of their spirits can be performed. I do not understand precisely, but it is terribly romantic."

Slowly, Justin began to massage Sarah's shoulders. "I cannot envision Anh as a romantic."

"But he is. He told me that I ought not worry that you would think me a loose woman." She frowned. "Perhaps he was simply trying to give me confidence so that I could get through the ordeal."

"Ordeal?" Justin's restless hands stilled. "Is that what you think of our wedding night?"

Sarah flushed. "No. Of course not. Although Anh said it might be a bit uncomfortable at first."

"Is there anything you did *not* ask Anh?" Justin demanded, glowering.

"The venus root was my idea entirely," Sarah confided. "Or rather, Mr. Magnus's. I found the spell while I was looking through his book."

"Remind me to toss Mr. Magnus in the river at the earliest opportunity." Justin scowled. "What, pray, is the venus root?"

"A herb buried on one's wedding night to ensure that one will have many children. I buried it amid the rosebushes at the side of the house. I hope you do not mind."

A smile transformed his features. "Let me guess. You envision enough little Trents to make an acting troupe."

"Only if they are so inclined," Sarah conceded.

"Then, my dear," he murmured, nuzzling her ear, "we had best bring the curtain down on this performance."

"We had?"

Justin tossed the lodestone onto the floor. "Most assuredly," he confirmed, pulling her down with him onto the plump comforter. "It contains entirely too much dialogue—and far too little action."